THE
WHISPERING
GALLERY

THE WHISPERING GALLERY

A NOVEL BY

RICHARD H. FRANCIS

W·W· NORTON & COMPANY
New York   London

First Edition

Library of Congress Cataloging in Publication Data
Francis, Richard H., 1945–
   The whispering gallery.
   I. Title.
PR6056.R277W5   1984   823'.914   84–15211

ISBN 0-393-01926-8

W.W. Norton & Company, Inc., 500 Fifth Avenue, New York, N.Y. 10110
W.W. Norton & Company Ltd., 37 Great Russell Street, London WC1B 3NU

1   2   3   4   5   6   7   8   9   0

For Jo
And, in due course,
for William and Helen.

And then a Plank in Reason, broke,
And I dropped down, and down–
And hit a World, at every plunge,
And Finished knowing–then–
(Emily Dickinson, *Poem 280*, concluding stanza)

Wovon man nicht sprechen kann, darüber
muβ man schweigen.
(Ludwig Wittgenstein, *Logisch-philosophische
Abhandlung*, concluding proposition)

THE
WHISPERING
GALLERY

PRELIMINARY

The experience had been so shocking, so appalling, so horrible, that on the following morning Anthony Manley summoned up his courage and decided to buy a newspaper so that he could read about it. On the basis that he might as well be hung for a sheep as a lamb, he chose a tabloid, the *Morning Sky*. He walked back to his house with it in his hand, not even giving it a glance, aware of the soft black print rubbing off on his fingers.

When he arrived home he placed the paper on the side in the kitchen and, as if to prolong the agony, made some coffee. Then he picked up cup and paper and went through with them into his living-room.

The room was immaculate as always, everything in position, everything clean and ready for use. One of Manley's central tenets was, your house is a form of clothing. He meant it literally: a brick and mortar coat that covered you, protected you from the elements, made a certain statement about you to the world at large. If your body was the temple of the spirit, then your home was the temple of your body, within the limits of your mortgage, of course.

Nevertheless Manley's living-room felt not-quite-right first thing in the morning, as if despite being in a state of full preparedness it hadn't yet been switched on. The morning light, schoolchildren passing the window, a sense of milkmen on their rounds, combined to make him feel anachronistic, too early or too late, as if he were occupying the wrong slot while a vacuum waited to suck him in elsewhere. Work, presumably, although his feeling of being misplaced was more severe than the fact of missing work, resembling rather the unproportioned reaction you have when you make a mistake in a dream. Anyway, there was no question of going into work this morning and he had phoned his secretary and told her so. Not after yesterday. . .

The story wasn't on the front page as he'd rather expected, but it wasn't hard to find. It occupied pride of place on page five.

Once his eyes had found the headline, they switched to one side in order to postpone the actual reading. He felt a kind of self-consciousness, as you do when you look in a mirror in a department store, wanting to avoid your own eye. However, he was also able to put a dignified gloss on his motive: perhaps, he told himself, he needed to find a context in which to place what had occurred, a world for it to happen in.

Certainly page five of the *Morning Sky* was rich in context:

Shocked parishioners are calling for the unfrocking of a vicar who untrousered himself at a church social on Wednesday night. The Rev Stephen Bright, 32 and unmarried, said yesterday: 'I went over the top in the heat of the moment, and am deeply sorry for any offence I may have caused.' Women screamed as. . .

Pensioner Alice Lovett, 84, died yesterday for the moggie nobody wanted. . .

The naked truth about those padded bras. See centre spread for details.

Brezhnev health rumours scotched. Soviet boss Leonid Brezhnev, 74, appeared in public yesterday. . .

Super-pig Mark Sutton, 21, has eaten nineteen pork pies in ten minutes. . .

Schoolgirl Ginnie Henderson, 15, who announced yesterday 'Sex is my hobby', is today being carpeted by headmaster Arnold Carter, 42. . .

Manley didn't laugh at all, not even in some remote corner of his brain. He couldn't allow himself to be taken in by the jolly style, any more than concentration camp inmates should have let themselves be bucked up by those positive and assertive notes of Wagner over the tannoy. Tannoy, tabloid, swirling music, chuckling phraseology, it all added up to a noose around your throat, or rather, to the gathering numbness of the sort of death that is insidiously absorbed into your system, breath by breath. Note the ages, like price-tags, after each person. Except that they are never people, simply names. Names and actions, minus always the human beings who should mediate between the two.

But it was the real world, all the same: that was the whole trouble. It was pushed through a million letterboxes simultaneously, pushed into a million lives. It was, above all, believed; and what *was* reality but a consensus, an agreement by its participants that life was so-and-so? Nobody else seemed to mind the abitrariness of the juxtapositions, the squeezing together of large and small, bosoms one column, people burned to death the next. Surely, surely, argued Manley, sitting in his lifeless living-room, the world should be a smooth continuity, not a dizzying jumble; the universe should be large enough for its own contents, they oughtn't to be heaped up, as in some warehouse.

The other side of the argument would be, of course, that the newspaper did precisely hold it all together, that underlying the black print was a white continuum.

Manley let his mind play over the possibility for a while, the possibility that life was actually woven out of a fabric in which Leonid Brezhnev was somehow involved with the super-pig, and the two of *them* implied the old lady who died for her cat and a precocious schoolgirl who was about to be carpeted by her headmaster. It was difficult to accept. Despite, or perhaps because of, certain oddities in his own background Manley had adopted the notion that the domestic was the essential environment of human civilisation, and that maturity was the value towards which the whole cumbersome machinery strove. True, his domesticity was of the minimal kind available in a bachelor household, and by the same token his maturity had to be of the vague sort associated with a broad outlook on life, since he didn't have any close human relationships to focus it on, but he had never felt that his solitary status needed to conflict with his basic position. You could affirm the values of life while dying; surely then you could nail your flag to the mast of the nuclear family while you yourself confronted a solitary destiny?

The *Morning Sky* stood neither for kinship nor for any form of human solidarity; and maturity was the last value it concerned itself with. Its stance was effectively that of the psychopath, celebrating an instant response to any experience, whether gargantuan, and measurable in pork pies, violent, and measurable in suffering and death, or sexual, and measurable in cup sizes and bust dimensions. It affirmed that perspective by the very language it employed. Manley found it intolerable to imagine that the structure of life actually conformed to its treatment, filled, in other words, the glass slipper or the padded bra which the *Sky* offered to its readers every morning.

On the other hand he had indeed seen what he had seen at the Regency Restaurant in Prince Street, Manchester, yesterday. In that respect at least he could endorse the *Morning Sky*'s rendering of experience.

1

Mr Wilkins was telling a story. It was about an Irishman who went to the optician's to be fitted for a pair of glasses. The optician asked him to cover up one of his eyes with his hand, so that he could test the other, but the man was completely unable to understand what he had to do.

First of all he covered the wrong eye; then he covered the correct eye but removed his hand so that he could see better when the optician asked him to read the test card; finally he gave up and stared at the optician with both eyes uncovered. Both eyes blank, for that matter.

In exasperation the optician sent his secretary into the inner office for an empty cornflake box he happened to have there. When she brought it back he cut out a single hole in the box with a pair of scissors and then placed it over the Irishman's head so that only the required eye could see out.

'All right,' he asked, 'could you please tell me what's written on the card?'

The Irishman didn't reply, and after a moment the optician made out a snivelling sound coming from inside the cornflake box.

'What on earth's the matter now?' the optician asked.

'I wanted a pair of gold-rimmed ones like me friend,' the Irishman sobbed.

Mr Wilkins looked across the table of the Regency Restaurant at Ed Pointon, the *Morning Sky* man who was sitting opposite. Pointon didn't look amused.

'They have those kind of floppy cakes,' Wilkins went on after a moment. 'I can't eat junk like that. I don't know why they've got to ruin a good lunch.'

Pointon leaned forward over his dirty plate.

'Mr Wilkins,' he said, 'are you trying to tell me that you feel no responsibility at all for what happened to those men?'

'I was trying to tell you about the blessed gateaux,' Wilkins replied, unable to maintain his charm.

'But don't you think —'

'Talking of blessings, have you heard the one about the bishop and the jar of cold cream? C of E, I only believe in one Irish joke at a time.'

There was a pause. Pointon stared doggedly into Wilkins's face.

'All right,' Wilkins conceded, 'but I'd thank you for not harping quite so much on the theme of responsibility. It's a meaningless term in this connection. I'm employed by a giant corporation, the Hautbois Company.' He pronounced it H-o-r-t-b-o-y-s. 'There are thousands of us in it. Its policies are corporate policies, nothing to do with one man. It's just struck me, I might stretch a point, there *is* another good Irish one that's come to mind. About a little cottager who had to sell his pig.'

'Let me put it this way, then. Does your *company* feel no responsibility for what happened to those men?'

'My company *has* no responsibility for what happened to those men. Listen, this Irishman loved his pig like a brother. It had a—'

'My paper's done its homework, Mr Wilkins.'

'Has it really? Done its homework, eh? I wish your paper would keep to the area it's good at, the tit and bum feature on page two.' Charm had been forgotten altogether now, as had the Irish cottager and his pig. Wilkins's voice reached a quiet monotone of sarcasm: 'Perhaps you could tell me how many space scientists you've *got* on your staff?'

'Don't you ever think about it?' Pointon asked. 'Don't you ever try to imagine what it was like for those poor bastards, all those miles up there? Just the two of them? What it might be like for them still, for all we know?'

'Don't be silly,' said Wilkins matter-of-factly, 'they've been dead for nearly two months.'

'So we're told.'

'I think about it,' Wilkins suddenly allowed. It was time to let a bit of sincerity intrude into the proceedings. In this case, within certain imaginative limits, it was sincere sincerity. He had been stationed in remote parts himself, and knew what it was like to feel at a distance from the rest of mankind. Even when you were a bit of a bastard, he'd noticed, you needed other people to be a bit of a bastard to.

He took his eyes off Pointon and stared abstractedly out of the restaurant window. 'Of course I think about it. Who doesn't?' Despite the restaurant's plush interior the street outside was bleak and run-down, conducive perhaps to depressing trains of thought.

2

The launch had been fine.

Fine was something of a technical term of course, like 'the patient is comfortable'. You didn't need to take it too literally.

As a matter of fact one of the two American astronauts *had* felt fine, or almost. Finn Malke had suffered no serious side-effects at blast-off, although it was a maiden voyage for him as for his partner. He had always enjoyed the sensation of taking off, even as a child in a passenger aircraft: the pressure building up behind you, the sudden release as you fire forwards, like a bullet from a gun, the unnatural smoothness of acceleration.

Of course, in the space shuttle all those experiences came at you from below. What didn't come at you from below!

For a start you wet yourself. Actually, that wasn't quite right: it wasn't possible, technically speaking, to wet yourself in a space suit. But you certainly peed abruptly down the tube to which you were connected. Much worse though was the fact that seconds later your balls yo-yoed up from the scrotum to the places from whence they came. 'Growing backwards' in NASA parlance.

Other launch phenomena, all routine, all to be subsumed under the heading of 'fine' were: headaches, stomach pains, dizziness. However, Malke only experienced these symptoms mildly. He had a sensation of pressure in the ears, a buzzing noise in his head, and the desire, unfulfilled, to be sick, but they faded away within half-an-hour.

John Patterson, his colleague and the shuttle pilot, was not so lucky: he passed out shortly after lift-off, and stayed unconscious for almost ten minutes.

It was in the manual, there was no need to panic. In any

case their separation from the launch rocket and entry into an orbiting trajectory were both the responsibility of ground control.

Finally Patterson began to stir, with the slow, oblique movements of a thawing mammoth. Although the men were only two feet apart, space suit had to communicate with space suit via the intercom.

'Are you O.K., John?' Malke asked.

There was a pause of seconds, the sort of pause you associate with interplanetary intervals, not the arm's length distance of two men in the same cockpit. Almost, Malke thought fancifully, as if they had been rocketed *apart* from each other. That turned out to be an intuition.

Finally: 'Yeah bleep um O.K.'

His voice sounded peculiar, perhaps distorted by the communication system.

'You blanked out for a while there, John,' Malke informed him.

Pause.

'That so bleep? I sure feel like I bleep slugged.'

There was no mistaking it, Patterson's habitual New York gobble had been replaced by a lazy drawl. That should please ground control, who put great emphasis on being laid-back in space. They wanted nerveless zombies really, which was why they picked astronauts of fifty, hoping they were too mature, or past it, for their pulses to so much as race as the huge rocket engines fired. They were looking for a still point at the heart of the explosion, and there weren't many things stiller than an unconscious astronaut.

'How you doing bleep boys?' came the voice of Dan Leonard, Mission Director, from ground control.

Malke went stiff with impatience, seeing Patterson slowly try to focus in response. He almost replied first himself, but thought better of it. Even – especially – up here, the hierarchy should be observed.

'Jus' fine bleep,' Patterson came out with at last, cumbersomely perhaps, but spot on in his terminology.

'Great to hear bleep wriggle out of them suits of yours, boys,' Leonard replied. Then, knowingly, added: 'Bleep yourselves comfortable.'

It was easier said than done, because the most obtrusive and constricting of all the launch symptoms had still to be coped with. 'Chicken legs', it was called, and it was one undesirable side-effect that even NASA hadn't been able to keep the lid on. Space flights were edited with some care, on a moment to moment basis, for the benefit of the world's networks, but no amount of live censorship could conceal the fact that for several hours on each mission astronauts had to confront both their tasks and the onboard television cameras with much of their lower body wrapped round their necks.

Malke, naked except for his singlet, looked down at himself, at the empty pouch of crinkled skin where his balls ought to be, at the spindle-shanks below. Growing backwards was bad enough, but at least you could remedy it. As for chicken legs, all you could do was wait. Nobody knew exactly what happened, although the phenomenon was obviously a product of the forces of blast-off. Your frame stood its ground as best it could, but the softer parts of your body billowed upwards like a girl's dress when she jumps. Apparently several litres of blood, other fluids and fatty deposits slid up your legs, along your trunk, and wrapped themselves like a flesh stole round your neck and shoulders. The astronaut-as-hero found himself confronting the solar system on stick legs, with a newly-fledged floppy hump on his back, and with no visible evidence of testicles.

It was time to at least do something about this last problem. Malke placed a finger on the hairy groove each side of his penis, and pressed gently downwards.

As his balls plopped back into place he felt, from each in turn, a quick spark of pain, and then with Pavlovian immediacy he succumbed to a sudden shock of sexual desire.

It was ridiculous, but he'd been plagued by such feelings for several days now, all through the forty-eight hour count-down prior to launching. He had decided it must be to do with what a lot of people talked about, the space-ship as phallic symbol, but he'd also expected that he'd gain a sense of proportion when he left the surface of the Earth. What was so sickening was that he'd had his chances in the two years leading up to the mission, there were space groupies enough in Houston and Canaveral, but it had suited him then to remain faithful to his wife while other astronauts went cowboying through the available females, and to direct his drives austerely towards the sky, moon, stars, that awaited him.

As soon as he found himself in the 'sterile conditions' prior to launch his glands had begun jitterbugging, his abdomen whooshed with regret, the muscles of his thighs and buttocks ached with lack of use. Even then, however, he'd been able to console himself with some fifty-year-old maturity, and decide that he was subconsciously bringing on a deflection of attention in order to obviate anxiety about the Imminent Experience.

But now he had no such excuse. He was being asked by his own destiny to apply his intellect on the one hand to the immense amount of technical data he had to handle, and on the other to the imaginative challenge of coping with a dimension to which only a minuscule proportion of the human race had so far had access; and all he could think of was the delight of brutal and miscellaneous sexual intercourse, his mind a collage of breasts, of curved hips, soft buttocks, of genital mounds and crevices.

He stood, a hundred and fifty miles above the world, on eighty-year-old legs, and lusted.

3

Dressed in tee-shirt and slacks, Malke settled himself back in the flight engineer's seat and watched the earth rise in his porthole. How to describe it, he wondered dutifully, still trying to exorcise the graffiti in his head. A disc, a near-circle, like the moon only coloured differently, no, it was all too trite and obvious. Then it occurred to him exactly what he was seeing: the completed horizon.

Beside him Patterson settled back in his seat, also dressed in casuals.

Then NASA felt it was time to give them a cue.

'How does the old Earth bleep from up there, boys?' came Leonard's voice, smirking through the slight static, as if the world were something which he, as Mission Director, had pulled out of a hat.

Patterson turned slowly, like a great humped fish, to look through Malke's porthole. The planet seemed to take an age to sink in. Malke, having described it for himself already, felt his impatience return. At last, though, Patterson spoke.

'Jeepers,' he said, in a whisper that was relaxed and awe-struck at the same time.

'Jeepers' as it happened was one of the terms they'd been assigned in training. NASA had spent a good deal of time drumming innocuous exclamations into them in order, as they claimed, to avoid the expletive deleted problem. This tampering with reflexes was all part of an attempt, Malke had long ago decided, to produce a breed of cuddly bite-sized astronauts.

Patterson, aware that a simile was now required, embarked on one. 'I guess it looks like a big, blue, beautiful eye, staring at you from out the darkness,' he went on.

At this point Malke also turned towards the staring Earth, to its strange combination of clarity and cloud film. Suddenly he recalled an aged, rheumy uncle, head of the family during his teenage years, whom he and his cousins used to ferry to baseball in the summers, taking it in turns to give him a running commentary. Malke embarked on a simile of his own.

'It looks like an eye with a cataract,' he suggested.

'Ha bleep,' Leonard laughed angrily. 'We sure got a pair of bright bleep up there.'

'An uncle of mine had cataracts,' Malke explained, taking up, he felt, his obligation to be homey.

'Yep,' agreed Leonard brusquely. 'Look, kids, bleep you turned in for a while. You got a load of bleep and observations to get through during this mission. Bleep you say?'

Kids! Malke was fifty, Patterson forty-six, Leonard thirty-nine.

'Yes, boss,' Patterson drawled obediently.

They did indeed obey: peed into labelled bags, stood in their adjoining bunks, swallowed sleeping pills, slept.

Malke awoke to the pinging of the emergency signal. For a disoriented second he thought he was at home in bed, listening to his alarm clock. Then panic subsided as he became aware that he was confronting a space emergency, and his training took over.

'Rise and bleep fellas,' came the cheery female voice of Astronaut Horfitz. She was due to ride the mission after next, one of the handful of American women to be selected for space.

'What is it, Ruth?' Malke asked. Patterson stepped out of his cubicle, looking hung over.

'We're pulling you bleep early boys. Our data suggests we got a bleep in the set–up. Some little wrinkle, nothing to bother bleep take chances in a game like this.'

Malke, choked, couldn't reply for a moment. For two years he'd kept his attention fixed on this mission and now it was being aborted. For two years, while other astronauts had had a good time, he'd maintained an iron, neutral commitment, and now his big trip was going to end in fiasco. From what he'd heard, Ruth Horfitz had balled her way through training as hard as any fella. As hard as any fella but Malke, who'd been reserving himself for blast-off the way young girls used to save their virginity for the wedding night. With the result that could have been predicted.

'That sure is a shame right enough,' Patterson said in his new-found equable drawl, as though the voyage had been not to space but Oklahoma. 'We were just beginning to feel kinda settled in up here.'

'Bleep in mind one thing,' Astronaut Horfitz suggested, 'we learn more from these slight disasters than when everything goes bleep pie. When you have something playing up, bleep when you boys really are in unknown bleep.'

Patterson, painfully thoughtful in response to this rationale, raised his hand to his face and scratched his stubble in puzzlement. Your beard grew faster in space, nobody knew why, much to the irritation of the authorities, who disliked welcoming unkempt, jowly astronauts back to the planet, even if it was obvious that the essential man, beneath his recent growth, was crew-cut and clean-shaven. If not, like Malke, actually thinning on top.

Anyway, Patterson's hump had subsided. Malke twisted his neck and realised his own had also. They had had time to get over chicken legs at least.

'You got a point there,' Patterson at last told Ruth. 'Might as well look at the bright side.'

'What *is* the slight disaster?' Malke asked.

'The F.D. console suggests a fuel bleep forward retro jet. It may be just a dud warning light bleep take chances.'

'There's no way we can test it, is there?'

'No, sirree, except by firing it bleep coming home.'

'You do mean the liquid fuel? Not the electric cell?'

'No, the liquid fuel. Bleep old explosive mixture.'

'But what on earth can go wrong with that? We haven't sprung a leak, have we?'

'No, Finn we bleep.' Dan Leonard had taken over. Ruth

had been the reassuring Mother Earth; now it was time to give it to them man to man. 'How you boys doing up there?'

'Fine. What is it then?'

'Could be some sort of bleep in viscosity. It's a new fuel we're using this bleep space before. Could be a clogged bleep. Some stuff's getting through so don't lose any sleep bleep sure how much.'

'We already did,' Malke replied.

'Did what?'

'Lose sleep. Ruth woke us, remember.'

'Like I bleep,' Leonard said unhappily, 'we got a pair of clowns in you two bleep party than a space ride.'

'If there's nothing we can do about it,' Malke said obstinately, 'and if it's a re-entry problem, we may as well go through our program and worry about re-entry when the time comes. What difference does it make?'

There was a pause.

'Bleep attitude on your part, fellas. But we'd bleep things go now. In just over four hours we got a slot. Bleep our emergency rota. This is a c-level emergency bleep c-level slot. So you bleep hammer down the groove.'

'Get it over with, you mean,' Malke suggested.

'Something like that,' Leonard replied quickly.

Patterson gave Malke a peculiar, almost wistful look, which seemed to say, I'd be worried about this if I could take in what's going on around here.

4

It was Patterson, as pilot, who had his finger on the onboard-computer program–override button, which would in effect instruct the forward retro jet when to make its single firing, and how long for. Seven seconds, just under, was all that was required.

It didn't fire at all. All that happened was a warning buzz, as thin and disappointing as the sound of a car on a cold morning, when the starting motor doesn't quite catch.

'Aitch cow,' Patterson said, 'the dummie's struck out on bleep.'

Both Patterson and Malke were in full space suits, and Patterson's voice, purged of violent expression, nevertheless hit Malke's ears abruptly from the hiss and crackle of their intercom. Patterson's great blunt head leaning over his console looked crude and prehistoric to be in charge of a computer. However, he reversed the firing of the after jet efficiently enough, and although of course there was no sensation of movement the dials indicated that having bounced Earthwards from orbit they'd now bounced back, slightly beyond the orbiting line in point of fact, the computer not having fully compensated for their lack of a forward source of power.

'We'll have to set bleep configuration on what we have,' came Leonard's voice. Of course, it was inevitably smaller than Patterson's, but Malke couldn't help wondering if it hadn't developed a certain amount of remoteness in its own right. The Earth had been remote ever since they achieved their orbit, but now the distance had turned from spectacle to reality. A completed horizon was one that cut you out.

Ruth's voice came chiming in: 'Don't worry boys, we got the big electric brain bleep on it. A bit of improvisation never did bleep.'

Malke suddenly thought: they're using her as a pin-up. Soldiers traditionally looked at two-dimensional nudes before going into battle with three-dimensional enemies; in space by contrast the erotic element turned out to be a variation on the theme of oral sex. Back on earth, confronted by actual women, he'd turned his attention to distances so great that physical reality became abstract. Now he was up among those distances and all he could do was imagine the women who weren't there. And try to trace appropriate contours within the accents of Astronaut Horfitz. She was well-built physically, if somewhat muscular, but her voice had a bony flat-chested timbre.

It took NASA half-an-hour to produce a d-level program, which left them with a margin of over seven hours before the slot arrived.

Less than three hours later they'd twitched the shuttle plumb into its original orbit; then Patterson programmed the override, and they did a couple of trial run-throughs, not merely of the tacking procedure that had been evolved for the two after-jets, but of the whole re-entry program. It was as well that they had time to practise, since Patterson still occupied some mid-western nirvana which slowed down every thought, every movement. No, Malke suddenly realised, that wasn't the image any more, it wasn't a question of hayseed casualness. There was now a subdued earnestness behind Patterson's leaden actions, as if he were operating in the teeth of a private gale. Oklahoma in deep winter, with a blizzard sweeping the land.

Nevertheless patience won out, he mastered the program with half-an-hour to spare. On Astronaut Horfitz's instructions, they then relaxed. That is they sat side by side in silence, looking alternately through one porthole at blackness and through the one opposite at radiant blue Earthshine.

A whisper: 'Bleep boys trigger-time.' Ruth Horfitz's voice had become intricate, detailed, nuanced, quite different from before, a voice in lacy underwear. 'I'm with you all the way,' she added deliciously.

For a few moments you could almost see Earth growing bigger as if, taking some cue from Astronaut Horfitz, it had become a ripening fruit. Then dials all over the console did an abrupt thumbs-down and they were bouncing far far back into space, having missed their re-entry window, the d-slot, altogether.

Patterson's voice came harshly into Malke's ear: 'I just filled my shit-bag bleep diarrhoea.'

'The starboard rear jet's died on us,' Malke told Earth, trying to be more businesslike. 'Not enough juice to get a firing there, either.'

Ruth's voice came back, harder than before, obviously offended by Patterson's explicitness. 'Bleep worry fellas we'll figure out another program bleep jet left.'

Patterson sustained his recovery from obliqueness. 'Jeez we bleep back on one engine. We couldn't bleep of the fucking block on one engine.'

Malke knew he was right. They couldn't in fact halt their lurch into deep space with what they had left. Even if they got the port rear-jet to fire – and the chances were it would rapidly succumb to the same infection as the other two – the shuttle would only revolve slowly as they continued to proceed in the wrong direction. He found himself wondering, quite coolly, whether to disobey standing orders and panic. There didn't seem to be anything to panic for.

Leonard began a long litany: 'Now listen boys, you gotta bleep this cool. . .' He gave them advice about switching off half their onboard systems and saving power. Why, Malke couldn't work out. To make them live longer? In any case NASA always left a neurotic margin for error, providing six months' internal power and supplies. The logic was impossible to fathom – error was simply given a larger territory to happen in.

'Christ Jesus,' said Patterson, interrupting Leonard's flow. 'We've had it.'

'That's right,' Malke agreed.

As if in response to their growing insubordination, Astronaut Horfitz played a trump card a little later.

'Bleep fellas, the President would like a word in about five bleep.'

How weird, thought Malke. They seemed to think, in the absence of technical control, they could use the President to bring the shuttle to heel through sheer political authority, as if he were president of the solar system. A pity, in the present situation, that he wasn't. Malke pictured him at the White House, preparing to come on the line, dyed hair, features ashine with cheek gloss but crumbling visibly, like a brightly painted ventriloquist's doll with dry rot.

'Fellas,' came Ruth's voice suddenly, desexed and once more functional as a spanner, 'the President of the United States would like to bleep. . .'

'Now men, proud to bleep Americans, calm in the face of danger, bleep example.'

It was like being addressed by the mayor of some hick town you've never heard of. Patterson, redeemed from the provincial, replied first.

'Shit off,' he said, his voice crisp and alive as it had not been since they entered space.

The President, as if acknowledging the strict parameters of his mandate, shat off.

'Fuck me,' Patterson added, and took off his helmet. Malke did likewise.

'. . .let yourselves crack bleep,' came Leonard's voice, out of the console this time, now that they had removed their earphones. 'In the medicine unit find something bleep you down.'

'I know what else is in that unit,' Patterson said, 'a coupla poison pills.'

'Boys bleep.' Ruth this time, panic-stricken.

'Surely not yet,' Malke said, instinctively.

'Why the hell not? What difference does it make? I'd sooner cop out now while the Earth's still in sight. We're just going to get further away for ever, for God's sake.'

At last, Malke couldn't help noting ruefully: it takes a situation like this to get the *authentic* homey touch.

5

Malke had expected that Patterson, dying, would relapse into his earlier trance but it didn't happen like that. In the minute or so it took he twitched and scratched irritably.

He had gone into his sleeping capsule to do it, but his instinct for privacy had been countered by the coffin-like appearance of the unit with its door closed, so he'd left it open. Malke, unable to dissuade him, felt he ought to show some sort of solidarity, so he stood at the entrance and watched.

At the last moment Patterson looked at him with hot eyes and opened his mouth to say something that would obviously be obscene, but then his lips settled back and he died, the word still in his mouth.

Back at the console Leonard's voice was coming out of the tiny speaker: '. . .come in fellas, god's sake doing bleep?'

For the first time in an hour, Malke spoke to Earth: 'John's got a —'

'Is bleep Finn?' Ruth asked. They'd obviously been waiting to plug her in as soon as Malke's voice came through.

'Yep.'

'Wow, that's great. We were beginning bleep lost contact.'

'Patterson's dead.'

'Oh gee that's terrible bleep. That's just *aw*ful news, I'm so *sor*ry.'

There was now something nakedly unattractive about her frank and sympathetic tone. The way she elongated the 'aw' in 'awful' and the 'sor' in 'sorry' was like a sudden strip by someone who didn't turn you on.

Leonard, calculating perfectly, came in: 'What happened, Finn?'

'What do you think? He killed himself.'

'My God.'

'Listen honey,' put in Ruth, 'play it cool, bleep? We got all systems on the job down here. You bleep —'

'John had a last message,' Malke interrupted.

'Oh.' Doubtfully, as if she somehow intuited: 'Did he?'

'Yeah, he sure did. He said you were a bunch of piss-artists.'

Malke didn't speak to them again. They cajoled and pleaded, but he remained remorselessly silent.

Days passed. The ship careered on. There was, of course, no sense of movement, perhaps it would have been easier to comprehend if there had been, something equivalent to that vertiginous drop as a plane hits a hole in the sky and plunges towards the ground until the engines find something to bite on once more. The only index of the shuttle's progress, regress, was the adjustment of stellar configurations, and Malke, sitting in his flight engineer's chair at the cockpit console had nothing else to do but watch that dance being performed. The Earth dwindled until it was no more than a star.

Malke rarely moved. He got up once to jettison Patterson, ignoring the manual, which advised on a form of service suitable for both Christians and Jews. Patterson had ended up trying to curse, which seemed as reasonable a stance as any, although Malke, blank after two years of aspiration, felt it was too positive for him. He himself was simply an agnostic, with sexual inclinations. He found disposing of his captain a cumbersome and long-drawn-out business, since, as with any activity involving the airlock and outer doors, he had to do it in full space suit.

Otherwise he did nothing, except eat and relieve himself when necessary. He peed and crapped into the appropriate bags, labelling and storing them as required, as if he were saving it for a rainy day. Apart from that he just looked out of the portholes – and listened to Dan Leonard and Astronaut Horfitz, of course.

After twenty-four hours or so NASA began to change its tune.

'Listen, Finn, I guess we gotta face bleep,' Leonard began. 'Things are not gonna get any betta bleep.' His tone and delivery had become terser, more hard-hitting, in proportion to the difficulty he found in getting to the point. 'What I'm driving bleep erson got on the right bus, after all. Sometimes something like bleep way out.'

'It'll take guts but that's exactly what bleep got,' Astronaut Horfitz put in. 'You saw how quick bleep John.'

Soon they were pleading with him to take the poison pill, the final solution. Malke listened cynically, as if this change of tack proved something he'd always suspected without even knowing he did. Since they couldn't control him any more they wanted to kill him. There was something ludicrously impotent about the request. Certainly it did nothing for Astronaut Horfitz's sex-appeal – her voice had become whining and monotonous.

In any case, distance, interference, static soon began to take their toll. Zoom howl wee joined bleep as forms of celestial punctuation. Leonard and Horfitz began to belch, slur, do funny voices, break off unexpectedly. The speeded-up gabble of foreign broadcasts began to intrude. Eventually the shuttle's receiver lost its fix on NASA altogether and began to pick up a broad, blurred band of signals which tended, as the days wore on, inexorably towards gibberish, a sound-jungle with clearings of silence. The distinguishable fragments gave Malke a vivid picture of the busy monotony of life on earth: a few moments of boxing commentary, a d.j.'s introduction to a country and western song, what appeared to be the news in German, somebody telling all his pals to 'keep truckin''. At one point, with sudden clarity, a warm English voice made an announcement:

. . . Radio Three, and this is Patricia Hughes in London. Our next programme is a performance, on records, of. . .

It wasn't long after this that the broadcasts became inaudible and even silence gave way to a thin continuous whine of static.

Patricia Hughes's words therefore gained something of the quality of a farewell message; that fact, and the contrast between her rich tones and the strident, cheap-skate timbre of Astronaut Horfitz, gave a retrospective poignancy to her announcement, as though she had spoken on behalf of the human race at large. Or at least its female component. Malke, still watching drearily through his porthole, realised that outer space was so austere and oppressive because it was essentially celibate – no, not celibate, neutral. A perspective that includes everything leaves no room for intercourse. He understood why, during training, he'd managed to confuse his space mission with religion and the monastic life.

Malke squirted down a roast turkey from its tube and looked out of the porthole once more at everlasting night. It was impossible to tell which of the myriad points of silver was Earth, if indeed it was still visible at all. He turned back to look wistfully at his radio receiver.

No more communications would take place. As he looked, however, Malke began to feel an odd tension developing in his chest, as if some time or other, soon or in the far future, the static would be broken once again and a further announcement made to him. He was aware of course that on an aural level the prospect was as delusive as the mirage of palm trees and water that appears to a dying man in a desert.

6

'I think I'll have one,' Pointon said suddenly, pulling Wilkins back from his reverie.

'Of course,' Wilkins replied, flicking over the waitress with the cake trolley. 'I wasn't trying to put you off. Hautbois can still run to the price of a nasty gateau or two. With as many international interests as ours, these recessions cut both ways, you know.'

Pointon silently indicated a creamy orange blob and the waitress slid her cake knife underneath and deposited it on a plate, which she put in front of him. Pointon watched the process carefully. You could just imagine him taking a forkful and then spitting it out into a bucket of sand, like one of those wine connoisseurs. Humourless so-and-so, thought Wilkins.

'I looked you up, of course, before I came here,' Pointon said, prodding his gateau carefully with the fork, as though it might go bang.

'Oh yes?'

'I found out one of your responsibilities was security. It's an interesting thought, that, isn't it?'

'Is it?'

'What I mean is, you'd have expected that a huge company like Hautbois, with a finger in every pie so to speak, would be able to run to a press officer, wouldn't you?' A sphere of cake appeared on Pointon's fork, and he ate it with a single, abrupt action, no chewing, like a goldfish swallowing an ant's egg. 'I mean how much is a security officer going to give away? Funny sort of publicity that is.'

'What you've got to bear in mind,' Wilkins said, 'is that Hautbois is not based in Manchester. All we have is a small office and an even smaller research unit. London's where the joggins is. But I'm in charge of administration up here. That's the basis of me being with you today. I'm a big fish in a small pond, I suppose you might say. I crank the handle. If you wanted to interview the washer-up, it'd be me, like as not. Security's got nothing to do with it.'

Pointon was halfway through his gateau. Wilkins was longing for a cigar. He got the pack out of his pocket, took one out, and fingered it.

'What I'm saying,' Pointon said, 'is that I don't need any flannel. I like to put a bit of the truth in my articles.'

'That's very commendable. Especially for a representative of the *Morning Sky*. You'd better not let your editor know how you feel.'

'Ha ha,' Pointon replied sourly. He was eating his gateau rapidly, greedily even, and yet maddeningly it seemed to get no smaller. Wilkins's cigar was clutched between his fingers like a drowning man's straw.

'Not a bad meal, was it?' he said, trying out his powers of suggestion. 'By Manchester standards, I mean. I feel quite pogged.'

'You what?' Pointon's unintelligent eyes narrowed shrewdly. He continued to work on the everlasting gateau with the persistence of Sisyphus.

'Ozzie term. I've spent a bit of time in the southern hemisphere, one way or another. And I've always had a soft spot for Australians, between ourselves. Stonkered's another one, meaning the same. It's like the way Arabs have got forty-seven words for camel. You have a lot of words for whatever happens to be important to you. The Tibetans have a million names for God. Pogged means full up. Eaten elegant sufficiency. To tell you the truth, I've got to the point where I'm longing to stick this cigar in my face.'

'Go ahead,' said Pointon. 'I've nearly finished.' Obstinately, though, he continued to work on his gateau until the bitter end, as a drip of water will erode a stone away.

Wilkins lit his cigar and puffed. 'It was the fuel pump gaskets.'

'You what?' repeated Pointon in disbelief.

'Yes, well, no kidding, that's the truth of it. They have them, you know, even in rocket boosters. They degenerated slightly and the resulting sludge clogged the doings up. It's as simple as that.'

'What you mean is that your fuel corroded the gaskets,' Pointon suggested.

'Not really, no, it's more the other way round. That's the way the responsibility lies. The chemical structure of the fuel and all its characteristics were made clear in advance to Fisher Thoms, the people who manufactured the gasket. We sent them a tanker-full to put in their paddling pool. That was one time when I *did* have my security hat on, let me tell you. You can't put that stuff in a poly-bag and post it. Dynamite in more ways than one. Anyway it was Fisher Thoms's obligation to produce something that would cope with our product, that's the way round it actually happened, I can assure you. Their gasket was a no-no from the beginning, they must have just tested it on the previous mixture. Engine knock wasn't in it, ha.' He took another puff at his cigar and became sincere for a moment. 'If you come back to our office afterwards, I'll let you see some of the report. Not the equations etcetera, all top-secret of course. Fat lot of good they would do you in any case, same as they do me. But you'll get the general drift.'

'If what you say is true, why are NASA introducing a new system for their next launch?'

'Because the world is full of journalists like you, sowing doubt and despondency.' He leaned forward towards Pointon. 'But I'll tell you one thing, if you write this up to make us the villains of the piece, we'll sue you through every court in Europe.' He settled back in his chair. Time to make a gesture: 'How about coffee and a cognac?'

Pointon nodded.

'When you're ready, duck,' Wilkins called across to the waitress.

While she brought the order, Wilkins thought about what came next, the difficult bit. It was a matter of balancing the

34

necessity for secrecy against the need for publicity: Pointon had already put his finger on that delicate problem.

On the one hand was the fact that Hautbois was pouring all its resources, more than all its resources, into what was virtually a one-man laboratory discreetly situated in Salford. Not into the lab itself, of course, that ticked over quite nicely on a shoe-string. It was the implications of the research in that lab which cost the money. The Project, if successful, would revolutionise not merely the company itself, but the economy of the U.K., indeed of the world as a whole. The investment in processing-plant and distribution network was on a corresponding scale.

The problem was that the bad publicity which had been generated by the space shuttle business was affecting both the resources and the credibility of the Project. It was ironic really, since the rocket fuel in question was merely a sophisticated version of a conventional product, nothing to do with the devil's brew Murgatroyd was working on. But the fate of those two astronauts had caused a world-wide trauma and had done appalling damage to the Hautbois Fuel Division. The drama had been so agonising: a few garbled messages, and then radio silence. NASA claimed they would have died peacefully but you didn't have to believe it.

On the other hand, unfortunately, was the fact that the only weapon Hautbois could pit against this disaster in public confidence was the Project; and it was the Project they were trying to defend. The devil and the deep blue sea.

The waitress fussed with coffee and brandy. Pointon had got the message that Wilkins was deliberating on something important and looked at him expectantly.

'I've got something else you might be interested in,' Wilkins said, as soon as the waitress had gone. He spoke as if he were making a difficult admission. 'I've got to be fairly discreet at this stage, of course.'

'Oh yes?'

'We're working on a major development. A very big Project.'

'Everybody knows Hautbois have got a project,' Pointon said, possibly improvising.

'Well, you'll know that much more than anybody else, because you'll know that the Project is in our Fuels Division.'

'What is it, another mix for space engines?' Sarcasm, possibly, it was hard to tell.

'Good God no. That space business was never more than a pimple. We only went into it in the first place for the sake of good publicity, ha ha, sick joke. We ended up as popular as a mastectomy surgeon in a bunny club. No, this is a new kind of fuel altogether, not just a variation on the old theme.'

Pointon swilled his brandy round while he took this in. 'You mean like solar heating?' he asked finally.

Wilkins almost exhaled his coffee. 'Solar heating, heavens above! Solar heat provides about as much transferable energy as a vicar's dick, excuse my French. No, this is the real thing, something you can use like petrol. We're going to be able to manufacture it in unlimited quantities, without having to use oil, and at almost no expense. How does that grab you?'

'Jesus,' said Pointon. 'What's it made of?'

'Don't expect me to open my mouth and hang myself. But I will tell you this, it's a biological process.'

'But surely —'

'Watch this space, that's what you lot say, isn't it?'

'But we can't start a story like that without following it up. When will we know something more?'

'Not long,' said Wilkins. He glanced towards the next table where their waitress was bending over a customer. 'A year at most.'

'A *year*! That's a lifetime in the newspaper business.'

'Really? Short-lived lot, aren't you?'

The waitress's form was fuzzy against the grey oblong of the window, dim Manchester light curling round her outline like soft hair or ruffled material. Not a typical observation on the part of Wilkins: he was horribly practical and pragmatic as a rule, more horrible than he even knew, although he took a pride in it.

The last thought that ever came into his mind was also strangely imaginative. It was: the window's screaming.

He watched it in slow-motion, beginning as a sharp oh and extending outwards into square yards of newly-frosted glass. The sound in point of fact wasn't exactly a scream, more a high-pitched rapid creaking as every splinter of glass rubbed irritably against the ones around it. And then the window wasn't there any more.

7

Superintendent Rostris was a thin depressed man who sat hunched like a question mark behind his desk. He suffered from chronic flatulence, and while he spoke to Inspector Chapman he emitted a series of small controlled farts to which he listened intently, as if they were coming from somewhere else.

'Did you shut him up?' he asked Chapman, who had come in to report.

'God, no, he's not a suspect.'

'His big mouth, I mean.'

'Oh yes, I suppose so, for what it's worth.'

'It might be worth an open and shut case for you.'

'Yes.'

'Squeezed him dry first, of course.'

'For heaven's sake, give me credit.'

Pointon hadn't particularly welcomed the squeezing process, as it happened. The pips squeaked noisily.

'I've told you the bit that counts,' he'd declared. 'The rest's just chit-chat.'

'I want to hear every last word. Every chit, every chat. All the jokes, even,' Chapman had answered him.

'If I miss my deadline —'

'You've already done that bit.'

'Jokes, you said. Jokes, Jesus Christ, jokes. You don't know what you're asking. Listen to this, "What's the difference between a virgin and a light-bulb?" he asks. "I don't know," I say. "You can unscrew a light-bulb," he says. "You what?" I say, not realising that was it. "I'm not sure that works on this side of the Atlantic," he says. "I heard it in America. They have screw-in light-bulbs over there. We have those sort of spring-loaded fitments, don't we?" Then he suddenly says, "Ha, ha, that's a good one that is, spring-loaded fitments." A laugh a minute, it was his way of softening me up, a bit like hitting a steak with a mallet.'

'You prefer a sophisticated approach, then.'

'I don't like crap,' Pointon agreed.

'High standards, the *Morning Sky*.'

'You and all,' Pointon said wearily.

'I want jokes, the lot.'

'I can't remember everything. I'll be here for hours.'

'You're a reporter, report.'

'There's such a thing as editing.'

'Leave the editing to us.'

In the gaps, while Chapman fiddled with his written report, Pointon roughed out the story as it ought to be told.

Mr Wilkins leaned confidentially over the table,

no, no, open with a splash, give the action, don't scene-set. Also, bear in mind the advice of Jock Griswold, figure from the past, editor of the *Rotherham Charger*: 'If you were there, you reacted. If you reacted, let's have the reaction, good and strong. Show you're a human being.'

I screamed with terror,

no, human being not ponce,

I cried out in horror as a quiet business lunch turned into a nightmare before my very eyes.

'Very eyes'? For Christ's sake, who has very eyes? You either have eyes or you don't have eyes.

Eyes.

Hang on,

a bloody nightmare,

make them understand it's a crunch item, not a three-line whip. A three-line whip was a basically boring news story which had been worked up till it sounded interesting. Given the kiss of life. A crunch item, Jock would say, was called a crunch item because it had bite.

I had been invited,

hang on, perhaps better not get bogged down in details yet, need some way of anchoring the 'bloody nightmare' to reality.

It had been a luxury meal,

earn a few noshes sur la maison,

but for my companion death was the final course.

A touch of your Agathas. Why not, sells like hot cakes.

Mr Wilkins had invited me to lunch to give me details of, exclusive details of, his company's latest earth-shattering project.

O.K., O.K., there weren't any details, but nobody would notice, not now there was a story: Wilkins's death was the detail.

He took a sip of his cognac,

no,

brandy,

we're in prolesville remember,

and then there was a huge smashing sound as the restaurant window fell into a million pieces. A waitress who came within an inch of being struck by the bullet screamed,

she cried out 'Shit!' as a matter of fact but there was a sort of scream in her tone,

and fainted to the floor,

that she did do, just like somebody acting a faint, with that soft fall so that they don't damage themselves on impact, but actually they discovered she really was out cold,

40

and Mr Wilkins keeled over, shot in the head by an unknown assassin,

wait, the late lamented wasn't a politician or a diplomat,

unknown killer.

He wondered what Wilkins would think. A paucity of jokes, of course, and possibly of the truth also. But you had to be realistic. If he told it how it was, people would think he was making it up: you had to talk their language. And what good would it do poor Mr Wilkins to describe how he suddenly took off backwards and shot across the room, bizarre as a penguin in flight, to end up sitting, dead, against the far wall?

'I'm afraid you won't be able to mention what Wilkins told you,' Chapman said, putting his pen down.

'He told me damn all.'

'I mean about the fuel.'

'Oh no!' Pointon sat in stunned silence. The next paragraph had been bubbling up, speculative in tone of course, something around the theme of *the answer lies in the oil*. The *Sky* ought to erect *some* kind of tombstone over the grave of a dead comedian.

'It'll deepen the mystery,' Chapman pointed out. He had very dark eyes which always made him look as if he'd been overworking, although they'd presumably be exactly as dark if he'd just come back from a fortnight in St Tropez. His face though was creased and leathery: it showed his age. 'Intrigue your readers,' he concluded.

'I don't have to take orders from you,' Pointon said. 'It's not a police state. Yet.'

'True. But our relationship is based on mutual co-operation, isn't it, Mr Pointon?'

Pointon knew well enough what he was driving at. As northern representative of a national newspaper he had to be a Jack of all trades, and most of them took him into Police

Headquarters sooner or later. If the police blackballed him, he'd be finished.

'We'll let you know in good time when you can take the lid off,' Chapman went on. 'Well before any other rag can get its hands on it.'

'What a world we live in,' Pointon said bitterly, as he left. He cheered up a little in the corridor below when he saw a ravishing young policewoman hurrying into the Ladies. She gave him a moment of disinterested pleasure, the sort a garden-lover might feel coming across a well-tended window-box in some dismal office where he had to transact his business.

'He wasn't very happy about it,' Chapman told Rostris.

'We're not in business to make reporters happy. I sometimes think they're more our natural enemies than criminals are. You know my philosophy about police work. Keep it pure and simple, that's what I believe in. This Wilkins invites a reporter to lunch to tell him that his company have invented something to take the place of oil, and promptly gets bumped off. The chances are he's not too popular with some of the leading oil companies. Dirty business anyway, from all accounts. I always like to start from square one. Don't misunderstand me, it's your case of course.'

'What about this letter we got this morning, telling us something was going to happen today?'

'Oh yes, what was it? The Green Something. Might as well be the Green Slime, for all I know about it.'

'The Green Principle.'

'We get that sort of claptrap every day, full of vague threats, you know that. It's like reading your horoscope.' The series of individually formed farts had given way to a continuous hissing, like steam in an old-fashioned central-heating system. Chapman got the impression Rostris was taking such an aggressive interest in the case, spinning out what he had to say, in an attempt to drown the sound. 'It'll tell you you're going to be cheerful or depressed or something, and somebody somewhere always is. But they always avoid saying you're going to win the pools or be run over by a bus. But some people do,' he concluded. 'Or are,' he added. The sibilance, despite his efforts, overlapped what he had to say, and left him no choice but to lay claim to it. 'Do you know anything about ulcers?' he asked.

'No. I don't think you're supposed to drink.'

'I'm sure that's what I've got. It's always the same, isn't it? Getting promoted out of the area where the action is, never being able to get your teeth into anything. I'm sure that's what's buggering up my insides.' The hissing had died away.

'Yes,' agreed Chapman unsympathetically. He had enough on his plate without Rostris's internal difficulties.

'Anyway,' Rostris said unenthusiastically, 'you'll have to tackle it the way you think best.'

'I'll think it over at home. I said I'd be back by five. They'll ring me if anything else turns up.'

'Don't apologise,' said Rostris, suddenly almost affable. 'And give Margaret my love.'

Chapman looked at him narrowly, but there was no trace of irony or unpleasant humour on the thin, wracked countenance. Rostris was obviously still concentrating on the apparently endless goings-on in his insides.

8

Margaret splashed her arms up and down on the surface of the bathwater. If you smacked it hard enough and at just the right angle it felt almost solid, like jelly, not like water at all. Some would always come out, though, and Mikey would say, 'Stop that, Margaret, you're getting water all over the room.' 'And over my trousers,' he said also, looking at her with his blobby eyes, so that she knew he wasn't really angry, just sad again, always sad. She tried to explain to him what she was doing, but there were too many words involved. The middle one was jelly, so she contented herself with saying that.

'Jelly,' she said.

'Not now, Margaret,' he replied. The blobbiness went out of his eyes, and she looked at them carefully to see what had come in its place. A message came to her from heaven. She couldn't recognise the voice although she knew it was a voice she knew. It said 'Our Margaret's got a talent for reading people's expressions.' She didn't understand what 'expressions' meant but she knew it meant sort of eyes. She read Mikey's eyes. The left one said 'Fed' and the other one said 'up'. 'You've had your tea,' he added. 'You enjoy your bath.'

'I like shooshing water,' she explained and his eyes switched again, click. 'I'm,' clock, 'pleased.' It was because she'd said a whole thing, that always pleased him. She knew how to please Mikey, always had, especially in heaven. She couldn't do those sort of things now, she was too young, but she could still please him by getting a whole thing out, or dressing herself, or wiping her own bottom.

'Just be careful, that's all,' he said warmly. 'I don't want to change my trousers.'

She was tired of doing the word she'd now forgotten with

water anyway so she picked up her sponge and started wiping herself with it. She watched her slow-moving heavy breasts under the sponge. They'd lost their youthful zest, all right, their sparkle. No, you couldn't say that, you couldn't say tits ever exactly sparkled, there were so many things you couldn't say. But her breasts didn't poke out as much as they used to, they more hung, that was the point, you could almost feel gravity pulling at them.

'That's a good girl,' Mikey said, even more PLEASED than before AS PUNCH.

She kept looking at him out of the corner of her eyes as she wiped away at her bosom with the pleasantly coarse sponge. He settled back on the stool that he sat on while she took her daily bath, and the pleased and punch gradually faded from his eyes while he didn't notice she was looking. In their place came fed and up for a moment again and then they in turn evaporated leaving nothing at all behind except the eyes themselves. They weren't looking at anything, they were just sitting in their sockets while thoughts went on in the brain behind. That was exactly what Margaret couldn't do: think thoughts. She could still think, of course, but only when she didn't know she was thinking.

She spoke suddenly. It was like those times when she didn't want to get into the hot bath, but in fact got straight in and hesitated afterwards. Then she would think, 'But I'm here already,' and it would be all right. It was the same with speaking. If she spoke immediately it would sometimes come out without any trouble, like speaking in heaven. She asked: 'What are you thinking about, Mikey?' and the old button was pressed so accurately that he answered:

'I was wondering if it could be anything to do with ecology, love.'

'Echo-collogy?' she asked, puzzled, and his eyes went beyond fed up, beyond sad. They were dark eyes and they looked like full-stops now, indicating nothing except the end of the line.

9

'I can't see it myself,' Rostris said, his fist clenched against his stomach. 'It doesn't seem very ecological to shoot someone in a restaurant in Manchester. Reclaiming some rubbish dump would be nearer the mark.'

'I suppose so,' Chapman replied thoughtfully.

'You don't sound as if you do,' Rostris grumbled. 'Hang on a minute.' He pressed a button on a little intercom console on his desk. 'Sergeant Hopwood?' he asked.

A woman's voice, miniaturised as if to fit the tiny grid in the middle of the unit, replied: 'Yes sir?'

'What's the latest on that Middleton Road business?'

'Three dead, sir. Oh no, hold on a minute. Four dead, that's the latest information, sir.'

'Four dead? Christ Almighty, what do they think they're doing over there? They're supposed to be administering medical aid.'

'Four's the latest count I've been given,' Sergeant Hopwood replied in a neutral voice, taking no responsibility.

'What about the injured?'

'Believed to be four also, sir, all seriously. The tanker driver's only got abrasions.'

'It's a mess, Sergeant.'

'Yes sir, it is, sir.' Rather plaintively: 'I'm just telling you what's come in.'

'All right, Sergeant Hopwood. Keep me informed.'

'Yes sir. Oh, sir!'

'What is it?'

'Another one's dead, sir. A message has just come in. Five dead at the last count.'

'Hell-fire,' Rostris said, and switched his intercom off

smartly, as if to stop the rot. 'Five teenagers dead,' he explained to Chapman. 'Usual bloody silly situation, van packed with drunk kids coming home from a party. Took that narrow bridge on the Middleton road at ninety miles an hour, I have no doubt. Slap into a tanker.'

Chapman wondered if he could detect an element of gloating in his superior's tone.

'Yes,' he replied unenthusiastically. Probably just being paranoid: when you had a catastrophe of your own you became somewhat protective towards those of other people.

'Anyway,' Rostris said, 'back to the matter in hand.'

'Well, what about "green?" ' Chapman suggested.

'What about it?'

'It's a suggestive colour, isn't it?'

'Is it? It suggests being seasick to me.'

'You could say a green principle is believing in nature and whatnot.'

'You could, you could.' Rostris's expression didn't change – it was acidic enough to start with – but the top part of his body bent over his desk, as a metal rod might bend, with the slowness of strain. Then there was an abrupt noise, like a distant gunshot, and he relaxed. 'Shit,' he said, as if in explanation, and moved a little more upright. He never sat up straight: his body always seemed to be describing some sort of orbit round its chronic misery.

'You ought to get yourself looked at,' Chapman said.

'I've been to the quack. He told me to stop worrying so much and take some indigestion tablets.'

'See a specialist then.'

'Yes,' Rostris said uninterestedly. 'I've never been much interested in nature,' he went on. 'We used to have a nature table at school. You know, you had to bring in a bag of shells or a squashed hedgehog or something, to put on display. That's about as far as my interest ever went. I might be old-fashioned but I'm a great believer in motive. People don't kill each other because of principles, green or otherwise.'

'What about the IRA?' Chapman asked. 'They do.'

'For heaven's sake, the IRA wouldn't touch those ecology creeps with a barge-pole.'

'I suppose not,' Chapman conceded. 'But there were those people who picked some soil with anthrax in it from that polluted Scottish island, and went around leaving it on park benches and places.'

'But nobody was daft enough to sit on it, were they? Or eat it or whatever you have to do. That proves my point, they couldn't knock the skin off a rice pudding.'

'I had a word with Pointon this morning,' Chapman continued obstinately. 'The *Morning Sky* did an in-depth article on the Hautbois Company a few months back. All about how they were clearing away millions of square miles of Brazilian jungle to get at the minerals that are deposited underneath. The trees there make most of the earth's oxygen apparently. The *Sky* claimed we'd all be suffocated to death in a few years.'

'The *Sky*'s a rag.'

'It might be true, for all we know about it. It needled Hautbois enough to run a full-page ad a couple of weeks later. Pointon gave me a copy of it.'

He took the paper out of his briefcase and passed it across to Rostris.

The headline read: HAUTBOIS OPENS UP THE WORLD.

Below it was a photograph of an anonymous-looking stretch of jungle; below that another photograph, this time of a field of some sort of tropical crop, with a pot-bellied native standing in the middle of it and looking pleased with life. Underneath was a short explanation:

Hautbois is proud to assist the Government of Brazil in opening up large areas of hitherto intractable Amazon forest and converting it into a useful and habitable landscape. Mineral utilisation and agricultural development are providing a decent way of life for many of the world's poorest people. The resources thus made available will finance education, the eradication of disease, and a secure future for tens of thousands of people who up till now could hope for little else than basic survival.

'I said to him,' Chapman explained, 'how can you publish this sort of rubbish if you're already supposed to have taken the lid off the organisation? He said it was to do with free speech. He also said he thought Wilkins had decided to confide in the *Sky* because of all the bad publicity it had given Hautbois. So they got advertising revenue *and* a scoop out of it. Well, nearly a scoop. It's a funny way of working.'

'That's what I mean. I'm not interested in funny ways of working.' Rostris gave Chapman a sour look. 'I believe in routine, I do. Your case, of course.'

There was a buzz from his desk console, and he pressed it savagely.

'Jesus Christ!' he almost shouted.

There was a baffled silence from the other end.

'I'm in conference,' Rostris explained. 'Surely I could be left for a minute?'

'I thought you'd want to know,' Sergeant Hopwood explained in a martyred voice. 'Another one's died.'

'No,' Rostris said in a suddenly quiet, almost resigned voice.

Sergeant Hopwood was new to HQ, and as it happened, Chapman hadn't yet met her. It was obvious though that she was someone with a knack of getting on the wrong side of Rostris.

10

As Michael Chapman watched his wife Margaret going her way about the sitting-room on Sunday morning, he suddenly realised he kept thinking of her as acting. He knew she wasn't, of course, but he couldn't stop imagining she was. He had no choice, she was a middle-aged woman behaving like a two-and-a-half-stone three-year-old: how *else* to look at her?

'Would you like to cut out?' he asked.

She didn't reply or even seem to notice, but lumbered over to her pile of bricks by the fireguard. She had so much else wrong with her, perhaps her ears had stopped working as well.

The idea reminded him of a car his father had bought just after the war, a 1930s Morgan three-wheeler which they'd nicknamed Eric the Relic. It was open-topped, with the single wheel at the back, and it made a harsh stuttering roar like a motor-bike – in fact, since there was no reverse gear it was actually classified as one. Things happened to Eric. Once his father put his foot on the clutch and it disappeared through the floor; another time a headlamp fell off and was returned by a sarcastic lorry-driver who made various remarks about prams belonging on the pavement. They didn't care: the more Eric broke down, the more affection they felt for it. Not working properly made it seem human. Funnily enough, now Margaret didn't work properly she seemed like a machine.

She had begun scrabbling with the bricks. He couldn't face having them all over the floor. Mrs Hodnet didn't come on Sundays so he had to cook the food *and* keep the house afloat. It was good of Rostris to make sure he always had Sundays off, but the consequence was weekly purgatory.

'Margaret, would you like to do some cutting out at the table?' he asked loudly.

This time he got through. She dropped her bricks and turned towards him. She ran her fingers through her hair and for a golden second she looked like a harassed housewife.

'With . . .' she began, and stopped immediately, lost for the word.

'Yes, with scissors,' he said.

'Yes. Pongy snappers,' she replied.

She often replaced normal speech with semi-nonsensical dream words. They tended to spark off in Chapman a strange kind of false memory of experiences his marriage had lacked: babyhood, nappies, smeared turd, talc and bawling. There was something perverse about the fact that when a woman in her early fifties began behaving like a toddler they put it down to premature old age: senile dementia was one of the terms the consultant used.

'You sit at the table and I'll get the scissors,' he told her.

He went to her toy-cupboard and took out a pile of old Christmas cards and a pair of round-ended children's scissors.

'Here you are,' he said, putting them in front of her. 'What do you say?'

'Fank you,' she replied obediently, in a loud sing-song voice.

She put her finger and thumb through the scissor holes and picked up a Christmas card. It featured a robin on a fence-post. The latter had a blob of tinsel on the top of it to highlight the snow.

'Pretty ca-ard,' she said. Her pronunciation was still exaggeratedly musical – she sounded like a tasteless individual making fun of imbeciles.

'Yes dear,' he replied.

She put the card between the scissor blades, and closed them. The card bent. She tried again, and again. The scissors were a bit tricky to use, obviously, because they were so blunt, but she'd found the cutting-point without much trouble a week ago. Now it was beyond her.

He watched her struggle with the card, moon-faced, tongue poking out with concentration. It was funny how her looks had gone immediately her features lost the underlying discipline of intelligence. She wouldn't cut again. Like Merlin, she grew backwards, day by day.

'Shall we play at something else?' he asked.

She looked up at him and for a fraction there was in her eyes, not intelligence certainly, but awareness, as though she were saying to him: 'It's still me, you know. I can't help all this stupidity that's got in the way.'

Chapman thought to himself, illness isn't a reflection of your personality, I mustn't forget. What about Rostris's indigestion, he then wondered. Even that?

'What would you like to play with now?' he asked.

'Lorry,' she replied.

He helped her off the chair, and then got her big plastic lorry out of the cupboard, remembering as he did how horrible it had been to buy it, along with her other toys. It had made him feel exposed and vulnerable, like buying a sex-aid. Nevertheless he'd had an intuition she needed toys, even though she hadn't asked for them, just as in the old days he'd had an instinct about when she was due for a little present, a bunch of flowers or some underclothes. They'd both been thoughtful about each other, in the way couples without children often are.

When he brought the toys home she looked at them in silence, with rapt joy. He'd tiptoed to the lavatory and was sick.

The telephone rang as he passed her the lorry and she jumped so it fell out of her grasp. Perhaps in her present state she'd never heard the telephone before.

'It's all right,' he said. 'It's the telephone. I'll answer it. You play with your lorry.'

She relaxed in instant trust, and squatted on the floor to play. He went into the hall and picked up the receiver.

'Hello,' said the voice at the other end, 'it's Rostris.'

'Hello,' Chapman replied grudgingly.

'Sorry to bother you at home. Margaret O.K.?'

'Yes.' What else could you say?

'It's just those Green Principle pests have sent a letter to the *Morning Sky*. Must have pushed it through the letterbox overnight, since it's a Sunday. That man Pointon came rushing round with it, big fat smile on his face, trying to butter us up. It turns out to be strictly drivel, luckily. No mention of oil. I imagine it's inspired by all that Brazil business you were talking about. Obviously just trying to jump on the bandwagon, they're too far round the bend to actually *do* anything off their own bat. At one point they describe themselves as antibodies, would you believe?'

'Anti-bodies?'

'I tried to persuade Pointon to do a big feature on it, to give the readers something to chew on while you're getting on with the case, but he didn't fall for it. After that Yorkshire Ripper business the press are getting canny about confessions. Shit!' The exclamation was ambivalent: irritation at the shrewdness of the press, onset of wind. 'Anyway,' he went on, 'I suppose you ought to have a look at it. I'll have a xerox taken and get someone to bring it over to you. The original had better go straight to Forensic.'

'Oh,' Chapman said. He was about to object but then he remembered that it was he who had favoured the Green Principle in the first place. Rostris, routine Rostris, was only going through the motions like a puppet on a string. Chapman would be cutting off his own nose if he turned down the opportunity to get a prompt look at that statement. And there was no way he could go to the station this afternoon. 'Oh all right,' he concluded after a pause. 'Thank you very much.'

11

Chapman was determined to let whichever constable they sent round with the document get no further than his front door. There would be no cup of tea, even though it was raining. Margaret wasn't for public display. He had a fear of loud ho-hos echoing round the police canteen later, even worse, expressions of sympathy, tut-tut, shake of the head, what a thing to happen, what a world, what a wife to be saddled with.

He knew his motive. He had so many motives these days he was becoming an expert on them. He wasn't trying to protect Margaret – she didn't need protection, she was impervious. He was trying to protect himself.

It was only natural, if that was any excuse. Everybody hated to admit they'd failed an exam, bought a dud car, married a dud wife. . . He was thinking of her as a piece of broken-down machinery again.

He looked at her scrabbling about on the floor with her big yellow plastic lorry. If he didn't think of her in that way he'd start howling with pity on the spot.

The doorbell rang.

Margaret looked up and cornered her eyes like a frightened horse about to bolt. Presumably she'd never heard the doorbell before either.

'It's all right, Margaret, only the front door. I'll answer it.'

Once again, the reassurance was immediate, and she turned back to her lorry. It made his heart sink, the way she took his word for everything. When she could make out what the word meant, that was.

He went through to the hallway and opened his front door the merest crack, as though he expected the constable to burst straight in in his eagerness to see the peepshow.

It wasn't a constable, it was a sergeant. And it wasn't a policeman, it was a policewoman, the most beautiful policewoman Chapman had ever seen. He had a glimpse of rose-pink cheeks, bizarrely delicate by contrast with the coarse gaberdine of her policewoman's raincoat, of bright brown curls coming from under her hat. She was in limbo, suspended in the rain, waiting, her face utterly relaxed.

She gave a little jump as she noticed him, a very different one from Margaret's raw expressions of surprise and fear. Her jump was controlled, amused, almost flirtatious. Chapman opened his door the proper distance, but stood squarely in the gap.

'You caught me on the hop,' she exclaimed. She had a light, amused voice. 'I was miles away. I'm Sergeant Hopwood.'

'Yes,' he agreed, suddenly confused. 'I don't think I've met you. Oh yes I have. No I haven't, I know what, I heard you on the intercom talking to the Super.'

'That was me. I'm handling internal communications for the time being.'

'You were reporting on that accident.'

'Wasn't it dreadful? There were seven killed at the final count. They say it's the worst accident in Greater Manchester for nearly ten years. I feel sorry for the poor people who had to clear up the mess.'

'Yes.'

There was a pause.

'I've got a copy of that document,' she said. 'The thing that Mr Pointon brought in.'

'Thank you,' Chapman said, putting out his hand. She passed him a large beige envelope she was carrying.

'Can I come in a minute?' she asked.

He flipped open the envelope and felt the pages inside. There were five or six sheets.

'Look,' he replied. 'It's quite long. I'd like to spend some time studying it.'

'It's not that. There's something I want to talk to you about.'

The twists life takes, he thought. Here I am, standing on my doorstep, trying to keep a girl who looks like that, *out*.

'Well, I've got a. . . my wife's in there,' was all he could dredge up.

'It's this bally rain. Just for a moment. There's something I want to tell you.'

'Come in, then,' said Chapman, giving up. He pushed the door open with his backside, and let her walk past him.

As he showed Sergeant Hopwood into the sitting-room Margaret looked up from her lorry in alarm. No doubt it was the first time she'd ever seen a policewoman. Everything she saw was for the first time.

Suddenly bitter, he remembered one of the late Mr Wilkins's jokes, as retold by Pointon. It concerned screwing virgins and light-bulbs. Wrong, he realised now: you could become a virgin again. All you had to do was contract senile dementia and everything you experienced was for the first time.

'It's all right, Margaret, this lady's come to see us.'

'Hello, Mrs Chapman,' Sergeant Hopwood said. Chapman squirmed – it seemed so close to mockery, using a grown-up address to a woman who was playing with her toys on the floor. And he shared in the name.

'Call her Margaret,' he said. 'It only confuses her.'

'Hello, Margaret.' Sergeant Hopwood said. Her tone was unaffectedly nice, not in the least patronising. Chapman wanted to tell her that Margaret hadn't always been like that, but he felt ashamed of admitting his shame.

'Anyway,' Sergeant Hopwood went on, turning to him. 'What I wanted to say was there's a man at the station asking for you. Or at least, asking for the officer in charge of the Wilkins case. He's very anxious.'

'Have you told Rostris about him?' he asked.

'That cunt,' she replied unexpectedly, a policewoman despite her looks. 'This bloke would run off, given half the chance. He needs to be handled carefully. It could be a confession for all I know, but we've got nothing on him. He's only got to open the door and leave. I told him I'd fetch you.'

'But I can't come in,' Chapman said aghast. 'I can't leave Margaret.'

'I'll look after her while you're gone,' Sergeant Hopwood replied briskly. 'Don't you worry about her.' She turned to Margaret: 'We'll be all right, won't we, Margaret? We'll have a good time together.'

Margaret, catching the confidence of her tone, nodded happily.

It had to be said, Chapman knew that, but it was hard, hard, to bring himself to say it: 'You don't understand, she might, she might —' he groped.

'That's all right,' the girl said. 'I can cope, I promise.'

Chapman felt like bursting into tears of relief, although it was hard to say exactly why. Perhaps it was because the girl's attitude implied that there was nothing so outlandish about the goings-on in his house after all, that Margaret hadn't taken him entirely beyond the scope of the human race. The girl appeared quite willing to enter into areas previously occupied solely by himself and Mrs Hodnet.

12

The man sat with his head slanted back and resting against the pockmarked plaster of the police station wall. His mouth was open slightly and his eyes were shut. Chapman guessed he was in that sort of imitation sleep into which you fall when you have to wait for a long time. He was probably perfectly aware of being looked at; but Chapman had a good look all the same.

The man had pink, stretched skin, rather lizard-like, with blood points on his cheeks where he'd shaved. Although he was only about the mid-thirties, his veins were near the surface and the sides of his sharp nose were covered in a lacy web. His short thinning hair was somewhere between grey and brown, no colour at all really, except that it wasn't colourless either – neutral hair. He was nicely dressed in a grey suit, white shirt, blue tie. Something in the combination of expensive clothes and spiky face suggested he was a pain in the neck, and Chapman looked at him without enthusiasm.

'Yes?' he asked abruptly.

The man opened his eyes with quite a convincing start and blinked up at him.

'I'm Inspector Chapman. I believe you want to speak to me.'

'Indeed yes,' the man replied fussily, and rose to his feet. 'My name's Manley, Anthony Manley.' He offered his hand, which Chapman dutifully shook. 'I'm a solicitor,' he added.

'That's not a crime.' Manley's hand felt as Chapman expected somehow, warm but dry, the sort of surface that would erupt into eczema or crack with chilblains at the slightest provocation. It was clingy, also. Chapman's own hand began to itch at the contact, and he pulled away.

'Perhaps it ought to be,' he finished.

'Oh, ha ha, yes,' Manley said without amusement. 'I don't think you policemen can talk.'

'I suppose not. I don't think we've met before, Mr Manley.'

'I don't have many dealings with the criminal side of things. I do conveyancing mostly.'

'I see. Well, how can I help you, sir?' Chapman was aware of being unpleasantly polite, but this was such a waste of time. Unlike Rostris he was a policeman who followed his instincts, and he had guessed immediately that Manley suffered from a kind of crime equivalent of hypochondria, converting trivial incidents or arbitrary bric-à-brac into conspiracies or clues. In any case, it was Manley's fault that the most delectable officer in the whole of the Greater Manchester constabulary was babysitting for Chapman's wife, perhaps at this very moment cleaning her up.

'It's about the murder the other day in that restaurant in Prince Street.'

'So I understand. The Wilkins case.'

'Yes. Could we go somewhere more private to discuss it?' Suiting action to word, Manley had dropped his voice to an ingratiating whisper. Chapman followed his gaze to Sergeant Stebbings, bent over paperwork at the reception desk, and shrugged his shoulders.

'All right, all right,' he said, leading the way to his own small office.

It was demoralising looking across the desk into Inspector Chapman's black irises, rather like looking down the barrels of a couple of rifles, the view the victim of a firing squad might get. Except of course that they always blindfolded you. Odd, the thoughtfulness of that, wanting to spare somebody's feelings when you were just about to fire bullets into them.

This train of thought reminded Manley of one of his favourite texts, George Orwell's essay 'A Hanging', in which the condemned man is described stepping round a puddle on the way to the gallows. Presumably it was just as unpleasant getting your feet wet when you were going to be dead in half a minute as at any other time. But the triviality of the detail reminded you of what an extreme thing it was to be killed. Manley had been very sensitive to that fact for the whole of his adult life, and what he had witnessed a few days ago had heightened his sensitivity to an almost unbearable extent.

Nevertheless a glance at Chapman's harsh, self-preoccupied face made him realise he'd been right to hesitate before coming here. He should perhaps have hesitated indefinitely. The story he had to tell was too strange and unlikely to be exposed to that black stare: in its starkness and surrealism it had the privacy of a dream.

He had been walking down Prince Street at lunch-time last Wednesday. On days when he managed to avoid a business-lunch he made a bit of a fetish about getting some fresh air and exercise.

Prince Street, despite the grand name, was a bit of a mess, like so many streets on the north side of Manchester town centre. Some of the original terraced shops survived, although a number of these were empty. Great sections had been pulled down, however, to be replaced by new office buildings, car parks, or nothing at all, just patches of waste land covered in bits of masonry, rusty tins and tough-looking functional grass. Although so uncared-for, the street was still an important part of town, and even at lunch-time the pavements were quite lively with shoppers and businessmen. And then it all went still.

Manley had just taken a glance at the Regency Restaurant on the other side of the road and was congratulating himself that he wasn't inside, stuffing. He turned back into an intense and unnatural quietude which had descended on the street in the interim.

He'd gone through a similar experience before. He was once in a crowded bar talking to a man he didn't know particularly well. For some reason, perhaps in fact in order to establish a friendship, he decided to confide to him certain domestic details he'd never revealed to anyone before. He had to raise his voice because of the hubbub of noise all round them. Just as he reached the nub of the matter the whole pub became abruptly silent. His details dropped appallingly into public view.

This time however the outbreak of silence led to the reverse effect, not public but private – a privacy so intense as to be ghostly, if you can have lunch-time ghosts. The passersby seemed to have been frozen in mid-chat, in mid-stride.

A fat man was waddling towards him along the pavement. It was a grey Manchester noon, with the sun gleaming through cloud, and the fat man looked an incongruously tropical figure, dressed as he was in a pale, baggy, light-weight suit. Manley, who took a pride in dressing reasonably, had often wondered how it was that fat people so frequently managed to buy clothes that were too big even for them.

As he watched, the man skipped with unexpected agility into the doorway of a disused shop, opened a leather briefcase he was carrying, took out the butt and barrel of a rifle, screwed the two together, raised it to his shoulder and aimed across the road. There was a sharp spitting sound, followed immediately by the earsplitting crash of a disintegrating window. At that moment everyone seemed to come alive again. A man threw himself to the ground, somebody screamed, most people span round to face the gaping restaurant. No one, though, seemed to have the sense to look in the direction from which the shot came – except Manley of course.

The time scales were reversed now: the street was busy, the fat man was still. Or at least, not still but certainly calm and methodical. Manley watched as he unscrewed his weapon, replaced the parts in his briefcase, fastened the flap, and then without a backward glance continued on his plodding way along the street. He walked right past Manley, who could have reached out and touched him.

Manley didn't though, he stood completely still and let the fat man go past, belly wobbling, thighs flopping over each other, buttocks locked together under pressure from waist and legs. What could he do or say? Place his hand on the man's shoulder, announce that he was making a citizen's arrest? How could you undertake something so public, straight from cold? The action would be incongruously formal, stemming as it did from an essentially secret experience. Also suicidal, of course.

As soon as the fat man disappeared round the corner normality reasserted itself – at least, the normality you'd expect when somebody's been shot. People fussed around the restaurant, several women cried openly in the street, police cars, ambulances, inexplicably fire engines, finally appeared on the scene.

Manley stood in his place opposite the restaurant watching everything that went on.

He was fascinated by the fact that the plate glass had been completely destroyed by the impact of the bullet. He would have expected it to pass straight through, leaving a tiny hole surrounded by a small frosted aureola. Manley was a man preoccupied by such issues as the trajectory and destination of bullets.

No doubt everything depended on the angle of impact; in such circumstances the angle was all-important. Perhaps that explained why nobody else had seen the fat man: he had inserted himself into the scene at exactly the right angle to achieve invisibility.

13

'I didn't think anyone would believe me,' Manley said in a wingeing tone.

'No,' Chapman agreed.

'Or I would have come before.'

Suddenly Chapman lost his temper at the sheer waste of time. 'You could at least have given it a try. In a case like this every little helps.' He was talking as if he believed Manley's story, which he didn't, but it was the only way he could show his anger without calling him a liar.

'It wasn't a little. I saw the whole thing.'

I give up, thought Chapman. He wondered if WPS Hopwood would have the sense to give Margaret a sandwich. She had her main meal in the middle of the day, school-dinner style, but would need a little something as the afternoon wore on.

'And what,' Chapman asked, 'made you change your mind?'

'Oh, I don't know,' Manley said evasively. He crossed his legs and looked down to inspect his highly polished shoes. Foot mittens rather, the leather was so soft and fine. 'I realised I had a responsibility.'

'Being a solicitor, you mean?'

'Good lord no.' Manley had looked up in genuine surprise. 'That's neither here nor there. I'm talking about a matter of principle.'

That was a word Chapman had heard before. 'And what principle in particular?'

'When all's said and done, of being on the side of the Wilkinses of this world.'

Chapman thought for a moment of the Wilkinses of this

world. From what he had learned from Pointon, they were not necessarily a prepossessing bunch. 'And what do you know about the late Mr Wilkins?'

'There's only one thing I *have* to know. He was a victim.'

'I see.' There were times in an interrogation when it would be nice to whimper. 'Can you describe this man to me?' Chapman asked wearily. 'The Fat Man, I mean.'

'There wouldn't be much point in coming here if I couldn't, would there?'

'I suppose not.'

'He was quite tall, getting on for six feet, I should think. He was a big man all over. I expect he weighed seventeen stone. He was dressed in a very light-weight suit, fawn. Expensive, probably, but it didn't fit him very well. He was bald, with one of those shiny heads.'

The last detail had suddenly come into his mind with peculiar vividness. With more vividness than the original impression, since he couldn't remember noticing it before. The sky had been overcast but with a sort of pearly light, and a small circle glowed on the top of the Fat Man's head, as though his scalp had the property of drawing an image of the sun out of the clouds.

For a second Manley wondered if the picture was *too* vivid; if he was experiencing a sort of retrospective hallucination.

No. He mustn't let Chapman demoralise him, shake his confidence. Pig.

'That's very helpful, Mr Manley.'

'Don't you —? I don't know. Get somebody to draw a picture?'

'I don't think that's necessary at this stage.'

'I see.' Manley looked long at Chapman. He *did* see. It was Chapman's dark eyes which were blind. Manley got up to leave. Just as he was turning away, Chapman spoke.

'Mr Manley, do you mind if I ask you something? Are you married?'

'What? For heaven's sake!'

Manley's exposed veins reddened further with indignation.

His facial skin was stretched so tight that you could imagine it abruptly shedding, like a snake's. Underneath would be goodness-knew-what, the absolute essence of being put upon.

But then the moment of indignation gave way to his characteristic whining: 'Let's say I *was* married, if you must know. What my private life's got to do with the murder of Mr Wilkins, I have no idea.'

'Just routine, Mr Manley.'

'Really?'

'Most of what we do is routine in this place. Anyway, I'll be in touch about developments. Could you leave your address with the desk sergeant on the way out?'

They shook hands again, Manley's as unpleasant to the touch as before. There was a quality of dehydration, like shaking hands with a mummy.

As soon as Manley had gone, that word came back into Chapman's mind. Mummy. Manley might not have a wife any longer, but he would probably have a mother. And a father, for that matter. Frankly or unintentionally, they would be sure to shed some light on their son's mental state.

Meanwhile he must be getting back to Margaret – and to Sergeant Hopwood. He was just about to go when the door opened and Rostris poked his head around it.

'What —?' Rostris began and farted simultaneously in surprise and indignation. The fart was so perfectly attuned to the beginning of the question that it sounded like some brass instrument providing background. 'I thought I heard someone. What are *you* doing here on a Sunday afternoon for heaven's sake?'

'Something cropped up about that Green Principle business and I thought I'd better come in. Ser—somebody's looking after Margaret for a few minutes.'

Rostris gave him a suspicious look, as much as to say, are you sure you're not neglecting her? It was odd, and irritating, to be rebuked by such an unpleasant man. 'I see. What do you think of that statement those Green Whatsernames sent Pointon?'

It suddenly occurred to Chapman that he hadn't got round to it yet. 'Oh yes,' he replied vaguely. He sniffed to imply a nod is as good as a wink.

'Strictly gibberish, eh?'

'Interesting, though,' Chapman replied hypocritically.

'Oh well,' said Rostris, turning to go. He didn't go, though, there was obviously more he wanted to say. He turned back. 'I've just heard the latest on that accident the other day. Another one's died.'

'*Another* one? That makes eight, doesn't it, all the kids there were in the van?'

'Yes. Clean sweep.' Rostris suddenly looked embarrassed. 'Pisses you off.'

'You mustn't take it personally,' Chapman said. 'That's the way to get indigestion.'

Rostris looked at him in astonishment. 'Well thank you very much,' he said, and stalked off.

Chapman listened to his footfalls retreating down the corridor. Rostris doesn't have the monopoly on cynicism, he thought. Anyway, the advice was sound enough.

14

He was hard. That was his reputation. That's what the girls said. She never trusted those conversations, the way they chattered together like big black birds: he's driven his wife round the bend.

She'd volunteered to drop the Green Principle manifesto round out of sheer curiosity.

It wasn't true at all. If Chapman was hard, it was because he was being baked in a hot fire. He was worlds apart, for example, from that bastard Rostris. Sergeant Hopwood thought for a moment of the latter's cunning eyes, his lemon face, calculating stare. Chapman's eyes were dark, possibly with suffering. They were brownish-black eyes but his skin was dark underneath them, almost as though the irises had run. But when he was trying to warn her that Margaret might dirty herself his eyes had flashed. Sergeant Hopwood was a passionate woman herself.

He was all apologies when he came in.

'I'm sorry to have been so long. They'll be wondering what's happened to you back at the station.'

'No, no. I came on my way home.'

'Oh I see. I was wondering why you'd come in an unmarked car.'

She screwed up her eyes. 'That's because I didn't want anybody to know where I was going,' she said in a funny voice, presumably hoping to sound like Humphrey Bogart. She was too beautiful to need to imitate anybody else, there was a kind of humility in it. Particularly as she did it so badly. 'It's my own little Fiat,' she went on in her ordinary voice. 'You should know the copshop wouldn't have one like that. It won't even pass its M.O.T.'

'I expect with a bit of. . .' Suddenly he remembered: 'Margaret.'

'She's all right.' Her voice had become confidential, as if Margaret were their secret. 'She's had her tea. I made her some sandwiches. I hope that's all right.'

'That's very all right.'

In a bright brisk tone, presumably for Margaret's benefit: 'Margaret's in the kitchen, working. Come and see.'

Margaret was standing by the working surface as they went in, fiddling with some grubby-looking scraps of pastry. There was a pleasant smell of cooking coming from the stove.

'Oh, you've got something in the oven,' Chapman said, addressing the remark automatically to Margaret.

'Yes,' Sergeant Hopwood said from behind him. 'I thought, if Margaret wants to play in the kitchen I might as well get on with something too. I found some bits and pieces in your pantry and the fridge.'

'That was very nice of you.' Feeling a little awkward he turned back towards Margaret. Beautiful policewomen who cooked for you. Perhaps his sufferings were making him hallucinate. 'Did you help, Margaret?' he asked.

'Yes,' Margaret replied in her terse way. 'Bath,' she added bluntly.

'All right,' Chapman replied. He turned back to Sergeant Hopwood to explain: 'She needs to go to bed early. She likes a bath before she goes.'

'I'll give you a hand.'

'No, no,' he said, unable to bear the thought.

'Susan will,' Margaret stated, blandly disagreeing.

'It's all right,' Sergeant Hopwood assured him.

'She calls you Susan, does she?'

'Well, that's my name.'

He paused for a moment in embarrassment. They couldn't be Sergeant and Inspector while bathing his wife.

'I'm Mike,' he said finally.

'Hello, Mike.'

'She's suffering from Alzheimer's Disease.'

'Oh. Yes.'

'Premature senility.'

'Yes.'

'I wish she'd die a premature death,' he suddenly whispered, tears starting to his eyes.

'Come into the sitting-room a minute,' Susan replied, practical, unshocked. 'Margaret'll be all right.'

Margaret was in fact absorbed in her pastry for the moment, taking no notice of either of them. They went into the other room and sat down side by side on the settee. Susan rested her hand lightly on his wrist but neither of them spoke. It was the first moment of stillness he'd known for a year.

After a while Margaret came in and stood in front of them. She raised her hand and scratched her moony cheek, obviously trying to remember what she'd come to say.

'It's time for your bath, isn't it?' Susan suggested in a soft voice. Margaret looked down at her gratefully as the word rang a bell in the confusion of her mind.

'Bath,' she repeated confidentially.

'All right then,' said Mike, and they all went upstairs for her bath.

Margaret looked enormous, naked in the water. Because it felt so much that he and Susan were parents, bathing their daughter, Margaret's sexual parts, her breasts and pubic clump, seemed comically exaggerated, like a seaside postcard. For a second Mike thought Margaret might be dimly aware of that too, and his anguish returned; then, suddenly, he found himself shaking with suppressed laughter. Beside him, Susan began to shake too, as if blown by the same wind. You sod, he thought of himself, but it's better than blarting. For Margaret's own sake. No doubt Susan took that line too.

After the bath he dried Margaret, put her nightdress on her, and tucked her into bed. Susan meanwhile went downstairs and made her a hot drink. Being separated calmed them both down, and Mike was as comforting and tender to Margaret as he could be; so was Susan when she came up with the Horlicks. Margaret sat up in bed and drank it obediently. Then she said 'Night, night,' and offered her cheek to be kissed. Mike kissed it; after a moment's hesitation, Susan did likewise. Then Margaret settled down snugly to sleep. They turned off the light and left the room.

Instead of going down the stairs Susan opened the next door on the landing.

'What room's this?' she asked.

'It's the spare room. At least it's the spare room in normal times. I've been sleeping here since Margaret became ill. I only wake her up otherwise.'

'I see. It's the spare room.' She eyed the bed and then turned to him. 'Do you know something?'

'No.'

'*I'm* spare.'

Her face was delicate. Almost, it seemed to shimmer before him in the evening light. I'm a man of fifty, he told himself, there's no need to react like some adolescent who can't believe a woman is going to be so good to him. My luck's in, that's all.

Luck wasn't a strong enough word. A beautiful policewoman who cooked and took you to bed with her, dreams came true after all. Why not? He'd discovered that nightmares did.

Suddenly they were both overtaken by bathroom mirth once more.

Afterwards, while they were lying in bed, Susan asked: 'Have you and Margaret any children?'

'No. I don't know why. They just never came along. It's as well, perhaps.'

'Well, they might have helped out. You wouldn't be so isolated now.'

'I don't feel isolated. Not at the moment, anyway.'

'Good,' she said quietly, and there was a pause.

'That's what makes it so strange,' he continued. 'Now that Margaret's become a child herself.'

'I suppose it must.'

'Having to treat her like that. Sometimes it seems almost perverted.'

Susan twisted round and looked at him earnestly. She was naked but her face seemed as bright and delicate as before. Often when people were naked, their faces looked inappropriate, as though the wrong head had been attached to the body. Susan, physically, was a single event.

'You mustn't think that. It's just an illness, that's what you've got to remember.'

'I know,' he said. 'That's what I keep having to tell myself. It's just an illness.'

It was a relief to bring the matter into the open, as though by describing the situation you began to resolve it. He relaxed back on to the pillow; then he sat bolt upright.

'Christ,' he said, 'I've just remembered. I haven't read that document you brought round yet. The Green Principle statement.'

'Oh well,' Susan said, 'you've had a lot on your mind in the interval.'

'Not just my mind,' he suggested.

'I expect it's a false confession anyway. There are a lot of loonies about, aren't there?'

'You sound as if you're dancing hand in hand with Rostris,' Mike said jocularly as he began to leave the bed.

For a moment there was a total change of atmosphere, as if a cold wind had blown across the room.

15

In a sense the Green Principle confession *was* a fake. But Miss Clare, its author, wasn't aware of that fact. Miss Clare was sincere enough, sincere to the core.

Always, defiantly, Miss Clare, never Ms. Neologisms didn't appeal, changing words in the hope they in turn would change reality. Like saying Black instead of Negro. What you had to do was change what it was to be Negro or Miss. Then if the word was inadequate, a new word would come. You didn't invent computers by coining the word computer. You invented the machine and then fixed on an appropriate term. Also Ms was a word without a pronunciation, and you couldn't imagine anything more bodiless, less convincing, than that. Unless you said Miz, to rhyme with Massah. Irony upon irony.

Miss Clare certainly believed the Green Principle had killed Mr Wilkins, just as it would kill Dr Murgatroyd. Two deaths were an unpleasant commitment, but they were a small price to pay to avert catastrophe. The Green Principle 'confession' was necessary precisely in order to demonstrate the logic behind that point of view.

It wasn't a position she'd always held. Only in recent years had she made the switch from the social cause of Marxism to the total one of ecology. It was a relief for her not to have to devote any more intellectual effort to justifying the waste and suffering involved in socialist class-struggle. The doctrine of evolution and the general laws of biology made the deaths of individuals inevitable in order to prevent the destruction of species.

Strange to think it was Dennis who'd brought her round to this position. The teacher taught. And by a less than gifted pupil. She remembered how mad he could make her in class. There'd been that stupid French exercise, random accents, a male cow, above all the invention of *walker*, a regular verb meaning to promenade, which had filled her with rage bordering on hysterical laughter. She'd flung the book at him with such force it disintegrated in mid-air, the pages fluttering over the classroom like confetti. He was just the normal type of nuisance, blackheady nose, unkempt hair, slight smell, but he must have had some sort of quality about him even then, to make her react so strongly.

Of course what happened to Dennis's father had been the catalyst. She remembered how Dennis had come round that evening, looming enormously out of the rainy night, strangely transformed in the two years since he'd left school from a spindly pest into a phenomenon impressive and chunky. As soon as she saw him she had a sense of an impending shift in perspective, consciousness, way of life, a cataclysm as intricate, silent and overwhelming as, say, sexual awakening. He was the unlikeliest protégé to return.

Not of course that the sexual was her arena, at whichever end, the awakening or the falling asleep. She had never succumbed and never would, despite the occasional mute accusations and suggestions from headmistresses, colleagues and most of all, pupils; especially, as far as the last were concerned, from those perennial teenage females whose brains are firmly and irrevocably located, like some simple form of monitoring equipment, a weather-gauge perhaps or theodolyte, amongst the various protuberances of their developing bodies. Nor did she subscribe to Freudian claptrap about transference or conversion of drives – that was just part of a conspiracy to deflect the concentration of the people. No, Miss Clare's intensities were strictly revolutionary; but she had occasionally to resort to analogies in order to get them across, even to herself. A true vocabulary was not yet available because the true reality had not been inaugurated.

So when Dennis had appeared on her doorstep, damp, tumescent almost, if you can have tumescence of the body as a whole, large certainly, Miss Clare experienced her equivalent of falling in love. As she showed him into her modern boxy lounge she realised that, brawny as he was, in jeans and tartan windcheater, he was desperate, ashake. From the severity of his trauma came the motivation for the Green Principle.

The process wasn't one-way of course: indeed the mutuality of their commitment was exactly what gave the sexual analogy its point. Dennis contributed his current emotions; she brought to bear her general preoccupations; together they achieved a proposal to help humanity at large by directing their attention at a specific institution, to wit the Hautbois Company, Manchester Division.

Their attention was all they *could* direct, at least for a year or two. And then one day Dennis brought a friend along, a man who suddenly made everything miraculously possible. He was, quite simply, a Mysterious Stranger, although as a matter of fact he went under the name of John Outram.

Miss Clare didn't probe John Outram too deeply. Not that she was religious – she had as much contempt for the people's opiate as for the body's anodyne; the only mysticism involved, as far as she was concerned, was that of not looking a gift horse in the mouth. She did discover, nevertheless, that he'd led a bitter emotional life, military discipline, marital desertion, ideological emptiness: a waste land but fertile, into which a seed had fallen. A seed consisting of certain information about the nature of the research in a small Salford laboratory which operated under the Hautbois aegis.

John occasionally shook or made oblique gestures. How odd that the two men who had done so much to establish the Green Principle should begin by vibrating involuntarily in her presence. Miss Clare couldn't help thinking of that ominous stasis of a Chinese jar, which seems to tremble out of sheer centrality. Of course Dennis's shivers had been strictly temporary, a product of shock and rainwater; under the influence of John in fact, he became hard as iron. John's tic remained; but there was nothing nervous about it.

Dennis contributed the original momentum; John the focus

and the means; but Miss Clare had her own part to play. She provided the rationale.

As far as she was concerned, a manifesto was the *sine qua non*. The *non* of death, the already achieved death of Mr Wilkins, the death in prospect of Dr Murgatroyd. Without a manifesto those men would be dead indeed.

To her astonishment Dennis disagreed.

'I think we've done our bit,' he said. 'We've taken the credit for it. I think we should leave it at that.'

She turned on him, the Miss Clare of the old days: 'Dennis, what do you think you're *saying*?'

'I'm saying,' he began, and then became tongue-tied again. Not like Dennis the schoolboy, though, luckily unable to articulate that French language which he ill-treated so sadistically with his pen. This was the new Dennis, seated as impressively on her *TV Times* special offer as Rodin's Thinker, taciturn as a Hemingway hero, pondering the dilemma of ecological assassination with Sartrean commitment.

John fumbled towards his cup and saucer on the coffee table. 'We've got to say what we stand for,' he affirmed, to Miss Clare's relief. 'The whole thing becomes pointless if we don't.' He finally succeeded in picking up his cup which immediately began to clatter quietly on its saucer.

For some reason the sound made Miss Clare think of those clockwork false teeth which you could buy in joke shops and she had to stifle a laugh. How strange, to want to giggle at a moment like this. And yet of course in the classroom it was always at the most serious part of the lesson that some child would lose control. The same thing, she remembered from her own childhood, happened in church.

'Anyway,' she said, pulling herself together, 'if we don't make our reasons plain we won't come out of the Wilkins phase cleanly. In which case I for one will vote to cancel Murgatroyd.'

'I'm saying,' Dennis continued doggedly, 'that the action spoke for itself. That's the whole point.' He paused again. 'A revolution has a language of its own,' he concluded.

She marvelled at how he was able to say such a thing. It was so aphoristic it actually sounded pretentious, yet Dennis had worked it out for himself, unaided by any sort of imagination or much intelligence. Perhaps revolution did raise one's consciousness.

Nevertheless, she was still the teacher.

'I'm sorry, Dennis, the manifesto's already written. Our reasons *must* be spelled out. For heaven's sake, after all my years as a schoolteacher, if I believe in anything I believe in reasons.'

In the end they compromised. Dennis modified her manifesto, abbreviating whole passages of the careful document into what he himself was the first to admit was 'plug-ugly' writing.

16

THE GREEN PRINCIPLE:
A STATEMENT TO THE PUBLIC

For the information of the public, the Green Principle is composed of a number of observed truths:–

1. Nature operates in a practical, not a sentimental manner.

2. Diversification is at the heart of Nature's method.

3. Nature insists on equilibrium rather than domination, so that ultimately an ant balances out a lion . . . .

The three basic truths remained in Miss Clare's words; even Dennis had to admit they were pithy enough to have force. The only thing he hadn't been sure about was the reference to the ant, on the grounds that it was belittling.

'What do you think we should call ourselves, "the flying ants"?' he had asked.

Miss Clare burst into angry laughter, as she so often did at Dennis's combination of simplicity and sarcasm. *Walker*, to walk, was his comment on the gratuitous complexity of foreign languages, or at least the dry-as-dust way in which they were taught: this word equals that, this problem in English is handled that way in French, the old old fallacy of not seeing that things were themselves, that there were no equivalents, that French wasn't English converted but absolutely French to the end of civilisation. Similarly, 'flying ants' was his gibe at her revolutionary humility, her belief that the story of three or four men in a darkened room was a parable of the truth that nature could use the smallest of agencies to advance its processes, an amoeba in the primeval soup, a lung-fish gasping on the sea-shore. For him the three or four men would testify to the power of will and muscle, to the scope of sheer masculine toughness. It was the difference between utopianism and struggle.

Still, he accepted the essential truth of her formulation and let it pass; she avoided telling him that the reference was inspired by the tale of Androcles and the lion, as dramatised by Bernard Shaw, one of the O level texts she'd taught in his day (English being the second string to her bow), or rather, taught *at* him, while he got up to mischief at the back of the class. She found him masturbating there on one occasion but had reacted calmly, with that live-and-let-live attitude which ironically enough only someone outside the sexual rat-race, a confirmed spinster like herself, could adopt.

'Pull yourself together,' she'd hissed at him. 'And your trousers, for that matter. Beastly youth.'

Onanism, actually, was a phenomenon a teacher of secondary males had to get used to; the girls seemed less explicit. Sometimes Miss Clare wondered that the boys' loos didn't glow red-hot, or begin to rise gently from the ground. What energy people had! How inert society was! Perhaps this perception anticipated her subsequent switch of allegiance from class dynamics to local action.

It was the next section of the document which caused the difficulty. This was the one in which she tried to make it clear that when you realised the existence of the 'observed truths,' they – or rather, the realisation – altered the way you lived your life. The complex that made up the Green Principle was not for paying lip-service to. She knew that the only way she could effectively demonstrate the reality it had for her was to be autobiographical; but that wouldn't do because the document was for public consumption, and her autobiography was hers alone. Perhaps as a result she had become too involved and tortuous – too literary; Dennis was no doubt right to hack away at the passage until it was 'plug ugly', and her over-complicated reasoning had given way to straightforward fulmination against the 'shits' and 'bastards' who were in charge of the military-industrial exploitation of most of the world.

Miss Clare had made the point, for example, that nature is a continuum, and that it is therefore wrong to see civilisation as its alternative or enemy since, as she'd put it, 'Nature has no door marked Exit; indeed, no door at all.' She had then gone on to say that a government or multi-national corporation, in laying waste to the environment, wasn't conquering nature or even pitting itself against nature, but rather modifying and perverting its processes just as a cancer cell did: turning nature round on itself. Dennis's version of this was an attack on the way radiation, pesticides and napalm destroyed forest growth and induced cancer in animals and people.

In this way, all her arguments became sledge-hammers; but as Miss Clare told herself, the Green Principle wasn't in the business of cracking a nut, so perhaps it was just as well.

Her concluding paragraphs remained, though:

In removing James Wilkins, . . .

(surprisingly, John Outram had made only three contributions to their discussion of the document: one of them had been to wish that Wilkins had a 'more rounded' name)

Director, Manchester Research Unit, Hautbois Corporation, we were not performing an act of revenge or punishment because such concepts are alien to the operations of the natural world; we were simply eliminating a dangerous presence, as anti-bodies do. The policies of Mr Wilkins's company . . .

(John had pointed out that there was no need to bring their actual motivation into sharp focus at this stage. Why indicate that it was the specific project being carried out in the Manchester laboratory which provided the trigger for their action? After all, Hautbois was a world-wide company; and they were opposed to it in general, as well as in particular.)

. . . contradicted two of the three basic truths outlined above; those truths, since they are truths, don't need to be defended, and we are not their defenders. They will take effect inevitably and we are simply the agents of their manifestation. Because at this stage of evolution natural events take place in the medium of conscious decision, so Mr Wilkins's death had to be planned and organised; nevertheless it was as necessary and amoral as the control of species by predators, drought, etc., in the wild. The operations of the Hautbois Company did, however, conform to the first of the truths we have listed. In removing one of those responsible for its administrative structure, so did we.

This document must be considered as neither a warning nor a boast . . . .

(John's final, most important, contribution to the debate had been to insist that no mention should be made of the Murgatroyd proposal. The Green Principle had removed the public face of the Hautbois Research Laboratory in Manchester; at least, they believed they were the ones responsible. Their next target was the organisation's scientific heart. But the person contracted to carry out the operation wouldn't proceed if the proposal became public knowledge. In any case, John argued, the effect of inevitability would be enhanced if Murgatroyd's death followed Wilkins's in an abrupt and unexpected fashion. 'It will look like the beginning of an epidemic,' as he put it.)

What has to happen will happen. Our statement has been issued simply to assist the police in their enquiries and to prevent inconvenience to those who are not involved. Although, as we hope to have made clear, there is a sense in which we are all involved.

(At this point Miss Clare wanted to insert John Donne's famous line about no man being an island, but Dennis just sneered. Anyway, she realised it would give away the fact she was a schoolteacher.)

Nevertheless the authorities should give credit for the event that has taken place specifically to

THE GREEN PRINCIPLE.

The historical inevitability of Mr Wilkins's death (and therefore, by extension, the absence of a moral dimension to the action) was brought home to Miss Clare most succinctly in the fact that she was able to sign the manifesto with a phrase that was not merely a name, but a description.

17

Rostris was obviously right: the Green Principle manifesto was the work of lunatics. But the moral he drew from that conclusion didn't have to be accepted, Chapman realised. Because Rostris had a logical approach to crime, and made his obeisances to the great God routine, he expected criminals to be guided by sweet reason likewise.

Chapman of course went through the routine procedures, on this case as on all cases: they wouldn't be routine procedures if you didn't follow them. He had officers take statements from all the witnesses; that is to say, from all the people who were on Prince Street at the time; there *were* no witnesses, unless you counted Anthony Manley.

You wouldn't have thought it was possible: they had tracked down twenty-six people who were either in the restaurant or on the street outside it at the crucial moment, and no one except Manley had noticed anything of significance. Still, practically everyone in the world had watched the assassination of President Kennedy, and nobody had seen what had happened there, either.

Two people remembered seeing a fat man, as it happened, but neither had observed him shooting anybody. Nevertheless Chapman put a sergeant on the task of inquiring about the sales of tropical-style outsize suits at any tailors in the Greater Manchester area, on the off-chance that a name and address would materialise. They didn't.

Chapman had also questioned Dr Murgatroyd, the chief scientist at the Hautbois Research Laboratory in Salford. Actually he was the only scientist, although his solitude seemed to confirm his status rather than diminish it. Murgatroyd told Chapman no more than Wilkins had told Pointon.

Chapman had done his best to squeeze further information out of him and had even made vague threats about the penalties for obstructing police enquiries. Murgatroyd had simply reminded him unpleasantly that he wasn't implicated in the crime, and had referred him to the London bigwigs of the Hautbois organisation, who had been similarly evasive, and had made threatening noises about the Department of Trade and Industry.

Chapman also followed up what Rostris regarded as the most fruitful line of motivation, and visited the Manchester representatives of the various oil companies. To a man they were sceptical, even contemptuous, about the possibility of creating a substitute for petrol; and they were amused and/or incredulous at the suggestion that rivalry might have brought about Wilkins's demise. Chapman was aware of the danger of looking for confirmation of his own opinion; nevertheless, after due consideration he was confident they were telling the truth.

He had no more luck with his own hunch, that the Green Principle might, as it claimed, be responsible for the crime. The organisation had never even been heard of by any of the local or national conservation groups. He was determined to pursue this angle, however. The writers of the manifesto might be mentally ill, but then any chain of reasoning which culminated in murder was, by ordinary standards, insane.

In the meantime Chapman decided to do some homework on Anthony Manley. It only took a few minutes to track down his mother to an address in Alderley Edge, North Cheshire. The father had disappeared from the telephone directory several years previously. Chapman decided to go on spec, without warning her. She had a solicitor only too close to hand.

Mrs Manley's house was less imposing than the address had led him to expect: a large terrace in a shadowy street on the north fringe of Alderley Edge, the sort of place that had originally been designed for tradesmen and skilled workers and was now usually inhabited by rising young business people who hadn't yet arrived at the top.

Not that Mrs Manley conformed to either picture. She was elderly and large, quite different physically from her son, with big hips and a bulky chest and bosom, but a very narrow waist in between, so that she appeared to be sectioned like an insect. She was also badly dressed, in a lime green crimplene suit that wasn't completely clean. She sucked a cigarette and looked at Chapman appraisingly with pale eyes; he couldn't tell which of two opposites she was, deadpan or humourless. She was wearing slippers that had given way in the toes.

'Yes?' she asked.

'Good afternoon, Mrs Manley. My name's Inspector Chapman.'

'Police, are you?' she asked.

'Well, yes, I am.'

'You'd better come in,' she said. 'You know what neighbours are like.'

'I *am* in plain clothes, Mrs Manley.'

'They'll smell you out, don't you worry.' Her expression suggested she was doing exactly that herself. 'No offence.'

'Of course not.'

He followed her into the front room. Although it was only mid-afternoon and – at least everywhere but this street – a sunny day, the room was dark and cavernous, full of looming forms: a battered piano, a shapeless three piece suite, Mrs Manley.

'Sit down,' she said.

He sat down on one of the armchairs. He felt like a modern midget, sitting on the knee of an Edwardian giant.

'Can I get you a cup of tea, Inspector?'

'No,' he replied, feeling it was wrong to accept hospitality from someone when you were just about to embark on a series of questions which she was likely to find insulting. Then he reflected that that was an excellent reason *for* accepting hospitality, and he modified the decision: 'If you're having one.'

'No, I'm not,' she replied, unmoved. 'I can't be bothered, to tell you the truth.'

84

'That's all right then.'

'What can I do for you, Inspector?'

'It's about your son, Mrs Manley.'

She drew on her cigarette, eyes narrowing as she did so. Then she tapped the ash off over a loaded ashtray.

'What about him?' she asked. Her tone was carefully unanxious. Chapman felt sure she wasn't surprised that the police were taking an interest in him.

'It's a slightly delicate matter. Mr Manley came to me with some very important information.'

'Oh yes? Well, he *is* a solicitor.'

'It was nothing to do with that. In evaluating the information we have to take the teller of it into account, that's the problem.'

'My son's not a liar, Inspector. I *am*, as a matter of fact.' She gave him another of her appraising looks, obviously hoping to see her words have an effect. 'It's one of my little hobbies.' She had an unpleasantly rasping voice, perhaps from too much smoking. 'When I'm in a railway carriage I spin some fine old yarns to whoever is sitting opposite me. I tell them my husband's in prison, things like that. It makes life interesting.' She grinned finally, maliciously: her good teeth made her face look old and decaying.

'I'm certainly not saying he's a liar, Mrs Manley. It's just that when he was talking to me he seemed. . . to have an axe to grind. That's all.'

There was a pause. Then in a cold tone Mrs Manley said: 'In the circumstances that happens to be a rather unfortunate phrase.'

'Oh really? I'm simply concerned with working out how objective he is as a witness.'

She settled back in her chair. 'I see,' she said, and stubbed out her cigarette, her fingers staying aloof, in an untypically finicky fashion, from the other butts in the ashtray.

Somewhat disorientated by her manner, by her conflicting manners, Chapman almost pleaded: 'That's all.'

'Before I answer your question, Mr Chapman, I'd be very

grateful if you would answer one of mine.'

'Anything you like,' Chapman offered, with a willingness he would rapidly regret.

Eyes puckered, voice lowered, Mrs Manley asked her question: 'Have you ever been circumcised, Inspector?'

'I'm —' He felt as if the breath had been knocked from his body. The question came as such a shock that it didn't occur to him that he could refuse to answer it. 'Yes, as a matter of fact.'

She gave a sage nod, her eyes still scrutinising him narrowly. 'I thought so. I usually seem to be able to tell.' Then, suddenly, her manner became bright and breezy once more. 'Tell you what,' she said, 'let's have that cup of tea after all.'

She lumbered out to make tea. Chapman rose to his feet to acknowledge her exit and then wandered about the room in a daze. You never knew where the conversation was going next. No wonder Anthony Manley seemed disturbed.

On the hideous tiled mantelpiece was a photograph, obviously taken some time ago, of a middle-aged man. He was wearing a large woolly and holding a cat. Although the photograph was in black-and-white you felt the original must have been monochrome also. Mr Manley Senior, presumably. He looked so meek and mild he set your teeth on edge. A strange partner for the redoubtable Mrs Manley – it was hardly surprising that he was no longer in evidence. Dead, presumably. It was just the sort of mantelpiece, in point of fact, for one of those ornate little urns into which you put your loved one's ashes. If not dead, Mr Manley Senior was certainly gone. Good luck to him.

Mrs Manley came in, carrying a tray with two cups of tea on it. Chapman took his, and resumed his chair. Mrs Manley plonked the tray on a pile of magazines and sat down herself.

The tea was weak and – inexplicably, since she hadn't taken more than a few minutes – cold already. Chapman took a sip and looked up expectantly, waiting for her to continue.

'That's better,' she said. 'Where had we got to? Oh yes, circumcision. At what age were you done, if you don't mind my asking?'

'I don't know,' Chapman muttered in reply. 'A few days old I suppose.' He took a long draught of the unsustaining liquid.

'There you are, that's my point, a few days old. Anthony wasn't done until he was seventeen. We thought he was all right before then. That's a sensitive time of life, you know, Inspector. A boy that age doesn't like to admit to himself that there's been anything wrong with his what-do-you-call-it, his willy. He became depressed and morbid.'

'I see.'

'And once you start it doesn't take long to add fuel to the flames. You know what young people are like. He began to worry about the world. Nuclear explosions, people dying of starvation, all that sort of thing. The suffering of mankind. He read all those horrible books about the concentration camps. I think he felt he ought to share in all the misery. I suppose he's right. Most of us are too lazy in our emotions even to try. He's a very genuine person, Inspector.'

'I'm sure he is,' Chapman agreed.

'Yes. Very genuine.' Her crumbly cheeks concertina-ed back from her nice white teeth again. 'Like his old mother,' she concluded.

Chapman felt he'd had a heavy afternoon by the time he got back to the police station. However he still had enough presence of mind to put in train a small enquiry.

The answer came within minutes. Mr Manley Senior was indeed in prison, serving a sentence for grievous bodily harm.

18

Chapman didn't see Rostris for several days; the Superintendent was apparently preoccupied with his own concerns. Just as well: Chapman wanted to be left alone on the Green Principle business.

Finally, though, one lunch-time, he came upon Rostris sitting in the police canteen.

The canteen was a large, prefabricated building, with all the cosiness of a warehouse. The high, cavernous roof, supported by steel girders, ensured that the place felt chilly and deserted even when it was packed. The self-service counter was manned, or womanned, by the sort of fearsome dinner ladies you associate with school.

He much preferred to eat a sandwich at his desk, but you were expected to put in an appearance from time to time. According to a pompous notice on the bulletin board, the canteen was a place where all ranks could 'mix and mingle, to exchange ideas and information'. That didn't happen in reality, needless to say. Inspectors and superintendents clustered in one corner, sergeants congregated in another, and the proletarian mass of constables, who didn't possess desks of their own to eat packed lunches at, ate busily and noisily near the counter end.

Rostris was sitting at a table by himself when Chapman joined him, staring at a plate of fish and chips. The fish was an oval shape, strangely regular, and covered in a hard shiny batter.

'That's just what you didn't ought to eat,' Chapman said. 'It'll wreck your insides faster than anything.'

'My insides are wrecked already,' Rostris replied, obstinately sawing at the batter, which finally gave way with a sharp crack. 'How's the Wilkins case going?'

'Slowly, I'm afraid.'

'You're not getting bogged down with a lot of ecologists, I hope. Hiding to nothing, that lot, in my opinion.' Rostris ate neatly, loading his fork with a small piece of fish, a couple of segments of chip, each cut to the same length, and a terminating blob of squashed peas: a precisely balanced package each time. It was sad to think of the chaos towards which that convoy was travelling.

'We had what could have been a witness at one stage,' Chapman said, refusing the bait, 'but he turned out to be round the bend.'

Rostris looked up interestedly.

'You checked, did you?' he asked.

'Of course I checked.'

There was a pause.

'How is it with you anyway?' Chapman went on. 'Busy?'

'That road accident's begun to take up quite a bit of my time.'

'Oh yes. I remember you saying they'd all died.'

'That wasn't the end of it.'

'What do you mean?'

'It's as if the accident won't stop happening. Another one's gone.'

'But there were only eight in the van, weren't there?'

'In the van, yes. But the tanker driver's died as well.'

'Good God! I thought he just suffered abrasions.'

'So did I. So did the hospital. So did everybody. He's dead all the same. I don't know how he managed it. Died healthy, I suppose. Funny isn't it, my health's in ruins and I'll live forever.'

'But what the devil's going on?'

'Enough said for the time being.' Rostris nodded towards the constables. 'Don't want one of those boneheads quacking to the papers. The press haven't noticed anything weird as yet. They're just doing an O my paws and whiskers about the original accident.'

Nobody was remotely in earshot, and in any case the steady hubbub, a concerto for scraped plates, would have blotted out any confidences. But Rostris was a secretive man, and passionately hated the press.

Chapman concentrated on a surprisingly pleasant scotch egg. Rostris meanwhile, having finished his meal, sat hunched and quizzical over the empty plate, presumably monitoring what was going on in his insides. Perhaps not, however, because he suddenly said aggressively: 'There's been some talk about you.'

The egg turned to cardboard in Chapman's mouth. He thought of Margaret and felt a sensation like pins and needles in his cheeks.

'What about me?' he asked.

'The name Susan Hopwood has been mentioned.'

'Has it really?'

'It's said she's more or less moved in.'

Chapman's relief that the talk didn't concern Margaret directly somehow fuelled his fury.

'It's none of their business,' he said, quiet with rage.

To his surprise, Rostris lost his temper also.

'You silly bastard!' he exclaimed, loudly enough for several of the constables to look vaguely in their direction. He moderated his tone, but not his vehemence: 'There's an unwritten law. Detective inspectors don't go to bed with police sergeants. It screws up the whole promotion structure.'

They stared at each other in silence for a moment. Suddenly Chapman found himself laughing. How could you take this seriously? How could you take anything seriously?

Rostris gave him a long, disgusted look and then rose and left the table. Chapman watched him go, tinging his fork against his now empty plate as he did so.

His laughter didn't take long to subside, when the explanation for Rostris's priggish attitude suddenly entered his head.

19

Rostris sat at his desk wishing he hadn't bawled Chapman out like that. He'd made a bit of a fool of himself.

No, that wasn't strictly true. He was a fool already.

He'd begun being a fool two years ago, while he was still an inspector stationed at Tarporley in Cheshire, an upper class rural place where the farmers wore heavy Aran sweaters and had studied agriculture at university. There was quite a bit of crime there, as one might expect, but it wasn't like Manchester. Large amounts of money and valuables were stolen regularly but people didn't get knocked about: bucolic bliss.

One day he received notification that a certain Constable Hopwood was being transferred to the Tarporley station. For some reason they'd omitted her W from the chit, so that the effect of her beauty when she wafted into his office was heightened by the fact that he hadn't expected her to be female in the first place. Straightaway he felt an urgent desire to get her to bed, not so much to possess her as to get her down to a human level, to prove that however stunning she might be, in all essential respects she was much like everybody else.

He ought to be the last person in the world to blame Chapman for succumbing, particularly given all the trouble the poor man was having with his wife. He, Rostris, was a bachelor and not prone to making an idiot of himself with young girls. He was used to coping, keeping his end up. On the one hand there were cosy family units, where the domestic hearth was regularly stoked; on the other the great outdoors, where sexual opportunity would come lumbering towards you with the abrupt randomness of an encounter between two beasts on the steppes. Possibly his imagery of the open field was suggested by Tarporley experiences. Anyway Chapman, his household in crisis, had every excuse for seeking comfort where he could find it; he, Rostris, accustomed to the elements, had not. Police officers of an inferior grade had always been forbidden fruit, for obvious reasons. It was exactly those reasons which Rostris had decided to exploit, when he first encountered Constable Hopwood.

What a fool he'd made of himself!

As he thought about it his indigestion stirred into action. The pain came over his innards like waves approaching the seashore, long rolling surges which built up and up, that accumulated and gathered momentum until they seemed to be curving round on themselves and he waited with longing for something to break, to give way, deep in his bowel. Often the moment of striking would be an anticlimax, just as a wave could dissipate into nothing in particular when it arrived at the shore; but sometimes the process would generate enough force to dislodge some of his wind, and then there would be an eddy of relief for a few moments before the next wave gathered itself.

At the time he'd begun to take Constable Hopwood out his stomach troubles hadn't started. Or rather they had, but he didn't know it. He would soon find out. In retrospect, some of the almost agonising sensations she'd triggered off in him from his first encounter with her, sweet-smelling PC 250, in a uniform she wore like a fetish, had probably been caused by the ongoing rearrangement of his insides. Two years later, sitting in pain at his desk in Manchester HQ, he wondered if that was so. Talk about hindsight.

The great moment came within a few weeks, as he knew it would. Rank will out, that was the grim premise on which he had grounded their relationship. He'd been quite ruthless, leaning down to her from a height as if he were God. At least, God in a Tarporley context. Beauty she might be, constable she was – that made her attainable all right. He would insist on the truth of his conclusion.

They were in his cottage. He'd bought a Chinese meal in for the occasion, and some good wine. They ate, they drank, they went up to his bedroom. He contrived to make it a perfectly natural sequence, a mere succession of courses. She conformed perfectly to the notion of inevitability, slipping off her clothes with no attempt at coyness or teasing, and sliding rapidly under the bedclothes. It was exactly what he had wanted: her body wasn't to be admired, or even manipulated, just defused. He stripped and joined her in bed.

Yes, she was in just as much of a hurry as he was. She fumbled at him, caught hold, steered him into position. She was in a passion to have it, or to get it over with, there was no time to work out which.

Then: disaster. No sooner had he entered her than he experienced a sudden horrific desire to pass wind.

It came out of the blue, with none of the build-up that he was to endure subsequently. With no warning of any kind, since he'd never, until this second, been prone to flatulence. It was a moment of initiation.

He did what he could, which was just to tighten his bum and carry on as best he might, but to no avail. You couldn't concentrate on keeping the door shut in one direction and still make things move normally in the other. Anyway, the fart had become irresistible, he had to let it out.

It came with a bang, except that a bang isn't usually sustained. Loud and long, there was no way on earth to carry it off. He pulled himself out of her and curled up in shame at the side of the bed.

After a few seconds he realised that Constable Hopwood was laughing.

His first thought was that she was trying to let him off the hook, and he turned to face her and join in the joke.

At that very moment, though, the laughter changed without warning into a series of huge jagged sobs, the sort that begin as a hiccup in the chest and finish as wrenching shudders that run through the whole body. He got out of bed and sat on a chair beside his wardrobe, watching her while she cried on and on. The soon-to-become-familiar acidic tide began to rise within his stomach.

After an age her weeping calmed long enough for her to say: 'You bastard. Didn't you realise I was a virgin?'

The words were crushing, they filled him with despair. They had defined his life, wretched as it had been, ever since. Even now, as he cringed behind his desk, the very thought of them made him cringe further, beyond the distortions of indigestion.

The terrible part about it was that he didn't really understand what the words meant. In the two years since she'd made her accusation he'd never been able to work out exactly what connection she was trying to establish between *his* fart and *her* virginity.

20

Margaret had been put to bed, and Mike Chapman and Susan Hopwood were eating their dinner, a nice meal of steak cooked in some sort of wine sauce. Susan had got it ready while Mike gave Margaret her bath. It gave him a slightly uneasy feeling to eat so well when his wife had made do with a boiled egg and soldiers, but they had no choice. Margaret was always too tired by evening to cope with a big meal: Mrs Hodnet made sure she had something filling in the middle of the day.

'There's something I've been meaning to ask you,' Mike said. He hadn't meant his tone to sound portentous but Susan immediately looked at him alertly, a piece of meat, on the end of her fork, suspended a few inches from her mouth.

'Oh yes?' she asked.

'Yes. It was nothing really. The thought went through my mind that you must have known our Super before you were transferred to the Manchester station. Rostris.'

'What makes you think that?'

'Oh, I don't know, I think it was something you said.' He could hardly remind her that she'd referred to Rostris as 'that cunt' the first time she came to his house. 'I got the impression you don't like him very much.'

She eyed the morsel of meat carefully, almost as though she were a public health inspector examining it for taint. 'I think he's a pig,' she said.

'I suppose he is. He's got his points though. He's conscientious in his way.'

'I knew him at Tarporley,' she said, popping the meat in her mouth.

'Did you? Oh yes, of course, that's where he was before he

transferred to Manchester. But that was a couple of years ago.'

'Yes. I was a constable then.'

'And you didn't get on?' he asked.

'Well, frankly –' she took her eyes off her plate and looked directly at him. He sensed she was going to modify the truth – 'he made a pass at me.'

His heart, ludicrously, thumped. There was only one truth *that* claim could be a modification of. So what? Two years ago he was still having sexual relations with Margaret. Two years ago was a different world.

'I see,' he said. 'But that's only human nature, isn't it?'

'I suppose so. But I didn't, you know, I didn't like him in that way. It made things awkward.'

'I imagine it did,' he said, grim disapproval beneath a coat of sympathy.

'Luckily,' she began to speak rapidly, wanting to get the story over with as soon as possible, 'he put in for a transfer shortly afterwards, which was a great relief. I'd forgotten where he'd gone to, and it was a bit of a shock when I came to Manchester and found he was here.'

'But he hasn't tried anything since you arrived?'

'No, no, he's kept his distance.'

'Oh well, I suppose a lot of water's flowed under the bridge in the meantime.'

'I suppose it has.'

She put her knife and fork down decisively, as if her verdict had gone against the meat. Chapman intuited that however much water had flowed under the bridge it hadn't been enough to wash away whatever Rostris had deposited there. He was just about to make some comment about the deliciousness of the casserole when the phone rang.

'I'll take it,' she said, beginning to rise from the table. Chapman got the impression she was glad of an excuse to go.

'No, I'd better. It's probably the station and we ought to be discreet. There's an unwritten rule: inspectors aren't supposed to have affairs with the lower ranks.'

She pinked acutely as she settled back into her place.

He managed to catch the phone before it stopped ringing. It was, surprise, surprise, Rostris.

'Sorry to poke my nose in,' Rostris said, unmistakable sarcasm in his voice. 'I couldn't help wondering about this London bang. I suppose you heard about it on the news?'

'Yes, of course I did. I've made some enquiries but there's no earthly connection. It was a car bomb of course, not a rifle job. And there's not been a squeak from the Green Principle. Nobody's taken credit for it yet. At least, they hadn't an hour or two ago.'

'As far as I'm concerned, the Green Principle are neither here nor there. This is another terrorist incident and it could be part of a pattern.' Rostris did like to discover patterns. 'I think you ought to go down there and look into it.'

'For heaven's sake,' Chapman replied, irritated, 'I can't investigate every terrorist outrage that takes place on the off-chance.'

'Look, can you come over for a few minutes? I mean, have you got . . . someone who could babysit for a while? Oh hell, I didn't mean to put it like that. You know what I mean.'

I know what you mean, thought Chapman. For babysit read: look after your wife. And for someone read: Susan.

'Why?'

'There's a bloke named Manley to see you. Says he's got some important information concerning this London business. Something that links it with the Wilkins murder. He wanted to tell me all about it as a matter of fact but I told him it's not my case. I'm too effing senior to have cases, you know that.' Rostris always spoke as if his promotion to superintendent had been a malicious trick on the part of the authorities designed specifically to give him indigestion, alienation, ennui and other discomforts.

'You've got that road accident,' Chapman pointed out.

'Only because it wasn't diagnosed as a case when it was first reported. If it had been I'd have had to assign it to somebody else. Do you know what the latest toll is, by the way?'

'Yes. You told me all nine had gone.'

'Not nine. Eleven.'

'For heaven's sake, how can you have eleven casualties when there were only nine involved in the crash?'

'That's a very good question.' His tone made it clear that the good question wasn't going to receive an answer.

'Anyway,' Chapman went on after a pause, 'I suppose I'd better come in for a minute. This Manley's the one I told you about, who's mentally disturbed.'

'Oh yes? He certainly doesn't like you very much. He wanted to tell all to me. Anyway, I think you ought to give him a listening to, to get him off our plates if nothing else.'

'All right,' said Chapman. 'I'll be in shortly.'

'Well, don't expect to see me here. I'm just off home.'

I'll bet you are, Chapman said to himself; you don't want to meet your rival in love. He wondered how a grown man could be so childish. No, no, not childish, that wasn't a word he liked to use.

When Chapman arrived at the station there was nobody sitting on the bench where people usually waited. Perhaps Manley had got tired of hanging about and gone. He looked quizzically at Sergeant Stebbings. No such luck. The Sergeant pointed with his pencil stub at the door of the Gents, and a second later Manley came out.

He was dressed smartly as before, this time in a tweed Norfolk jacket and cavalry twill trousers. The clothes were well cut but rather bulky for such a lean man, particularly on a warm evening, and they had the effect of making him seem pin-headed. He didn't offer his hand, and Chapman was glad to be spared that dry contact.

'Good evening, Mr Manley,' he said, hoping that a hearty tone would keep repulsion at bay for a moment. 'How are you?'

'I've got something I must tell you about.'

'Come along to my office then.'

As soon as he was seated there, Manley said accusingly: 'You obviously believe that the sins of the fathers are visited unto the children.'

'I beg your pardon?'

'Don't worry, I heard all about your inquiries at my mother's house.'

'Mr Manley, in cases like this we must —'

'Try to smear me as much as possible, that's what you must.'

Chapman invoked Rostris's catch-word. 'I have to follow the routine, Mr Manley.'

'And the routine is to dig up family ghosts so you don't have to take any notice of what I have to tell you. My father was an alcoholic.' Manley thought for a moment and then said bitterly: 'He was a drunkard. In the pub he used to drink at, there was one of those people who finish up other people's drinks when they've left them. He was known as Robert the Rubbish. My father left the bar for a moment to go to the toilet and when he came back he found Robert the Rubbish downing his drink. He hit him, on the spur of the moment. It was just a drunken blow, nothing more would have been thought of it except that this Rubbish man staggered backwards against the cellar door which hadn't been shut properly, and fell down the steps. Father should never have been found guilty of grievous bodily harm, the defence made a botch-up.'

'Perhaps you should do less conveyancing and more criminal work yourself, Mr Manley.' Chapman didn't mention the fact that according to police records Mr Manley Senior had beaten up a fellow punter in an argument over the disposal of their winnings on a horse-race. 'But I can assure you I'm not the slightest bit interested in your father's case. The only thing I'm interested in is the murder of Mr Wilkins. I understand you've got something to tell me about it.'

'It's about that explosion in London.'

'That case doesn't concern me, Mr Manley. I'm —'

'I think it does concern you, Inspector. Do you know who the dead man was?'

It was time to show Manley who was boss.

'Yes, I do as a matter of fact, Mr Manley. His name was Fox. Frederick Fox.'

'And –' defiantly unruffled, indeed insistent – 'and what does that name mean to you?'

'I *do* read the newspapers, you know. Mr Fox was a leading heart transplant surgeon. It's one of those stupid —'

'That's not all Mr Fox was, Inspector.'

'No?'

'No. Mr Fox was a Zionist. One of the most important and influential English Zionists. By any standards.'

'I'm afraid I just don't see the relevance of this, Mr Manley. Mr Wilkins wasn't a Zionist, as far as I understand. He wasn't even a Jew for that matter. Perhaps you could tell me the connection?'

'*I* don't know the connection. Surely it's your job to find that out. There *is* a connection, that's for sure.'

'How do you know?'

'Perhaps you'll be so good as to listen to what I have to tell you.' He gave Chapman a long look, which strangely combined bitterness, hostility, complacence, glee and nervousness, all at once. 'And then you'll understand.'

21

In the early hours of that morning Carole Shearer had sat in the cubby-hole on Men's Surgical, drinking a cup of tea with three other nurses, and listening to them talking about Mr Fox.

'If he thinks Israel's so great,' Liz Boffey asked, 'why doesn't he go and live there?'

'His wife won't let him,' claimed Angela MacLeod. 'Hasn't she got some kind of arty-farty job on a newspaper?'

'That's probably how he gets so much publicity,' Miss Piggy claimed.

'My God, that's a great reason,' Boffey put in, 'not going to the promised land because the missus won't let him.'

Nurse Shearer had to say something. 'Most of the time you go on about female equality. Then you talk like that. I don't understand you.' She wished it hadn't come out so seriously and sincerely, with a quiver in it. The other girls were just lightly chatting.

'But I believe people should have the courage of their convictions,' Boffey said in a suddenly self-righteous voice. 'How can you believe so strongly in somewhere like Israel and not go there to live?'

'People believe in heaven,' Nurse Shearer countered, 'but they don't necessarily want to go there for the time being.'

'Who's in love with Mr Foxkins then?' Piggy tweedled.

Nurse Shearer wondered why she didn't tell the girls she was Jewish and get it over with: they were nice kids at heart and wouldn't talk that way if they knew. But of course that was the point. She didn't really want them to talk differently. Nobody had ever been unpleasant to her in any conscious way on the subject, but people, when they knew, talked to you with a certain amount of care, even on neutral matters. She couldn't bear that. It was as if you were half in, half out, of their world, as if you were just to one side of the centre of things. But it wasn't the Jews' fault; perhaps in the end it wasn't even the anti-Semites' fault. It was history's fault. No, no, it was geography's fault.

'Israel's a long way away,' Nurse Shearer said, hoping to conclude the discussion. She didn't attempt to answer Nurse Sowerby's allegation, how could she? She *was* in love with Mr Fox, after all.

But Miss P. wouldn't leave the subject alone. 'Perhaps Foxy-loxy loves her back,' she claimed. 'He's given her a post at a porthole, after all.'

'I'd better go now, anyway,' Nurse Shearer said.

'Is it time already?' Boffey asked. She sounded irritated and it suddenly occurred to Nurse Shearer that she was jealous.

'I'm not sure when it will start, but I don't want to be late.'

'They're bringing the new one from Windsor,' Angela MacLeod said authoritatively, 'so it shouldn't take long.'

'How do you know that?'

Airily: 'Oh, I just do. It belonged to a motor-cyclist. A pal of mine gave me a ring, just. She said he was a real toughie, with a skull and crossbones on the back of his jacket. He seemed all right after the accident. The ambulanceman said he was standing at the side of the road complaining that he'd torn his trousers. Then he took his crash-helmet off and his head sort of caved in. The shock wave had got in underneath somehow. They managed to get him on life support before his heart had a chance to conk out. He was brain dead by then, of course. He never said a thing after he took his helmet off, just collapsed on the pavement.'

There was a moment of silence. Nurse MacLeod realised that she had failed to keep the glee out of her voice. 'Horrible, isn't it?' she asked.

'I'd better go straightaway,' said Nurse Shearer, 'if it's only coming from Windsor.' As she left she revolved in her mind the point that Piggy had made. Perhaps it did mean something that Mr Fox had given her a post at a porthole. There were so many other nurses he could have chosen.

The theatre only had four portholes, and three people were assigned to each. Medical journalists took up one, Mr Fox's fellow consultants, along with some junior doctors, another two, and the remaining one was for Nurse Shearer and two of her colleagues. The other two girls were there already, so it was just as well that she had hurried. Nothing was said – they just made small talk – but all three girls knew that they were being groomed for a future heart transplant in this very theatre. Only three nurses were used at a time because the team always included three surgeons and an anaesthetist, and with the risk of infection it was important to keep numbers down.

The patient was trundled into position, and a few minutes later the team arrived – all except Mr Fox. As she watched the preparations, Carole Shearer continued to think about what could have made him pick her. She had never done anything dramatic in the wards, like performing an emergency tracheotomy, or even giving somebody the kiss of life. Mr Fox had always been a forbidding figure, sweeping past in his dark consultant's suit or his white coat, hardly noticing her.

Somehow, though, she had been selected. Her name must have come up at a meeting, and been approved of. She felt herself go pink as she thought about it. Why? Why? In some invisible way she must fit the bill, she must have some quality that even she didn't know about. Or perhaps it wasn't because of a specific quality, perhaps she just added up, in an accidental way, to the totality they needed.

Her blush deepened. To be exactly the right person, without even trying. . . it was almost a medical equivalent of being someone's wife. That must have been what the Pig was getting at.

There was a sudden stirring of excitement. Nurse Shearer looked along the corridor to see two porters approaching with a small trolley – actually a little refrigerator on wheels. The motor-cyclist's still-living heart would be inside it. Mr Fox accompanied the porters, matching their pace stride for stride. They all disappeared into the antechamber of the theatre.

A moment or two later the porters returned to the corridor. Shortly after that you could see the trolley being received into the theatre itself. Another five minutes passed, and then Mr Fox appeared, gowned-up and ready to begin the operation.

Everybody said the surgical procedures in a heart transplant were relatively mundane, and Nurse Shearer realised the truth of the claim as she watched. But that made no difference to the feelings it aroused in her. You might just as well say amputating somebody's head was a routine operation: that wouldn't stop it giving you a funny sensation as you witnessed it. The basic purpose served by porthole observation was not so much to learn what to do as to get used to the idea of doing it. And of course, as with all transplants, the nursing side was of the utmost importance. The two contributions a nurse could really provide, speed and sterility, were paramount.

Anyway, watching Mr Fox at work filled Nurse Shearer with awe. As he got deeper into the patient it was as if he revealed depths in himself. She found her gaze continually travelling from the neatly exposed chest cavity, up the nimble arms, to those intensely concentrated downward-looking eyes. Just as a surgical incision got you down to basics, so did surgical garb: a face-mask didn't so much conceal the face as simplify it, enabling you to confine your attention to the eyes, which were the soul, or the heart, of the man.

Suddenly everything changed.

Even from this side of the porthole you could hear the alarm buzz from the anaesthetist's monitoring equipment. One of the nurses scurried round to thump an oxygen mask over the patient's face. The anaesthetist switched and twisted his controls like the pilot of a crippled aircraft. Mr Fox, elbow-deep, was manipulating, stimulating, pumping the man by hand. Another nurse rushed to one corner and rushed back with a defibrillator. For a few seconds there was a blur, in green.

Then as suddenly as it had started, it stopped. It was odd, she had noticed it before in operations, to see a person die without any change taking place in him. One moment the patient was worth concentrating all your attention on; the next, he could be completely ignored. The anaesthetist irritatedly flicked off his switches; the nurses began to collect the instruments together; Mr Fox looked up, surely straight at her porthole, and gave the thumbs down sign. The observers began to disperse, talking together quietly. Nurse Shearer, however, walked off by herself.

She didn't feel like talking to anybody: certainly not the girls on the ward. It was funny not to have to clear up, scrub and change after being in on surgery She went to the locker room and had a smoke. Technically speaking there were another couple of hours till the end of her shift but nobody would expect her back. When she'd finished her cigarette she put on her cloak and left for the nurses' home.

Dawn was coming up as she walked out of the hospital and the darkness was giving way to that chilly shade of grey that you get for a few minutes even when a nice day is in the offing. Birds were singing in the loud, panic-stricken way that they had at this time in the morning. She made her way across the car park towards the dormitories on the other side. When she was about halfway across she noticed that Mr Fox was getting into his Mercedes, which was parked on the far side of the area, near the hospital wall.

Then she realised the dimness had deceived her. It wasn't Mr Fox getting in, it was somebody else – a big, fat man – getting out. She hurried a step or two forwards, and then hesitated.

The fat man began to stride away. At that very moment Mr Fox appeared round the side of the car, and opened the door. The fact that it wasn't locked obviously didn't strike him as suspicious. Perhaps he didn't bother, despite the fact that it was such an expensive vehicle. If you have heart transplants on your mind the fate of a Mercedes probably doesn't mean a lot.

'Mr Fox!' she called, unable to keep the timidity out of her voice.

He looked up, saw her, recognised her. He gave a little sad smile and shrugged his shoulders. Then he did something astounding. He raised his hand to his mouth and blew her a kiss!

Even at that moment she knew it wasn't exactly sexual, it wasn't a pass or anything like that. But it was the next best thing. It was a rueful kiss, it seemed to say: oh well, love, we were in that operation together, and it didn't work out. You win some, you lose some.

Then he got in his car and closed the door. She heard the starting motor turn.

She never actually heard the explosion.

The Mercedes roof bulged upwards as if it were made of rubber, and then Mr Fox rose through it. For the fraction of a second he stayed almost in one piece, and then he seemed to disintegrate in mid-air. Still lyrical from his kiss she watched his body radiate outwards, the pinks and reds bursting into bloom, a meat flower.

Then the blast struck her, too.

22

How do you make people believe what you've seen?

The problem had dogged Manley all his adult life, ever since his perception, via his red-raw, unbearable-to-look-at penis, that the human body was soft, vulnerable.

Everybody knew that. Everybody had always known it. But there were qualities of knowing, degrees, gradations. Everybody knew that they were going to *die*, but some people conducted their lives as if they were, and others lived as if they weren't. Some people knew their mortality as a fact; others had grasped it as an imaginative reality.

Manley had grasped that imaginative reality when he was seventeen. He had had to go into hospital to be circumcised. To soften the blow, presumably, everybody assured him this would be the answer to all his problems. Even his father took a day off from the races, and placed his bets instead from a telephone in the hospital waiting room. As a result of all this support and comfort he'd gone into the operation under some sort of childish delusion that it would turn his equipment into a magic wand extruding glitter, like one waved by a fairy godmother in Disney. After a puberty of bent erections, he would be given leverage on his world. Instead, he had been trundled out of surgery with a disaster area between his legs.

Of course it had healed. But he had seen what he had seen.

Whenever, subsequently, he looked down at the strange purple bulb which had been exposed, he felt he was seeing it still. He couldn't escape the sense that an obscure internal organ which ought to be lurking out of sight had been ruthlessly brought into the light of day. To be male was to have a discoloured boil at the end of a mottled piece of tubing, as though the Almighty were offering an explicit warning not to convert masculinity into aggression.

And to be female! He had discovered what it was to be female when he'd got married.

He was now alone, a kind of witness, an observer, of the cruelty that seemed to have been embedded in the very nature of things. But like other such witnesses he had a tendency to be unconvincing.

Inspector Chapman, fascist bastard, hadn't believed a word he'd told him about the occurrence on Prince Street. Unless Manley was very careful he wouldn't believe what he had to say about the assassination of Mr Fox either.

The one chance was to be as circumstantial as possible, to locate the bizarre amidst a dense tissue of detail. So, in Chapman's office, ignoring the impatience that seemed to crackle in the very atmosphere like electricity, ignoring, above all, the unsympathetic stare of those dark eyes, Manley began at the beginning.

This morning he'd gone to work intending to complete a house transaction on behalf of a client. The deal had temporarily run aground, however, because he discovered at the last moment that the vendor hadn't been keeping up his chief rent payments. It was absolutely ridiculous, a forty thousand pound conveyance being held up over a matter of ten pounds or so, but that was the law. The law, Manley believed, was one and indivisible, unlike the human body.

The problem had left him at loose ends. It was late morning by the time he discovered it, and he didn't have another appointment until three-thirty. Since the incident on Prince Street he'd lost his appetite for lunch-time walks. He decided, therefore, to drive home for a sandwich and perhaps a quick nap instead of trying to kill time at the office.

When he arrived home he switched on his television for the lunch-time news.

There had been an explosion, but when wasn't there an explosion? A reporter stood in front of the blackened ruins of a car and gave the details.

Manley didn't take a great deal of notice at first; not, at least, to what the man was saying. He did listen to the manner in which he said it, however. He was always amazed at the way television reporters could make all news, big or little, personal or political, sound the same. Here was a medium which could actually humanise the news, which could make it sound as if things happened to real people and concerned *you*, which could guide the listener through the labyrinth of what took place in the world by means of the continuous thread of the human voice, and what happened? All newspeople, male or female, studio voice-over, wind-blown commentator on the street, chose, or, presumably, were made, to speak like zombies.

Manley had long ago worked out how they managed it; why was another matter altogether. They did it, he realised, by the simple technique of using pauses instead of modulations for emphasis. Before the important word or phrase in any sentence they hesitated: always for exactly the same amount of time. You could measure it with a stopwatch, though Manley had never tried. Point seven five of a second, something like that. Where they learned the technique heaven knew: some sort of pause gymnasium run by the broadcasting authorities, where you practised until you could fracture a sentence with a single blow, as a karate expert can break a brick by striking it with his bare hand.

In a language which had traditionally used pauses to enforce the grammatical and logical structure of a sentence, and tone to establish its emotional content, the effect of this combination of monotonous delivery and emphatic pausing was confusing to say the least. Reporters and newscasters contrived to sound uninterested and excited at the same time; what they were being bored and enthusiastic about was sometimes difficult to establish.

Manley had thought long and hard about why this perverse form of delivery had been brought in by those in control of the media. Finally he'd decided there could be only one satisfactory explanation: it was intended to further the totalitarianism of the state. Certainly on the level of that most precious of all acquisitions, language, the blandness of *Nationwide* was as cruel in spirit, as fascist in intention, as the outrages committed by the bombers and machine gunners in the biological field.

Suddenly content splattered from the reporter's smooth delivery, like the yolk of a dropped egg:

'. . . Mr Fox had left the hospital earlier than expected because unfortunately the patient, a thirty-nine year old Bradford man, had died under surgery. Mr Fox, who was aged forty-two, and was well-known for his pro-Zionist views, died instantly.'

Mr Fox.

Manley had written to him once, asking how he could reconcile the need to stop the holocaust being repeated with one's duty to avoid persecuting and terrorising others. Mr Fox had sent back some xeroxes of newspaper cuttings that had done nothing to resolve the conundrum. As far as Manley was concerned, *the* conundrum:

SCHOOL-BUS CHILDREN INJURED IN PALESTINE BOMB ATTACK.

ELDERLY HOSTAGE SHOT AFTER NIGHT-LONG ORDEAL.

SUICIDE SQUAD FOILED IN CANOE RAID.

As Manley saw it: Palestinian A killed Israeli civilian B. The consequence was that Israeli C killed Palestinian civilians C,D,E, God knew how many, X,Y,Z. The old doctrine of an eye for an eye, which itself should surely have been outmoded by now, at least implied that you hit back at the person who had harmed you. This notion of moving sideways along a queue of victims, apart from being morally indefensible, seemed designed solely to escalate conflict and bitterness for ever. It exhibited the same tendency towards lateral thinking as that promulgated by setters-out of newspaper pages, or compilers of news bulletins. Always, always, juxtaposition without significance. We will kill you because a person in the next town killed somebody in the town beyond. British Leyland strike call. . .Unmarried mother (25) has triplets. . .We will kill you because a Jewish banker. . .Boy (19) Molested Girl (7), Prosecution Alleges. . .Wear this Yellow Star, to show what you are. . .A Pint and a Half of Full Cream Milk in Every Bar. . .Israelis Bomb Palestinian Refugee Camp in Revenge Mission. . .The Final Solution: We will eliminate you because. You are a Jew.

I am not a Jew. I am me. *I* am a Jew.

Anyway, the conundrum had not been resolved in Mr Fox's case, because he'd been blown to bits.

'. . . happened one of our film units was parked a short distance from the hospital awaiting news of the transplant operation. We apologise for the poor technical quality.'

There were some shots of the car ruin, this time with wisps of smoke curling upwards in the dim light. Then a snatched interview with a witness.

'There was a big bang and I fell flat on my face,' he said unhelpfully.

On the grainy screen, his face came into focus, the Fat Man.

Despite the poor picture, despite the spread of features, Manley's recognition had all the sharpness of a point of light. In this case it was the reflection of a hastily-positioned arclamp on the Fat Man's expansive forehead.

Cut forward to the drab reporter standing in the hospital car park some time later in the morning:

'The police would be grateful if that gentleman we interviewed would report to them as soon as possible, as they believe he might be able to give them further details of the incident.'

'He would have slipped off directly he could,' Manley told Chapman. 'Don't you see, he caused the explosion in the first place. It was the man who shot Mr Wilkins in that restaurant last week.'

111

'If that was the case, could you explain what he was doing being interviewed on television?'

Manley swallowed, calmed himself. He had to speak as if this was neutral business between easy-going professional people. An unshaded, calm tone. Newspeak.

'The operation finished earlier than expected. The patient died. The Fat Man must have been almost caught in the act. He was holding his left arm and his jacket sleeve was scorched. He was probably stunned by his own explosion. Before he knew what was going on, a microphone was being stuffed in his mouth. You know what these media people are like.'

Chapman looked amused, from a distance.

'You've been very helpful,' he said with all the emotion of a shutting door.

'I wish you'd take some notice of me,' Manley said, unable to keep a certain querulousness from his tone. 'It might stop people getting killed.'

'I've been listening to you for nearly half an hour. If that isn't noticing, Mr Manley, I don't know what is. I'll be in touch. Good evening. . .sir.'

Sir, from that source, had the force of an insult.

23

Chapman was due in Rostris's office at eleven, to make a routine report. Before he came in Rostris tried to get himself into a good frame of mind, or stomach. He drank half a tumbler of thick white liquid that he'd bought from the chemist's. You were only supposed to take a spoonful, but that was for stomach-ache. He was suffering from stomach agony.

He'd made an exhibition of himself with Chapman in the canteen the other day. The last thing he wanted, the last thing in the world, would be to make Chapman suspicious enough to ask Sergeant Hopwood if anything had happened between the two of them. The possible scenario made him wince.

CHAPMAN (those dark eyes which could look right through you at the best of times): Did you say, a fuck?
WPS HOPWOOD: No, no, not on your life. *A fart.*

Could you be jealous of another man's fart? And if you *weren't* jealous, what were you? Something violent, Rostris suspected. Almost hoped: because the alternative was worse, the realm of fecal comedy, of the bluebottle, maggot, dog-turd.

He mustn't make the mistake of being too conciliatory either. That would look suspicious. The best thing would be to be as normal as possible, businesslike. Routine Rostris.

Meanwhile, he could feel that white stuff sifting down. It had a slow texture, slightly gluey, like semen or wallpaper paste. Perhaps it would descend upon his rubble, rocks, gravel-pit, junkyard, like snow, blotting out all the angles.

There was a brisk knock on the door.

'Come in,' Rostris called, bending over some work.

Chapman came in. Rostris dropped his pen, a second after picking it up.

'Busy?' Chapman asked. 'I can come back later.'

'Just paper work,' Rostris replied. 'I have to *look* as if I'm working. That's my job, remember.' How to tell truth so that it comes out a lie. Or was it a lie that came out as truth? Either way, it was easy for Rostris to be a cynical man: he had himself to be cynical about.

Chapman made his report: oil company offices he'd visited, witnesses he'd reinterrogated, ecologists he'd grilled, a reconstruction he'd arranged. None of it had got him very far. He concluded by outlining his meeting with Anthony Manley the evening before. He was convinced that Manley was the victim of delusions.

'I wonder,' Rostris suggested, trying to achieve a certain academic disinterestedness, his hands pressed together, palm to palm, in front of his mouth.

'I don't,' Chapman said harshly. He was obviously prepared for a battle on this subject. Rostris realised he would have to be careful. There was a point he had to make, however. You couldn't ignore your only witness: and it was certainly perverse to do so on the grounds that no one else had seen anything. It would be like not posting your football coupon because you never won anything on the pools.

'It would do no harm to take him seriously. What *else* have you got to go on?'

'The man lives in a fantasy world. For example, he seems to have convinced himself he's a Jew. He believes in suffering the way other people believe in God.'

'Why not?' Rostris asked moodily. The snow had already begun to thaw. 'It's there.'

'I haven't got time to investigate the nightmares of a lunatic.'

'You've obviously been spending time investigating those statements from the Green Principle, and we've already agreed they're the work of lunatics.'

Chapman answered with the patience of bad temper: 'But

the Green Principle haven't even taken credit for this London bombing. What we have is a totally different m.o., and a totally different location. Also, the London victim was a prominent pro-Zionist spokesman while our Mr Wilkins had no Israeli connections whatsoever. There's absolutely nothing to link the two cases.'

'I wouldn't say that. Wilkins was into a substitute for oil, and oil means Arabs, and Arabs mean Jews. I would have called that a pretty good series of links.'

'You'd never even have thought of it if it hadn't been for Manley.'

'But for Christ's sake, that's my whole point. The link *is* Manley. That's what I'm trying to tell you.'

'Look, do you know the sort of things Manley talked about? He rambled on on the subject of the *Nationwide* programme, and how fascist it was. He even told me what sort of sandwich he had for lunch. No, it wasn't a sandwich, it was a couple of Ryvitas. With cheese. He had gone home for a sandwich and then found he had no bread in the house. He talked for some time about the anomalies of chief rent, and how the government should have abolished it years ago. How it fouled up conveyancing on property transactions. What kind of a witness is that?'

'You know the way *I* work. I go through them all, one at a time. See if they've anything to give me. The Green Principle have provided you with nothing so far except red herrings. Anthony Manley has suggested a line of investigation. You need to give everything equal weight at this stage, you know.'

'It's my case,' said Chapman, in a conclusive voice. 'I'll just have to get on with it in my own way.'

There was no denying it, at least without calling into question Chapman's competence to do his job.

'I suppose so,' Rostris agreed grudgingly.

Chapman became conciliatory. 'What about *your* case, anyway?'

'Fourteen dead,' said Rostris glumly, 'at the latest count.'

'*Fourteen?* God in heaven, what's going on?'

'As I said the other day, it's an accident that won't stop happening. The firemen who went to the scene are dropping like flies. We haven't pointed out the connection but the papers will be on to it by tomorrow. There's a limit to how long you can keep the lid on. Also one copper's ill in hospital. A lad called Bennett from the Middleton substation. I suppose he'll go too, it makes you sick.'

'But what in hell are they dying of?'

'Nobody knows. Some crap that spilled out from the tanker. They've never met up with it before. It's like that fake olive oil in Spain, it gives you a new sort of illness altogether. Imagine it, dying a new kind of death.'

There was a pause.

'What's the difference?' Chapman asked quietly. 'We don't know what the old sort's like anyway.'

'The point is,' Rostris resumed, 'we've been lied to up hill and down dale. The tanker had been painted with the name of a fake company, for a start. They were thorough, you've got to give them credit for that. The whole works had been professionally sprayed with a fictional logo, advertising slogan, the lot. It was a brand new lorry, as well. No expense spared. We still haven't tracked the real firm down. The tanker driver wasn't able to help us much before he died, poor bastard. It was a contract job, a one-off he got through some middle-men called Driver Hire. They knew bugger all also. The tracks have been covered knee-deep. That compulsory doodah that you have to stick on the back of tankers to say what chemicals they're carrying and what they're liable to do to you in the event of spillage claimed the load was something totally innocuous, some chlorate or other. Chlorate my backside. It was biological, that's what it was.'

'Biological?'

'Viruses. Or bacteria. The victims are dying of acute bronchial congestion, it's related to pneumonia. That tanker was full of something like Legionnaire's Disease.'

'My God.'

'Not to mention it was explosive as well. If anybody had lit a fag the whole lot would have gone sky-high. I'm going to put whoever's responsible through the mincer when I find them.'

'Remember you believe in being cool, calm and collected,' Chapman pointed out, taking his revenge for the earlier part of their conversation.

24

After his second abortive attempt to offer himself as a witness to the police Anthony Manley needed to think. Or perhaps he needed to stop thinking. It was a matter of clearing his head, or emptying his mind. He decided to go for a walk – not down claustrophobic Manchester streets but out and up, in wide open spaces. Perhaps they would invade his being and he would see with clarity, or see nothing.

He spent an hour getting his equipment ready. As far as he was concerned that was almost the nicest thing about walking in the Peaks. He polished his boots first.

He began by bringing them up to a high shine, not for the effect but to ensure the polish had really penetrated the leather; then he dulled it off with a little more polish, to make them fully waterproof. The polish had the sort of dark, fruity scent that wood sometimes has; it was always a bonus to Manley to get a sensual experience via the process of cleaning something. He had a theory that people nowadays didn't make an appreciative enough contact with the external world, and that that was possibly a cause, or at least a symptom, of much of the violence of modern times. You became almost numb, so in the end you hardly noticed when you were mutilating something – or someone. As he explored the leather contours, rubbing away with cloth and brushes, he felt that in some subtle fashion he was coming to terms, rather as an artist might, Van Gogh perhaps, with the intrinsic nature of his boots.

The next task was to rethread his laces (he always removed them first, to prevent them from getting sticky and discoloured). When that was done he put a specially bought bar of Milk Tray, his drinking bottle and a torch in the small rucksack he would wear on his back. Then he put a large-scale map of the Dark Peak and a compass in the appropriate pockets of his anorak.

His anorak was full of zip-up pockets – several of them ran, like stitched scars, along the sleeves. There were more pockets than you could possibly use, at least on the one-day expeditions Manley always went on. He didn't mind, though. For one thing they provided double insulation and conditions could be pretty elemental up on the tops. For the same reason it was nice to be within something so intricate – rather like inhabiting a mobile rabbit warren. This didn't contradict the aim of being in touch with the universe, which was of course the whole intention behind his hikes, but you needed a small secure domain, a territory of your own, from which to extend your arm and make your handshake with the world. He believed in domesticity.

He stowed his gear in the boot of his car and drove south and east of the Manchester conurbation towards the hills. They loomed out of the Cheshire plain in a series of grey humps, like a school of whales. It was a grey day in point of fact, though warm, with a great deal of tumbling cloud set against the paler, smoother cloud above, so that from certain perspectives you got the impression that the Peaks were nothing but a section of the sky that had somehow solidified. As he began to draw near, however, he became aware of the green of this year's grass modulating the greys and browns of old bracken, heather, and rock.

He drove into the small stone village of Hayfield, left his car in the car park, and walked along a road that rose out of the village until he got to the stile which marked the beginning of a footpath to the tops. The air grew noticeably colder within a few hundred yards of beginning the ascent, as if he were climbing from mid-summer through autumn towards winter. and the greyness intensified till he was walking through thin cloud the colour of the rather mangy sheep that hurried about these hillsides. His face began to get wet: you couldn't say it was raining because the drops of rain didn't fall, they seemed to distill themselves from the air all about him. It was like walking through a rain factory.

Conditions continued to worsen rapidly, so that the sphere of face that wasn't protected by his anorak hood was drenched by the time he reached the top of the first slope. Visibility was poor and there seemed little point in making for the Dark Peak. He turned right instead, and walked past a small copse of low twisted trees that had died at some remote date in the past and remained up here in an almost petrified state, like so many discarded antlers. After about a mile in this direction he would come to a slope which, though steep, could be scrambled down, and then he would be heading towards civilisation again.

As he walked along on level ground in his personal cloud, Manley found his worries returning. So much for Nature. True, the particular issue that had occupied him down below, the scepticism of the police, didn't come immediately to the forefront of his mind; instead came an equally disagreeable and, obscurely, related matter: his visit to his father yesterday.

Those monthly encounters were always purgatory. The prison visiting-room, with all its small tables, was depressingly institutional, and his father had gone from looking totally inconspicuous, as he did in civilian life, to disreputable, even though there were no signs that he was neglecting himself, and in some ways he must be living a more healthy life in prison than he had on the outside. At least he couldn't drink. But his jowls seemed to have darkened, although he was clean-shaven. Perhaps the different diet, or anxiety, or the change in regimen, had had some kind of effect on his hormones. His veins seemed redder and nearer the surface of his face than ever. Anthony Manley had the same problem himself – one of the reasons behind his attempts at living a healthy life was that he feared they could be a symptom of high blood-pressure – but nothing on the scale of his father, who looked as though a blood mask were gradually being superimposed over his skin. His cheeks had sunk a little and his eyes were correspondingly large; rolling eyes.

Manley thought to himself: he's not got long, poor old boy, but instead of stirring up any pity that thought only added to the contempt and bitterness he already felt, as though his father were making a point of betraying him in every way he could find. The old man looked so frail, but of course he'd never seemed exactly robust, with his sloping shoulders and mild-mannered, unimpressive demeanour. Manley wondered where he found the leverage to hit people so hard. It wasn't a matter of drunken brawling either, Manley knew that in his heart of hearts, despite his loyal refusal to accept the prosecution case.

Not that his father wasn't a drunk – or at least, in this context, a would-be drunk. Even as they sat there together, his father rolled his gaze round the room in that unpleasant way he had, as if his eyes had been oiled or greased in some fashion so that they moved more readily than they ought, and then asked confidentially: 'Can you get me any scotch?'

'What?' Manley asked in return, pretending not to have heard him.

His father leaned forward over the table and repeated the question in a louder whisper. Manley noticed how unpleasant his breath smelled, like stale milk, and he realised how often in the past that must have been disguised by the aftermath of booze.

'How can I?' he replied, meaning it to be a rhetorical question, but his father immediately answered:

'Pour it into a shampoo bottle. You're allowed to bring those in.' He paused a moment, to let the idea sink in, then added: 'A family size one would do the trick.'

'You're forgetting something, father: I'm a solicitor. I can't —'

'All the more reason. They'll never check up on you.'

'No, no, it would be disastrous if I got caught. For heaven's sake, my position's bad enough already. And anyway – ' He was going to say that anyway it was better for his father not to drink, but decided at the last minute not to rub salt into the wound.

'Anyway what?' his father asked aggressively.

'Nothing.'

Nothing was the word. He could get nothing from his father; he had nothing to give his father.

Nothing daunted his father rolled his eyes once more, and tried again with his other vice: gambling. He wanted Manley to lay some bets for him.

'For God's sake, that's what's got you in here, Dad,' Manley said brutally. He had the sense of his inheritance clutching towards him with hairy, atavistic arm, claiming him for its own.

As he trudged through the mist along the slightly boggy summit of the Peak, Manley once more felt the presence of his father as one might a monkey perched on one's shoulder, swivelling its gaze, chattering its teeth, pulling at your hair and ears. However elaborate your anorak, it wasn't monkey-proof.

How to make a fresh start? The other dilemma that had been so much on his mind intertwined itself with this problem, and he thought to himself ruefully, well, at least I tried to make the police do something. He felt that by making an effort to prevent some further tragedy happening in the future he had shown willingness to learn the lessons of the past, to exorcise history, to alleviate the long accumulation of suffering. To no avail, of course, the police hadn't been interested.

The only alternative would have been to go to the press but he hadn't been able to bring himself to do so. If the police were the agents of fascism, the papers were its consciousness itself. Anything communicated to them would be dirtied and distorted. Tragedy would be converted into triviality.

He had reached the scrambling-off point.

He turned off the path and began, half-running, half-sliding, to travel down the damp bracken. After only a few yards he came below the ceiling of cloud and suddenly there was the whole valley before him, green grass, bright, pearly light, the neat contours of a nineteenth-century reservoir tactfully inserted at the end of it. The elements were bracing in their way, but strangely it gave Manley a sense of relief to see something man-made.

As he drew nearer, he noticed the reservoir controller, the waterman, whatever he called himself, fiddling with a brass lever on some sort of sluice gate. Manley had been so cut off from people recently – by the turbulence of his inner problems, by the thickness of surrounding cloud. He felt he had been in that cloud not for an hour or so but for a long long time, ever since the murder on Prince Street, in fact. He experienced a sudden urge to go over and have a few words with the man. Why not? Passing ramblers must often go up to him and ask directions, or make casual conversation.

Manley walked carefully along a narrow stone parapet that ran between two sections of the reservoir. The man had his back to him, still intent on whatever it was he was doing.

'Not much of a day, is it?' Manley asked his back.

The man started, then slowly turned to face him. His gaze travelled up and down Manley's body in a calm appraising manner, and then he said slowly, as if weighing each word: 'This isn't a fancy dress party, mate, this is a reservoir.'

For a second the significance of the words didn't sink in, and Manley looked blankly back at the bland, cruel stare. 'I beg your —'

With his previous deliberation, the man put in: 'If you don't clear off right away, I'll set my bloody dog on you.'

As Manley hurried off, his mind suddenly achieved its wished-for clarity.

He would go to the press, cost what it may. The waterman's aggressiveness had brought him to a simple realisation. It was better to accept publication of one's story, however much that process perverted, brutalised, demeaned, its essence, than to remain silent. The final lesson of suffering: you should at least cry out.

As he came to his decision it struck him as strange that he should put his head in the noose just because someone had been unpleasant about his appearance.

Perhaps it was no coincidence that tailoring was a Jewish profession.

25

Ed Pointon, journalist and explorer of feminine charms, wasn't in fact a cynic. As far as he was concerned, his women were the cynical ones. They would climb into his bed as if they were stepping straight on to page two.

In any roomful of people he came to know exactly the ones who would respond to his modest announcement that he worked for the *Morning Sky*, 'that rag'. It wasn't the type the uninitiated might imagine, those jolly busty women who let the drinks go to their head, who laugh a lot and who stand closer to you than is really necessary while you're talking. Nine times out of ten they were a waste of time. But serene lean women with slinky hair and a cool aura, who look at you as if they've rarely seen such an uninteresting male, would get into your bed almost before you knew what was going on.

They remained cool, however, even then, wrapped up in themselves rather than in you. Pointon marvelled at their capacity to stay aloof, even snobbish, while they were being screwed. He, meanwhile, was a romantic, always ready to fall in love. As he told one of them once, in an effort to break through her shell, he wore his heart on his. . . (suddenly coy, in the face of the continued severity of her gaze, he glanced rapidly down at his nakedness and mouthed the offending word silently).

In other words it was both a blessing and a curse to Ed Pointon that such a surprising proportion of young women wanted to take up a career in modelling.

One of them was due to arrive this evening, fairly late. From his point of view, a romantic encounter, a sexual adventure, an opening of doors that could lead anywhere (even though experience told him you always arrived at the same place). Don Juan, in Pointon's professional opinion, had received a bad press. His promiscuity was a symptom of insatiable innocence.

From her point of view, of course, the encounter would have a rather different significance, a sneak preview, sample offer, loss leader, with the *Morning Sky*'s forthcoming 'Birds of Britain' series in mind. Women were such cynics.

The doorbell rang slightly earlier than he had expected, about nine o'clock. Pointon was just forking up a portion of Tyrolean honey cake he had baked himself. He was a well-built man with not an ounce of fat, despite his taste for such things: presumably, in the course of a busy life, he burned the sweetness off.

He put his cake-fork down, dabbed his lips, and went to answer the front door. He got something of a shock to discover it wasn't Marcia (so-called) standing there in the sunset but a small, intense-looking man in an elegant suit.

'Excuse me,' said the man, 'are you Mr Pointon of the *Morning Sky*?'

'Yes,' Pointon answered gruffly, 'but you've caught me at a bad time, I'm afraid. I've got a story I must work on.'

'I believe it was you who wrote that article about the murder of Mr Wilkins the other week.'

'That's right.'

Then, unexpectedly from such a lower-case individual, a scoop announced itself: 'I saw who committed that murder, Mr Pointon. And I've seen him since. My name is Anthony Manley.'

He offered his hand; Pointon shook it. The skin felt strangely dry, like paper.

After they had been in a huddle for an hour, Pointon made his suggestion.

'Look, the tape of that news bulletin will be at the BBC in London. I've got a friend there. Why don't we catch the overnight train, and have a look at it first thing tomorrow? Give you another chance to be sure in your own mind.'

Manley agreed without making any difficulty. He wanted to go home first, however, to collect some things. As luck would have it, just as they reached Pointon's front door Marcia rang the bell.

'Hello my darling,' Pointon boomed. He had noticed himself that his voice became deeper and more rounded when he talked to women.

'Hello, Ed,' she replied, her voice also low, and cool as toothpaste. She glanced quickly at Manley and then back at Pointon. One eyebrow, lean and sinuous as the rest of her, rose fractionally.

'This is Mr Manley,' Pointon explained. 'This is Marcia,' he told Manley.

'I'm pleased to meet you,' Manley said.

She nodded vaguely by way of reply and once more turned her attention to Pointon. 'Shall I go on in?' she asked.

'Sorry, love, something's turned up.'

'Has it then?' Her voice was even lower; cool to the point of refrigeration. Yet again her eyes referred to Manley; and back.

'Don't worry. You'll get your chance. One way or another. I mean, one way *and* another.' Suddenly he succumbed to impatience. 'Your tits will be admired by millions.'

She winced with shock. 'Thank you very much,' she replied.

'Only joking. Well, I wasn't joking, but I was joking. You'll be in the *Sky*, a promise is a promise. But come round in a day or two, eh? Take a rain check.'

'I hope he gave you a good time,' she said to Manley, swivelled on a tiny shoe, and hurried off.

'She wasn't. . .implying?' Manley asked Pointon.

'Mind like the gutter, that type,' Pointon informed him.

Pointon sold his soul to get a video of the BBC tape, after Manley had said he was sure, sure, sure, with curious mounting excitement for such a dapper man. The *Sky*'s northern photographer, pleased with the challenge of having to deal with something other than daily Marcias plus the odd fire or road accident, froze the best image and photographed it. The picture retained the blurred, *in media res* quality of a video-still, features vague and spherical face glowing like the moon. But however unrecognisable the shot was more than any other paper had got, it made the story concrete, took the reader, as Jock Griswold, editor of the *Rotherham Charger* would have put it, *'in'* to the news.

IS THIS THE FACE OF RESTAURANT KILLER?

Pointon's shorthand pencil asked his notebook.

I had planned a quiet evening at home,

the pencil went on to explain. Pointon paused to consider. Yes, the autobiographical – once again – was the right approach. 'If you've got it, flaunt it,' Jock had advised him during his long apprenticeship. 'Your old mum might appreciate a blush of maidenly modesty, but the rest of the world doesn't give a damn if you've your finger stuck up your nostril. As long as you deliver the goods.'

. . .when there was a knock at my door.

Better than a ring even if less true. Destiny doesn't ring the bell, it gives a few heavy bangs to announce its presence. When you hit a certain rarified level of journalism, the news arrives on *your* doorstep.

As a reporter,

no, flaunt it,

As an experienced reporter, I am used to running after,

mustn't sound like a groupie after a pop-star, a macho emphasis is required,

to hunting out the big news stories of the day. But for the second time in the strange and tragic case of the Wilkins murder, a scoop announced itself . . .

What the hell is happening to my style, wherefore this peculiar tendency to ponce and pussyfoot, this slither towards *The Times*? Nasty Marcia must be putting ideas into my head:

> . . . a scoop came up and grabbed me by the . . .

On the other hand not even the *Sky* could wear the other extreme:

> . . . grabbed me by the lapels.

Then a quick reminder that he was there when Wilkins was shot. Then:

> Last night a stranger came to my house.

Give his references, make the reader realise we're not dealing with the sort of random big-mouth you can come across in any pub,

> a well-dressed, quietly spoken man. . .

Manley had made him promise not to give his occupation away, far less, of course, his name, so that would have to serve to identify him,

> who had some staggering news to impart.

Then came Manley's story, the second phase of the article: from scoop-trumpeting and the personal touch to Jock Griswold's famous crunch. Which left, for finale, the QUESTIONS OF PUBLIC CONCERN:

> Why have the police ignored this man's evidence? Do they understand these two cases are linked? If not, why not?

Don't forget in all the excitement, that there is always the *Sky*'s market to defend, remind the readers – and the editor, for God's sake – that congratulations are in order:

> The *Morning Sky* takes this witness very seriously. Surely it is not too much to ask that the authorities do the same?

At long last the climax – in tabloid journalism there must be nothing premature about one's ejaculations:

Do the police accept that they could be dealing with a mercenary
of terror?

And to conclude, a note of menace, God bless you Agatha:

Does our photograph

– 'our photograph', break your heart Beeb –

show the face of the British Carlos?

26

Late afternoon. The sunshine was as lukewarm and mellow as medium sherry, enriching the interior of the bus.

The little pleasures of life had returned to John Outram, as he was currently known, since the Hautbois operation had got underway. He even enjoyed the smell of his bus as it ground towards Cheadle: upholstery, plastic, diesel fuel, plus a certain other something, a generic bus scent that brought back, as he let it seep from the olfactory passages to his nostalgia organ, certain tram rides he'd taken as a child. Buses were all right. He couldn't be bothered to run a car, he couldn't be bothered to do so many things. What he *could* be bothered to do was arrange for the death of James Wilkins, which had already been achieved, and of Dr Leo Murgatroyd, which was still to take place.

It had better take place. He was on the bus, travelling towards Miss Clare's, to make sure it did, to defuse the threat posed by today's story in the *Morning Sky*.

That paper was a curse. Or rather, that reporter, Ed Pointon. He obviously had an instinct for demoralising Miss Clare.

At first he'd seemed to be handed to them on a plate, a media representative who'd obligingly witnessed the death of Mr Wilkins. He was the obvious person to receive Miss Clare's beloved manifesto. And what had he done with it? Squashed it into six column inches on page five, and played *them* for laughs. Any person of normal intelligence (Miss Clare had intelligence but she was by no means normal) could see the funny side, of course, which was why Outram had steered the document away from the upmarket press, *The Times*, *Telegraph* and *Guardian*, who liked to relieve their habitual pomposity with the occasional tract of dinosaur humour – you didn't go to the *Morning Sky* for penetrating satire and a sharp sense of the absurd.

Presumably his proximity to the actuality of Mr Wilkins's death had given the *Sky* journalist a critical frame of reference within which to judge Miss Clare's demented banalities.

That had been bad enough. This morning's contribution had been even worse. God knew how she would react to that.

One consolation perhaps was that you couldn't recognise the Fat Man from his photograph. He only came out as a pale but grainy blob. John Outram, of course, wouldn't have been able to recognise him anyway, never having met him, but a fat man, in the context of terrorist outrages, could only be *the* Fat Man. There was no point in pretending otherwise: even Miss Clare wouldn't swallow the argument that mercenaries of that build were thick on the ground.

The problem wasn't that the police might tighten up on security as a result and endanger their plans. The photograph had no features on it for a start; there might not be many obese terrorists but luckily there was a plethora of large, blameless individuals walking the streets. In any case, that was the Fat Man's problem. The contract had already been taken out. N.B. Make that point to Miss Clare. A contract is a contract. Honour among thieves.

The real difficulty was that the old crone might worry that the purity of her ecological motivation could be impeached if their actions were confused, via the agency of the Fat Man, with an irrelevant outrage, organised by some Abdul or Mohammed with a grudge against Zionism. Political crimes differed in one crucial respect from the secular variety: their perpetrators wanted the general public to know, at least to a certain extent, whodunnit. Miss Clare would hate the credit to go elsewhere.

What made the Hautbois case so extraordinary, of course, was that the credit actually *belonged* elsewhere, although she was unaware of that fact. The ultimate detective story: in which the murderer didn't do it.

The responsibility belonged entirely to John Outram, who

had been planning the operation long before the Green Principle had been thought of. Long before John Outram had been thought of, come to that: he was Gordon Chamberlain, alias Frobisher, in those days.

Rigorous early training had taught Outram how to put an impending crisis, or confrontation, out of his mind. Instead, as he trundled from stop to stop, en route to his meeting with Miss Clare and Dennis, John Outram, formerly Gordon Chamberlain alias Frobisher, who operated under cover of the Green Principle, luxuriated in the thought that whenever in his life he'd fully committed himself to a line of action the first thing that happened was that his name either disappeared altogether, or at least became obscure and equivocal.

That, of course, had been the great attraction of the SAS.

The media had done his beloved profession no good at all by equating it with glamour, excitement, aggression, the qualities associated with self-expression of one kind or another. Ignorant louts, bloodthirsty members of the other armed services, psychopaths, men suffering from superiority or inferiority complexes, unemployed night-club bouncers, superannuated boy-scouts, read their newspapers and thrillers and then applied to join, in the belief that they would let off steam, vent their frustrations, live a life of adventure.

That motivation disqualified the applicant immediately.

The love of adventure reflected a desire to gamble. In order to gamble you had to have something to lose. When an SAS man was on a mission the only loss he should fear was the loss of the mission. The vocation provided no opportunity for self-assertion. Indeed the first thing you relinquished was your name.

Anonymity was what Gordon needed most of all. When he joined the SAS he felt that a weight had been lifted from his shoulders. Not a huge weight: there would have been a challenge in carrying that about, taking on the responsibility of coping with genius or complexity or disturbance. But if the weight wasn't huge it was leaden: nondescript, dismal, grey. People were often described as being overfond of themselves;

by the same token you could dislike yourself also, just as you could dislike a colleague or relation, finding them dull or depressing company. When it was yourself, of course, you couldn't just walk out of the door. But you could, if certain factors were right, walk into the SAS.

He had walked into marriage on the same basis – that is, on the basis that his wife wasn't himself. Indeed she wasn't. She was beautiful.

No, Nicola wasn't beautiful, there was no point in being dishonest, even in retrospect, even on a 127 bus.

Perhaps when she was young, at first glance, you might have thought so. Certainly she was blonde, well-rounded, provocative. She could make your pulses race. But when you looked more closely you realised she wasn't quite what she seemed.

She was *too* blonde, for a start. Her hair was nearly white and was matched by a milky, almost anaemic complexion. Her eyes were on the small side, and because her lashes were so fine and pale as to be virtually invisible they reminded him of a hamster's. Her nose was a little too long, though straight (possibly on second thoughts it was too straight), and had the faintest sheen which she usually concealed with powder. She had a merry smile which she displayed frequently, obviously conscious that her lips were thin.

Her most important attribute though was her sexuality. It suffused her system, she thought of nothing else.

This didn't have the effect of making her seem monotonous or limited, however. She thought of nothing else in the way a cat thinks of nothing else but being a cat. Her features, taken in the abstract – except that in her case such a perspective wasn't conceivable, she was the least abstract person Gordon had ever known – would have suggested a shrinking violet, a woman for whom modesty wasn't just decorous but appropriate.

Not on your life. She looked at men – Gordon included – boldly, frankly, without any deference at all. Nevertheless, the effect was to make you, as a male, feel pleased, elated, at the thought of being regarded by her as a sexual counterpart. Of being, as Gordon tended to think of his role, useful to her. Thus the ideal of service, at one level or another, underlay both his military and married life.

There were then three stages in Nicola's appeal: the initial bowling-over, the secondary disappointment, and the subsequent bonus, piquant as the taste of a strawberry, when you realised that she was after all what certain SAS officers, the sort with bristly moustaches, public school accents, the sort who'd relinquished double-barrelled names, would call 'a real woman'.

Gordon had wanted nothing more than to occupy that third stage for ever. He was certainly not a vain man; nor on the other hand was he a man who needed to prove something to himself. Nicola, quite simply, was all he wanted.

She had been his for almost ten years.

He hadn't deluded himself that she was actually in love with him. What she loved was being an SAS wife.

She had had to sign the Official Secrets Act when they got married, promising not to reveal the nature of his job to anybody outside the service.

From that moment on she'd come to adore being in the company of outsiders, silently sharing the secret with Gordon. At such times she made a public display of affection, relishing the puzzlement people couldn't help feeling at the devotion of this sensual woman to such an undistinguished and insignificant man. Gordon was tall and fit, of course, in the SAS you had to be, but he contrived to give no impression of stature or athleticism. He was a six-footer of medium height; a strong man whose extreme slimness made him appear almost frail. In such groups nobody except Nicola could have any inkling he was a trained killer. She managed to give even her loyalty an exciting quality, as if it were adulterous.

It wasn't until she was approaching middle-age and beginning to get rather plump that she left him.

He could see it coming but there was nothing whatsoever he could do about it. She had always been rather impervious to suggestions, turned in upon herself. You couldn't call her introverted – it was by no means a matter of mental attitude. More accurate would be to say that she lived deep within her body and therefore any communication had a long way to go; and without a sexual vehicle the journey was an arduous one indeed.

She became restless, flirtatious, agitated by a sense that somehow she'd missed out on life's opportunities. In other words, she was reaching the age when those opportunities dwindled away and you had to stand by your commitments.

She was very tender to him when she broke the news, stroking his hair and cheek, looking sympathetically into his eyes, as a mother might when her child is in difficulties. She had never looked at him like a mother before.

She went off with a successful barrister, good-looking as a film-star. Until this point in her life she had wanted to be regarded as a great catch; now, less confident of her qualities, she required her man to be the desirable one, public testimony to her worth.

Shortly afterwards, as if they had some sort of tactful poetry in their souls, SAS Command sent Gordon on a mission to Antarctica. Specifically to Livingston Island, in the South Shetlands group; looming out of a swirling Polar Sea, the next island in the chain was called Deception.

It was here that Gordon met James Wilkins and Leon Murgatroyd, and thereby encountered the principle of pure evil for the first time in a life of varied experience.

27

On the Cheadle bus, on a warm Manchester afternoon, John Outram's thoughts turned towards polar regions. It had been January, high summer, when SAS Officer Gordon Frobisher, properly known as Gordon Chamberlain, later to become John Outram, alias the Green Principle, had stepped ashore on Livingston Island; a deep-freeze version of that season which you felt needed to be thawed and cooked before consumption. The packed snow had been worn away in places to reveal whitish-grey rock which itself looked like fossilised snow. A low asbestos building, perfectly calculated to suit the bleak environment, housed a laboratory belonging to the Germ Warfare Section, alias the Biological Research Department, of the Ministry of Defence, alias Antarctic Station 4Z of the British Meteorological Office.

Gordon Frobisher's party consisted of two other SAS men and, bizarrely, two meteorologists, to 'give authenticity'. It wasn't made welcome.

'We don't need security,' said James Wilkins, Laboratory Administrator, as they sat around the mess table eating canned stew.

'I gather you're engaged on high priority biological research,' Frobisher pointed out. 'Surely you —'

'Look at that weather outside,' Wilkins suggested. 'It's midsummer and cold as a nun's twat. We don't get a lot of holidaymakers, you know.'

'What do you think I am?' Frobisher asked. 'A nightwatchman? I'd prefer to be on active service myself, but when we do security, we mean it, and often the other lot mean it too.'

'All we have is the odd Jap or Argie whaler going past, no

problem. But when they see you lot crawling over the place they're going to start taking an interest. It's a low profile we need, we've got a bunch of bugs here, not Battersea Power Station.'

Wilkins was brusque, aggressive, convincing. Frobisher couldn't bear him. There was nothing worse, he felt, than another person's sense of humour when you were sharing his island. Wilkins's jokes were endless. They featured the thalidomide child who didn't feel well, the infantryman with the blunt bayonet, the fate of the frog in a liquidiser, the sex-maniac who thought that babies were brought by storks. Frobisher spent hours sitting in the calor gaslight of the dim small-windowed room, listening as the man milked experience for humour, kneading, manipulating, raping the world until it had a red nose and sticking-out ears. There was no warmth or friendship behind the jokes: Wilkins made it perfectly clear that he thought Frobisher and his men ought to go. He was so adamant on the subject that Frobisher began to wonder if his presence wasn't posing a threat to something that was being planned on the island, a touch of private enterprise perhaps.

Dr Murgatroyd didn't exactly inspire confidence either. He had a craggy face with an eagle nose and tufted eyebrows, a face that was all thrusting topography. Frobisher had his first meeting with him in a small ante-chamber to the laboratory; ante-hut was more like it, in terms of Antarctic architecture.

'Dr Murgatroyd,' Frobisher began, 'I need to be given more information about what's going on here.'

'What's going on here,' Murgatroyd answered testily, 'is a red herring. A cul-de-sac. Whatever you want to call it. A blind alley.' His eyes gleamed angrily.

'I don't believe that,' Frobisher answered bluntly.

'You've only just come. You don't even know what we're working on.'

'That's precisely why I'm asking you.'

'Look, what happened was this. An Antarctic research team were doing a routine borehole on the main continental shelf, a hundred miles or so south of here. Looking for minerals or oil, who isn't? They took the sample to their little laboratory and began analysing it. The next day all four of them were as dead as a doornail. The press were told they'd fallen down a crevasse; they were actually flat out on the floor of their hut. The autopsies revealed they'd died of an illness akin to pneumonia. Naturally the Ministry of Defence were interested – anything that can clobber four people that effectively is obviously worth looking into. Another sample bore was taken, this time with all the safety precautions. They thought it would be wiser not to send it back to civilisation, given that they didn't know how lethal it might be, but on the other hand they couldn't set up a sophisticated enough laboratory out in the howling wilderness. So that's why we're here. We've been isolating the organism. But it turns out to be no use for the M.O.D.'s purposes. It only thrives in very warm conditions. The bugs are mardy, as they say where I come from.'

'But I would have —'

'Anyway I'll see you later.' The animation called up to features and voice by the necessity for explanation dwindled away; a sort of lugubrious abstractedness spread over the craggy face like moss over rocks. 'Don't forget the do tonight,' he added, his attention already elsewhere: on whatever it was that seethed and popped in test tubes next door, perhaps.

'I'll make sure I don't have another engagement,' Frobisher replied somewhat sarcastically.

His tone was lost on Murgatroyd. 'I've got to get back to work,' he muttered, and sloped off. Frobisher picked up the contradiction. If the Antarctic bugs were, incomprehensibly, mardy and useless, why was the call of work so imperative?

Frobisher left the laboratory building and followed a narrow track down to the seashore. The frail sunshine of the morning had disappeared, and the whole sky swirled and eddied with grey clouds, as though the sky were the sea. The water in turn was as active, only in a more orderly fashion: grey-green breakers hurrying past as if they hardly noticed Livingston Island, with the occasional spume breaking ranks like a sudden scream. The scentless wind blew hard as iron. A few hundred yards away the Government Survey ship *Expedition* leaned away from its moorings. Beyond, the gleam of an iceberg, white as the white of an eye, and beyond that the dark hunched shape of Deception. Frobisher thought of Wilkins's words: 'We don't get a lot of holidaymakers, you know.'

What *did* you get, by the shores of Bellingshausen's Sea?

You got whatever Murgatroyd was brewing up in his laboratory.

Frobisher reminded himself that his own specific mandate was to protect the security of the scientific research being carried out here. It crossed his mind that he might need to protect it from Murgatroyd, the researcher, as much as from more explicitly foreign powers.

This task – this duty – was to formulate itself more clearly to Frobisher/Chamberlain/Outram/Principle, as the day, and the years, wore on.

Meanwhile even SAS officers could suffer from toothache. Frobisher turned from the bitter wind, and made his way to his quarters.

28

The 'do' was in honour of the *Expedition*'s company who, having delivered the so-called meteorologists to Livingston Island, would be going south on a tour of inspection. Lord Tetley, a junior Trade and Industry minister was on board, although Frobisher hadn't seen him during the week or two he'd been on the same ship. He had wondered whether his own mission was so delicate that contact was being minimised, or whether Tetley's was; possibly his lordship was just too comfortable in his specially furnished cabin to want to come out. The ship's steward had told Frobisher about that cabin. Plush as a Pullman car, rarely occupied, it was kept available for VIPs as though the authorities expected the *Expedition* to draw in alongside some iceberg and pick up a first-class passenger with a long distance season ticket. Anyway, for the time being Lord Tetley was that passenger.

He condescended to come to the 'do' however, huddled in the rocking but pennanted landing vessel along with the captain, ship's officers, and scientific complement of the *Expedition*. It gave Frobisher a malicious satisfaction, he wasn't sure why, to go over their security clearances with a fine tooth comb while they shifted from foot to foot outside the messhut. The clouds had cleared, and a white, low sun was shining faintly; the wind was still bitter, however.

Murgatroyd stumped over from his quarters, nodded curtly at the little queue, and walked on in. He was wearing a dinner jacket that shone faintly green in the pale antarctic twilight; indeed when Frobisher looked at it more closely, later in the evening, he realised it was as mouldy as a neglected cheese. Murgatroyd, by that stage drunk, disagreed.

'It's what they call rusty,' he claimed, his voice oddly free of the animus and testiness it had when he was sober. 'Haven't you ever read descriptions of rusty jackets in Victorian novels?' That itself was an eye-opener, sour Dr Murgatroyd reading Victorian novels. On the other hand evenings were long in Antarctica: in summer because the night never fell, in winter because it had already occupied the whole of the day. Frobisher couldn't bring himself to think of winter here; the strange summer was oppressive enough.

'But rust is brown,' he pointed out.

'Copper rust is green,' Murgatroyd claimed triumphantly.

'But your jacket isn't made of copper,' Frobisher concluded, feeling that he had been scrupulously logical but already uncertain as to what he'd been logical about. Who cared? It was just banter.

Banter with Dr Murgatroyd: the privilege had been dearly bought.

But as Frobisher checked in the *Expedition* guests the endless evening was still young and all was cold sobriety. Frobisher watched as Lord Tetley, small and toothy but with a brisk confident air, was introduced to Murgatroyd. Almost immediately the two men went to the far end of the bar and began to talk like old cronies. Lord Tetley poured himself water from a jug at his elbow, and sipped it as he chattered on.

Once more Frobisher's seismograph registered. He had checked on Tetley, of course: for the time being security was his duty. In addition to his government responsibilities his lordship was a director of the Hautbois Company (UK) Ltd.

The water jug provided an opportunity.

Frobisher poured himself a measure of scotch. Then he casually sauntered along the bar until he reached Tetley, said 'Excuse me,' and picked up the jug. Tetley looked up and started in surprise: confirmation possibly of guilty secrets. The conversation of course had stopped dead. The problem that had always plagued espionage and counter-espionage was that when you were near enough to listen, the subjects usually stopped talking. Modern technology could make life easier, but not, as it happened, on Livingston Island. Nobody had anticipated a threat from within.

Frobisher took a sip from his drink, and nearly spat. The jug didn't contain water at all but a liquid hot and aniseedy, an Argentinian spirit called aguila, he later discovered. It combined hideously with scotch: battery acid with a hint of vomit – shades of things to come. No wonder Tetley had looked startled. Frobisher had poured in a lot of the liquid too, with the intention of diluting his whisky.

He decided to sip away. Any repudiation of the drink, with Tetley watching him suspiciously from one side, would convert his low profile into a comic turn. Both Tetley and Murgatroyd were drinking their own aguila readily enough.

Tetley became distinctly merry. In not much more than an hour he was actually boisterous, in a public school sort of way, horsing around with several other members of the party, including one of Frobisher's genuine meteorologists who stood on the bar and forecast sufficient weather to freeze the balls off a brass monkey. Tetley himself managed to lose all the buttons off his evening blazer. Murgatroyd sat on his stool in the corner, looking lugubrious. By this time Frobisher was beside him, keeping them both topped up with the aguila jug.

'Upper crust bastards,' Murgatroyd said confidentially. 'They'll be poking it up each other next.' It was the most friendly remark he'd yet directed to Frobisher.

'Have you ever come across Tetley before?' Frobisher asked, a carefully contrived note of slurred innocence in his voice.

'No,' Murgatroyd replied, a little too quickly to convince Frobisher. 'I think we'd better get the food on the table, before these people begin to smash the place up.'

Frobisher managed to arrange things so he sat by Murgatroyd. Tetley, tie wayward, collar about his ears, looked beatifically about him from the bottom of the table, unaware of his demotion. Murgatroyd carved with the clumsy movements of a drunk. The meat was seal.

Frobisher topped up Murgatroyd's glass and his own. He

looked down at the evil, sweet-smelling drink and the great slice of fishy blubber before him and for the only time in his life felt a twinge of fear at the prospect of food. The important thing to remember was that Murgatroyd was in the same boat, at least alcoholically. Perhaps he would be able to take seal in his stride – he had the advantage of experience in that direction.

Frobisher cut off a small cube of seal and put it in his mouth. Dear God. The taste – a pungent quintessence of all the fish consumed in the seal's lifetime – haunted his mouth and even his nostrils, mingling with the after-gasp of aguila.

'Tell me about these microbes,' he said to Murgatroyd, rather earlier than he'd intended to raise the subject. He needed a topic to pin his attention to.

Murgatroyd, gobbling seal with quick, slightly smacking movements of his lips, was, however, far enough gone to co-operate.

'It's a breakthrough,' he said, his mouth still busy. The smell of Murgatroyd's seal, a fish equivalent of rancid butter, mingled in Frobisher's nostrils with his own. 'Not in M.O.D. terms, of course, it's a dead-loss from their angle. But from a Darwinian point of view. I forecast their existence you know, the bug equivalent of the missing link, although the gap between viruses and bacteria is far greater than that between men and apes. And these little sweethearts fit right in the middle of it. I never thought in my wildest dreams that I'd come across any that had survived. It's a bit like discovering that prehistoric fish, the coelacanth.' The deepset eyes twinkled in triumph. Frobisher's investment in aguila was paying off.

Murgatroyd took another mouthful of seal. Frobisher held his breath and did likewise.

'Why should they have died out?' he asked.

'Cold. Ice ages. They're very sensitive to the cold.'

'For heaven's sake, the only survivors were discovered in Antarctica. Under nearly a mile of ice.'

'Funny that, a paradox. We scientists are always coming up

against those little tricks in nature. They're like alibis, you know, when a criminal says he couldn't have done the evil deed because he was having his leg amputated at the time.' He swallowed, took a mouthful of aguila as if to wash the seal down, cut off another strip of blubber and put it in his mouth. A small piece of blackish-grey fat remained visible in the corner of his lips. 'I think they got frozen so quickly the little buggers didn't have time to drop dead. Suspended animation, you might call it.'

'It seems impossible.'

'They're a very primitive form of life, you know. Survive anything.' He paused, took a sip of aguila, continued chewing. 'Except the cold of course.'

Frobisher tried to collect his thoughts. They seemed to be running in every direction, it was like trying to pick up hand-fuls of water. Or aguila. That was another problem of espionage: when you got the opposition drunk enough to confide, you were sometimes too far gone yourself to take it all in.

Murgatroyd was continuing.

'That's why they're no use to the war machine. They love the human host, and they're highly infectious. But they can't survive in the atmosphere of even the warmest country. So they're not transmitted from A to B. Except in certain circumstances.'

Frobisher, with exaggerated calm, took another draught of aguila. They were so near the nub.

'Like what?' he asked.

'Like a heatwave, for example, when the temperature is a hundred degrees fahrenheit, or above. But apparently the M.O.D. don't envisage the possibility of high temperature conflicts in the foreseeable future. Too expensive. They're much more interested in temperate climates closer to home, like Ireland. That dump would be the kiss of death to my little bugs, of course. They don't seem to mind how *hot* it gets, just as long as it doesn't go below bloodheat or thereabouts. They'd thrive in an explosion, for example. But of course if you're being blown to smithereens it probably wouldn't worry you a lot that you were catching pneumonia at the same time.'

'So they're not a lot of use.'

'Not in that direction, no. But they've got another trick or two up their sleeves, that's the great thing about them. Not that the government gives a damn. You know how HMG operates – they ask a question, if they get the answer no, they give up. But not to worry.' He leaned confidentially towards Frobisher over the scraped black skin which was all that remained of his portion of seal. 'The great thing about bugs is there's no copyright on them.'

Frobisher had hit the jackpot. 'I see,' he said, trying to sound calm in the face of the undulating table. He almost slid off his chair, as if gravity were sucking at him from side on, or as if the outside wind were blowing silently within the mess-hall also. Murgatroyd, too, wobbled, and it wasn't merely an optical impression.

'Dangerous little perishers,' Murgatroyd said. It occurred to Frobisher that Murgatroyd, drunk, sounded oddly like his sidekick Wilkins, sober. Perhaps at the other end of the table Wilkins, drunk, was being as glum and taciturn as his master normally was. 'Make nuclear fission look like a kindergarten project.'

It was the nearest thing to a clue Frobisher was to get on Livingston Island.

Perhaps Murgatroyd would have communicated more there and then, if only Frobisher had been able to wait. That suddenly wasn't possible however. Instead, over-polite, bandy-legged, he stood up, made his excuses, and left the room.

Outside the mess-hut he picked out the rugged track he'd taken earlier in the afternoon, and hurried down it to vomit in Bellingshausen's Sea.

It wasn't dark of course, there was a midnight gleam, poised exactly between sunset and sunrise. The wind, as always, blew bone-cold, and breakers hit the rocky shore with what you could only call blows – the sound was midway between a clap and a thud and somehow seemed in tune with the contractions in Frobisher's belly.

146

He chose a tidal pool, hoping that the evidence would be washed away by the following morning. As he leaned over it he could make out clots of ice drifting about below the surface of the dim water, translucent as shrimps or crayfish. While he retched he remembered how Wilkins, cavorting before dinner, had made great play of the fact that one of the (genuine) weathermen came from Scunthorpe.

'Where's the cunt in Britain? Scunthorpe!' And so forth.

Then Wilkins faded and was replaced by the loss of Nicola, his own responsibility for guarding a germ warfare research installation, the possibility that Murgatroyd, aided and abetted by Lord Tetley, was engaged on a line of private research that was even more insidious and threatening than his official mandate allowed for.

'They make nuclear fission look like a kindergarten project.'

Frobisher, with the melodrama of seal and alcohol, suddenly understood that he'd encountered evil itself. Evil, evil, evil, the word became part of his heaving.

At last he could look up again. He stood on the tiny shore, facing ultimate south, and watching the hump of Deception Island as it stood out in the evening and morning sun. If Scunthorpe was a country's cunt, what in the name of sanity was this place?

Truly the bottom of the world.

29

Dennis gave Miss Clare a hard look. He'd known her for so long that he didn't usually see her. In the background John Outram scratched and gibbered. But this time, because he didn't know which way she was going to jump, Dennis saw her almost as if she was a stranger. Quite pretty, oddly enough, considering she was such an old bag. She had one of those old faces that look young even though they are covered in wrinkles, like a face caught in a net.

'*I* know the two deaths aren't connected,' she said. '*We* know the two deaths aren't connected. Of course. All they have in common is the Fat Man, and he is nothing but a. . .' Her voice trailed off as she searched for the word.

'A tool,' suggested John, and gave a sudden start. Then noticing that Dennis and Miss Clare were both looking at him, he unnecessarily explained: 'Goose walked over my grave.' Dennis had a sudden picture of an army of geese walking over John's grave. Like the sheep you were supposed to count in bed, only the geese kept him on the move instead of sending him to sleep.

'Yes,' Miss Clare said grudgingly, 'a tool.'

Dennis knew why she didn't like the word. Not because it was dirty, she probably didn't even know that, but because it was a capitalist idea, one person using another person as a tool. Dennis had had to learn a lot of revolutionary morality in his dealings with Miss Clare, and had found to his surprise that it was one subject he was good at. He had taken to it like a duck to water, or a goose to graveyards. Strange, really, considering he thought the whole business was a load of rubbish.

'But it's the general public,' Miss Clare went on. 'They

might not realise. And we don't want to be confused with whoever killed that Mr Fox.'

'Why not?' Dennis asked, unable to stop himself sounding sullen.

This time he *did* know which way she would jump. 'Use your head, Den,' she said.

The schoolmarm.

Her tone and expression brought back so many memories. The sound of her nail scraping across the blackboard, which she would do on purpose, reducing the class to nervous wrecks, while she grinned her self-satisfied little grin. The way she would ask a question and you'd know, before she ever said your name, that it was you she'd decided to give the black spot to. Even worse the time when with sudden inevitableness she left the work she was doing at the teacher's desk, hurried to the back of the classroom, and caught him before he had time to put himself away. (The bastard wouldn't fit back in his trousers, and the fact that she was standing there glaring at it seemed to make it more unmanageable than ever. He said magic words, tried hypnosis, thought sad and lonely thoughts in quick succession, until at last it dwindled and could be folded up. Then he shot a glance at her and realised she was bug-eyed with horror, pale-faced, on the point of throwing up.) Oddly, it was even worse, on another occasion, to see her gloating like a vulture while she tore his French exercise book to pieces after he'd made a mess of some homework.

They had become the unlikeliest of allies. He'd had his reasons for coming to her in his trouble, however. For one thing, her sheer aggressiveness towards him had a certain honesty about it. Also involved was the notion that when a woman, even a senile bitch like Miss Clare, came on so strongly as your enemy, it was because she fancied you in one way or another. Above all, he knew she was a woman who liked to espouse causes.

'We don't know,' she was continuing, 'what the principles are of the people who did this. They could be thugs for all we know. In any case, their aims, if they have aims, might be totally incompatible with ours.'

Thugs, Dennis thought. A heart surgeon is blown to bits, a nurse is critically injured, and Miss Clare worries in case the people who arranged for it are thugs. How pure can you get? The thought of being, in her terms, a thug, at least in relation to the late Mr Wilkins, and the soon-to-be-dealt-with Dr Murgatroyd, was precisely what gave the Green Principle its point as far as he was concerned. There were times in your life when a thug was what you needed most of all to be. Of course, from Dennis's point of view this was an essentially male standpoint: Miss Clare remained distinctively feminine even when she was killing people.

'If they knocked this surgeon off for reasons that are completely different to us,' Dennis said, 'I can't see how they would be confused with us.'

'It must have been an Arab or left-wing group,' John put in, 'what else can it be? Nobody's going to go to such lengths because they don't agree with heart transplants. It was anti-Zionists. Are we anti-Zionists? I've never even thought about it.'

'I have,' said Miss Clare, 'and I am. Israel represents an interference with the course of history.'

'Oh, for God's sake,' replied John irritably. He wrapped his right arm round the back of his head and scratched his left cheek with the hand that appeared from behind his ear. The manoeuvre, flexible, even telescopic, caught Dennis by surprise, used as he was to John Outram's fits and starts. 'Everything that happens in history represents an interference with the course of history,' John went on.

'Any rate,' Dennis told Miss Clare, 'if you're an anti-Zionist as well, it shouldn't matter being confused with them.'

As if, not having paid attention, he'd missed the whole point of the lesson: 'I said, Den, they *may* be thugs.'

But Dennis was no longer a schoolboy: 'But we *aren't* them, even if people might think we are.' Moral logic, unexpected resource of his adulthood, came to his aid once more: 'If it's right to do what we're doing, it's right to do what we're doing, whatever people might think.'

'I'm not so sure, Dennis,' Miss Clare replied reflectively. 'Do you remember that play we once did in class, *Murder in the Cathedral*? There's a line in there that we need to take to heart, it seems to me. "To do the right deed for the wrong reason." That's the problem. Not of course our actual reason, but what people might *think* our reason is, given that the press seems to mangle up everything we do.'

Dennis remembered the play. Miss Clare had sold it as a sort of crime story, but it had come out, perhaps because of the cathedral setting, indistinguishable from a sermon. Trust her to trot it out now. That was exactly what she herself enjoyed doing, converting murders into sermons.

'So?' he asked.

'So,' she replied, long-suffering. 'We are embarking on a revolutionary process, remember. We are trying to alter the way people think and behave. We're not in this for personal satisfaction, you know, or private vendettas.'

But, of course, Dennis was.

30

Miss Clare had tried to tart up Dennis's motives; she had insisted he should see events 'in context'. He'd gone along with her, what choice did he have? He would have liked to tear Wilkins and Murgatroyd apart with his bare hands, but then he'd be thrown into prison and he didn't want to give them, even dead, that satisfaction. Perhaps she was right, perhaps ecology would do some good. Ecology, for Christ's sake. Conquer the world with words, trust Miss Clare, like all teachers a paper tiger.

The worst thing about coughing yourself to death is the feeling that in a way it's your own fault. His father had kept apologising, as if he were coughing on purpose. At intervals, in the phlegm waterfall: sorry, sorry, sorry.

Wilkins and Murgatroyd hadn't said sorry. The nearest they got was, 'Your father was an excellent worker. We're very sad to have lost him.' Thus Wilkins, with the natural grace of an elephant on a bicycle.

There had been no doubt in Dennis's mind about where the blame lay. His father had worked for Hautbois Packaging for some years in the section that made foil envelopes for powdered soup and the like. On the day he fell ill he'd been asked to begin testing a new laminate that was supposed to provide an ultra-effective seal and prevent contamination of – or by – products that had to be kept apart from external conditions. Obviously it hadn't worked. Whatever garbage it was that the laminate was supposed to seal in had leaked out, and, as he described it, 'caught' the back of his throat. The coroner, in his pussyfooting way, said he'd succumbed to a 'severe bronchial inflammation'. He refused to commit himself on the subject of Hautbois's responsibility.

Dennis realised that the authorities would do nothing; or rather, that Hautbois International and the authorities were indistinguishable from each other. He therefore arranged a meeting with Dr Murgatroyd, the company's chief research scientist, and Mr Wilkins, its head of administration for the north of England.

'The laminate should have provided an adequate shield,' Dr Murgatroyd assured him, 'if the proper procedures had been gone through. It was designed to be totally effective with organic materials.'

'Organic materials?' Dennis asked, trying to keep his mind clear, to assemble the facts with care. This was a lesson he wanted to learn, despite his long history as a classroom dunce.

'Yes. It was designed to keep, shall we say, the contents of the envelope and your father's lungs separate from each other. In a sense they're both, both, organic materials, you understand.'

Dennis understood. The equation was simple. Your father equals packet soup.

'What Dr Murgatroyd is driving at,' Mr Wilkins put in, 'is the whole question of liability. We cannot rule out an element of mis-handling, you see. Possible carelessness.'

'But my fath —'

'Hautbois will be reasonable by their lights. But don't expect the moon.' Mr Wilkins adopted a confidential tone, as if he were talking about a nearby third person. 'You've got to realise what these big companies are like. They wouldn't piss in your ear if your brains were on fire. What I'm getting at is, an *ex gratia* in the hand is worth any amount of compensation in the bush. Hautbois have closed down their packaging plant anyway, part of their rationalisation programme. All that's left in the North of England is a small research unit. Demotion for me, of course,' he said, looking perfectly complacent. 'So the show's packed up and moved on. It's all history, see what I mean, very hard to build up a case. Nothing to inspect, dispersal of witnesses. If you take Hautbois to court, they'll hire some sod who'll end up putting the blame on the dear departed. I've seen those sort of bastards at work.'

So have I, thought Dennis, watching Mr Wilkins at work.

When his mother received the money it amounted to ten thousand pounds. Implied no admission of liability . . . Acceptance taken to mean acknowledgement of . . . etc., etc. She was quite pleased, as it happened. You can buy a lot of powdered soup for ten thousand pounds.

Dennis meanwhile had begun to dream about the stages of his father's catarrh. At first it had been a thick, opaque green, then pink streaks appeared on the surface; then came dark gobbets of almost undiluted blood, with tiny bits of tissue floating about in it, not unlike the crumbs of meat and veg you actually get when you add hot water to dehydrated soup.

Sorry. Sorry. Sorry.

He went to see Miss Clare. Who else could he discuss it with? His pals in the boozer, the girls he met at discos? He discussed it with Miss Clare for over a year. She was good at discussing things, she had a whole army of words, led by Ecology.

And then John Outram appeared out of the blue, armed with information about Murgatroyd's secret research, the conversion of germ warfare material into a substitute for petrol. He was the only outsider who knew what was going on. The stakes were beyond belief, but the project was also unimaginably dangerous, particularly as the germs involved stayed moribund until activated by intense heat. One miscalculation on the part of the Hautbois people and every internal combustion engine in the country could become a factory for producing bacteria. Or rather, not bacteria exactly. They were something rather different and therefore, like viruses, totally resistant to antibiotics.

A lot had happened since Outram explained what was going on. They had organised themselves into the Green Principle, dealt with Mr Wilkins, arranged the disposal of Dr Murgatroyd. They were too deeply committed to draw back now.

'It's very nice,' Dennis said, 'going round altering the way people think. Raising consciousness. But if we stop now there might not be any consciousness left to raise in a year's time.'

Miss Clare thought about it. She went from thoughtful to doubtful; her features sharpened to the point where she could split hairs.

Before she had a chance, however, John spoke, 'Have you seen the *Evening News*?' he asked.

Neither of them had.

'I bought one as I was walking from the bus,' he went on. 'After that story about the Fat Man in this morning's *Sky*, I wanted to see if there were any more developments. But there's another item on the front page as well. Look at it.'

He pulled the paper from his pocket, unfolded it, and passed it over.

The Fat Man featured on the front page, but only as a subordinate article. The main headline was:

HORROR CRASH TANKER HIRED BY HAUTBOIS.

'Good God,' Dennis said triumphantly to Miss Clare. 'You know what that means. People have been infected by those things already.'

There was a pause while Miss Clare accepted the point. The argument had reached its last stage.

'But what about the Fat Man?' she asked. 'The publicity he got this morning will make things very difficult for him.'

'That's his worry, not ours,' John said, 'that's what he gets paid for. My guess is that he'll make the Murgatroyd contract his last, at least for the time being. He must have earned enough to retire on by now, anyway.'

John wondered for a moment if he should mention what the chicken-chicken had once told him. 'The Fat Man is a master of disguise. He always looks just as he really is. That's his disguise.'

Perhaps not, it was the kind of remark that could bounce either way.

In any case, there was no need. Miss Clare had been talked round. He and Dennis had done what they set out to do.

31

Rostris sat not hunched but almost straight with fury, ignoring abdominal consequences.

'I think it is about time you went to London,' he agreed, eyes harsh as bile. 'Perhaps if you'd done a bit of legwork there in the first place, or even if you'd taken any notice of that Manley object, you might have made the connection before the papers did.'

'I'm perfectly capable of making connections. You seem to assume that Manley and the press have made the *right* connection. I don't. I think Manley sees fat men the way other people see giant rabbits.' Chapman felt calm, disinterested even. The only connection that concerned him at present was the one between Rostris and Susan. She had arrived on his doorstep cleanly, without implication; Rostris had become caught up in her train and acted as a sort of anchor on to the real world, real because it was ugly.

'That isn't the point,' Rostris said. 'I don't give a damn whether the *Sky* got their story right or wrong. All that matters is that they've got it everywhere. We ought to have proved their claim before they'd even made it. Or alternatively been in a position to say it's a load of balls. Why you can't simply work your way methodically through a case like a proper copper I just don't understand. We're not Red Indians you know, following our instincts. It's a matter of ABC.'

Chapman was tempted to suggest once again that if Rostris believed so strongly in behaving like Constable Plod he had no business getting excited. But on the other hand Rostris had a point.

'I'm going to London tomorrow,' he said finally. He couldn't however resist getting a small dig in: 'At least it'll help with the process of elimination.'

Ironically Rostris hadn't seen the article about the Fat Man when it appeared in the *Sky* yesterday morning. He didn't take the paper and he hadn't gone into his office first thing. Instead he'd done some legwork on the accident which wouldn't stop happening, culminating in a visit to Dr Murgatroyd's research laboratory in Salford.

Rostris had discovered late the day before that Hautbois owned the tanker that was involved in the Middleton Road crash. He had actually defied his own principles and rung up the *Northern Evening News* to give them the story as soon as the information had come to light. If Hautbois were so passionate about secrecy, perhaps a little publicity would help to get the oyster out of its shell. Meanwhile he wanted to see Murgatroyd before the story broke, and find out what he had to say.

Imagine cornflakes were made not of corn, but of razor blades. Then imagine you've just swallowed a bowlful. That's how Rostris's stomach felt as he sat in Murgatroyd's office, a small room partitioned off from the laboratory, and listened to what the architect of the Hautbois Project, and the ultimate cause of the Middleton Road accident, death toll eighteen, had to say for himself. The intricate and widespread sharpness in his innards provided a fitting backcloth to the web of pomposity, self-righteousness and deceit which Murgatroyd was weaving.

'Let me take you into my confidence,' Murgatroyd said, peering at him from beneath tufted brows.

'Yes, please,' Rostris replied cynically.

'I am evolving,' Murgatroyd continued, 'on behalf of the Hautbois Corporation, a biochemical method of transforming certain cheap and readily available materials into a fuel that is as adaptable as petrol.'

He paused in order to let his point sink in. Rostris, however, had become preoccupied with another point altogether. Inside him the razor blades were coagulating into a single, downward-pointing dagger.

He knew what would happen shortly. The dagger would make a sudden thrust in the direction of his rectum and he would experience the sensation of passing a motion under duress. Nothing would come out, however, but a fart.

What made the whole process so appalling was that it was impossible to tell in advance if the fart would be just a faint hiss or an explosion as loud and surprising as a burst paperbag. It was hopeless trying to organise any kind of social relationship without such information, even the minimal relationship involved in questioning Dr Murgatroyd, or at least in listening to what Murgatroyd chose to say.

'In other words,' Murgatroyd went on, 'some microbes are put in a tank of liquid, they eat, they reproduce like greased lightning, the offspring eat also.' He paused again. His features seemed to loosen slightly, his eyebrows became less bristling, his mouth relaxed. Even through the preoccupation of pain Rostris noticed that he was going to try the soft sell. 'As a late colleague of mine once put it, they breed like rabbits and eat like horses.' Businesslike once more: 'And before you know it the whole shebang's turned into something you can use instead of petrol.'

'I see,' Rostris managed to mutter guardedly, holding himself in readiness for the stab that could come at any moment.

'The liquid, incidentally, is mainly water. And the other ingredients cost hardly anything and are readily available.'

'I understand,' Rostris almost whispered.

'I wonder if you do?' Murgatroyd asked in his most bullying tone. He obviously felt he'd driven Rostris into a corner. 'I'm talking about the stuff the Third World War could be fought over. For God's sake, we've already had a diplomatic incident with Libya on the subject. This product makes North Sea oil look like a jumble sale.

'Let me tell you a true story. A friend of mine, not a well-off man, inherited some priceless antiques from some relative or other. Lovely stuff apparently, if you like that sort of thing. Of course he gets the insurance assessor round. But the premium's through the roof, my friend can't afford it. So the insurance man gives him some advice. He says, "Get bloody good padlocks on your doors and windows, be a bit choosy about your friends, and above all take down your burglar alarm as soon as possible. The last thing you want to do is advertise the fact that you've got valuable stuff in here."

'Do you see what I mean? You can get to the stage when your contents are too expensive even to allow for the normal precautions.' He paused to let the moral sink in, and then, with obvious contempt for Rostris's intelligence, announced it anyway: 'In other words, you don't go advertising the fact that you have the answer to all the world's problems on the back of some long-distance lorry.'

Just as a tight-rope walker might speak quietly, afraid that a loud word would knock him backwards: 'Dr Murgatroyd, I'm amazed that you can be so blasé with the law.'

'Me, Superintendent?' The eyebrows dutifully climbed his forehead and expressed surprise. 'I'm talking about my late colleague, Mr Wilkins. He was in charge of all aspects of the administration of our northern division, including both security and transport arrangements. I've got quite enough on my mind with this research I was telling you about.'

'This research you were telling me about,' said Rostris, hoping his diminished delivery would sound like low-key threat, an austerity evolved from the discipline of flatulence, 'has been responsible for at least fourteen of the Middleton Road deaths.'

'Superintendent, you can't make an omelette without breaking eggs. Think how many miners die in order to get us our coal. Think of all those drowned oilmen in the North Sea. Think of the dangers involved in nuclear generating plants. Fuel is a high-risk business, I'm afraid.'

'Now listen, Dr —'

'I'll tell you what, Superintendent. Our London headquarters is going to send a delegation to talk to you about these matters. Senior Management. Plus, I believe, a representative from the Department of Trade and Industry. Lord Tetley. I think that's a fair index of how seriously Hautbois take this problem. Now, really, I have a lot of work to be getting along with.'

Murgatroyd rose. So did Rostris's gorge. Restraint, at last, was impossible.

'It's time that you understood something, Murgatroyd. I'm not going to be deflected by government stooges and plausible business executives from London. I'm not going to give up until I've found out exactly what's going on. I'm going to accumulate enough evidence to stop your company manufacturing this poison. And I'm going to arrest you, whatever smokescreen Hautbois put up, and make sure you submit to the due process of the law. That's what I'm going to do. Or I'll die in the attempt.'

The dagger fell.

For once luck was on Rostris's side, however: it was the hiss, not the bang, which acted as postscript to his argument. He capitalised on this turn of events and walked straight out.

The laboratory was a huge windowless ex-warehouse in Salford. Revamped inside, the building's exterior was a depressing monotony of blackened brickwork that looked exactly as it had done in the days when industry and commerce still had a stronghold in the area, and it had been used for storing mail order goods or local textiles. A memorial to times gone by: with a monstrous future being distilled inside it.

The street was dazzling for a moment, a bright burst of dinginess. Rostris turned to the right and walked towards a patch of waste land, presumably the site of another warehouse, where he'd parked his car.

Strangely, an elderly and decrepit newspaper seller was standing on the corner, as though he'd not yet noticed most of the locals had gone to work elsewhere, if at all.

Rostris remembered the story he'd given the *Evening News*, and bought a copy.

The old man had patchy stubble, à la Desperate Dan, and his puffy features and cold red eyes gave a suggestion of viciousness in times gone by. Prison fodder in his day. Rostris felt a sudden solidarity with him, as you might with an enemy when the war is over.

'Keep the change,' he said. He'd given him a fifty pence piece. He'd noticed before in himself a tendency to be generous to layabouts. Probably because he despised most ordinary people.

'I owe you thirty-six pence.' The man's aggressive tone was oddly packaged in a wavering voice.

Rostris began to walk away. The last thing he wanted was for the old sod to start getting proud.

'I owe you thirty-six pence,' the vendor repeated. Suddenly it seemed almost bad manners to ignore the impotent cruelty of his tone.

The old man searched his pockets infuriatingly, and then handed the change over with arthritic fingers.

Rostris took it and walked off. 'Shit,' he said aloud to relieve his feelings. Then, still walking, he glanced at the front page to see what they'd done with his story about the Hautbois tanker. It was there all right, taking up most of the page. But Rostris's attention was immediately caught by something else, the *Evening News*'s grudging elaboration of the *Sky*'s claim that the Fat Man was involved in the Fox and Wilkins murders. Since he'd not come across Ed Pointon's scoop in the morning paper, this was the first Rostris had heard of it.

There was a grainy picture of a round face, a circle of light on the forehead but the features otherwise vague and dark. Above the photograph was the question:

IS THIS THE FACE OF RESTAURANT KILLER?

Shit, Rostris said again. Shit, shit, shit.

As though obeying an instruction the acid tide in his stomach began its journey to the shore again.

32

There was the jumble and fuzz of Mikey's explanation and then ping ping the eyes came on and shone through the tangle like a pair of black spotlights. The sounds, letters, stood up, shuffled together, and then fitted into each other with the tightness and niceness of the blocks of Lego that she played with: that she *had* played with once, in heaven. Heaven grew bigger with each day that passed.

She could see London. London was one of his words.

I, I, I, he kept saying. He pointed to himself. And then: London. He'd made London with his sounds as you might make a house. It was a box to put himself in.

His eyes went into reverse. They weren't spotlights now, but little black holes. What he wanted was for her to fall into them. All she had to do was to say yes. Yes meant stepping off the ledge and falling down and down. Down one eye; down the other.

Her yes would say: yes, I understand. That was the first eye. But he would take it as yes, I agree. The other eye.

He waited.

His eyes rose to the surface.

No further: they remained exactly on the surface, midway between the searching beam and the vertiginous well, slightly glistening. They waited for her to make the next move: to say the word.

Luckily she could no longer say it.

She still possessed words, queuing up behind her tongue, but had long ago forgotten how to get them out in one piece. Even worse, she had lost her capacity to surprise herself with language and speak without thinking. Her mouth was now strictly a machine for eating with.

His eyes dried, faded. He turned away.

Instead came Susan. She looked with her whole face. Her bright curls, her rose cheeks, her full mouth, all paid attention.

'Mrs Hodnet will look after you in the day, Margaret. Like usually.'

Susan's words had a faint perfume, as if they were an invisible, intangible form of confectionery.

'And guess who?' Susan asked. 'At night? It'll be me. You and me together.'

Margaret's heart missed a beat. A complicated excitement, such as she'd not experienced since heaven, gripped her chest, her groin, ran up her spine to the back of her neck. The sensation was cold and silvery, like the top notes of a piano.

A piano.

That was it, a piano. She would play her mouth as you would a piano. Operate it as if it were an instrument. Concentrate not on content but on sound and phrasing.

Margaret sat down at her mouth, stretched out her hands (knocking her mug of milk over in the process), ordered her teeth, tongue, lips into place, and tried to repeat Susan's last words.

'I think she wants to go to the lavatory,' came Mikey's voice from somewhere. No scent here: a secular voice.

Susan shook her head impatiently.

'She wants to say it,' she said, and then, to Margaret: 'You and me.' Her lips shaped each word delicately.

You and me.

How blissful that Susan should understand it also. Susan *was* you and me. Those were exactly the words for her.

Susan protected Margaret: she was mother.

Susan was young: she was child.

Susan had sex with Mikey: she was Margaret herself.

Or at least her twin, her second, radiant self. The self that remained in heaven.

You and me.

*   *   *

Susan turned to Michael. 'I'm sure she'll be all right,' she said. 'Don't worry about it. And it will only be for a few days.'

33

Chapman had arranged to meet a certain Superintendent Hewitt of the anti-terrorist squad of the Metropolitan Police. They had a building of their own near Marble Arch. When he arrived there, however, late on a hot summer's afternoon, he discovered that Hewitt had received news that the other victim of the hospital bombing, a nurse called Carole Shearer, was showing signs of regaining consciousness, and he had hurried off to her bedside at the Hammersmith Hospital. After a certain amount of badgering Chapman managed to get the use of a car and driver and followed him there.

There was an armed policeman outside the private room into which Nurse Shearer had been put. Once again Chapman experienced the irritation of being out of his own territory: he showed his identification and the guard merely looked doubtful.

'It *is* my case as well,' Chapman said. 'It's connected with a crime that took place in Manchester.' How ironic that he should have to explain his presence like that: it was just what he didn't believe.

Nevertheless the guard grudgingly stepped to one side. He shrugged his shoulders as he did so, as though saying, on your own head be it.

Chapman turned the handle; the door opened and then stopped abruptly after a few inches. What had stopped it was half of a nursing sister's bosom. It seemed to have the same absolute lack of give as another person's boot. The other half of the bosom was visible in the aperture, complete with crisp white bib front and pinned-on watch. Above, half a face eyed him steadily; behind its spectacle the green eye would no more blink than that of a fish.

'Yes?' Sister asked.

'I'm Inspector Chapman. I'm a policeman. Can I come in?'

'No,' Sister replied.

'Look, Sister, it's possible I can help find out who did this to your patient. Surely —'

'There's a policeman in here already.'

'I know but —'

'Mr Chapman, Nurse Shearer is very ill. Very ill. In fact, she's dying.'

'Oh. I'm very sorry to hear that.'

'Yes. Well.' A hand reinforced the pressure of the bosom, and the door began to close.

'Sister, if she's dying what harm can it do?'

'There are enough people in here already. There's your colleague Mr Hewitt for a start. Then there are medical staff. Also her parents and a rabbi. The young lady is Jewish.'

'I see,' Chapman said, trying to collect his thoughts. While he hesitated the door shut. It was quite a relief to face its cool oblong after the aggressive presence of the Sister. In any case Hewitt would no doubt tell him everything that was said.

He turned round to find a chair. The guard gave him a long look, that clearly said, I told you so.

There is a certain explicitness about being blown to bits. Your whole body comes out of concealment. It's an extreme way of announcing: here I am. Take me as you find me. Beneath surface whiteness, a sudden red.

No wonder people talked about their hearts when they fell in love. To have seen Mr Fox die was to know him. Carole Shearer enjoyed the privilege, the intimacy, of shared experience. Shared in more ways than one.

She lay upon her red bed. The raw, fragmented areas of her body were new dimensions to herself, were discoveries. She had seen into Mr Fox; and then, a fraction later, as though the pendulum had swung back, she had entered deep within herself, exploring fold after fold until she arrived at the centre.

166

She inhabited a completely flesh world, with no external projection, like a baby in the womb. Pain was a constant: you might as well settle back on the soft mattress of yourself.

As she lay the mattress became a raft and then that dissolved and she drifted with the stream. The reversal was almost complete: the blood outside; the person within. Mr Fox floated beside her. The medium was that of sexual attraction; of Jewishness; of the human race at large; of organic life in general. The stream grew wider and wider as it approached the sea, until it became indistinguishable from that ultimate entity, a chemical calm into which the biological evenly flowed.

At the final moment, a hook, an arrest.

'What did he look like?'

She shivered with the cold of the outside air.

'The man who put the bomb in the car. Did you see him?'

The detail of memory: it hurt as much as a sudden light in the middle of a night's sleep. Slowly the Mercedes moved towards her, along with a sense of the empty dawn atmosphere, the clear grey air of the car park, the birds squawking as if in complaint at the prospect of a summer's day to come. She could understand their complaining now.

'Tall or short? Middle?'

The door of the Mercedes slowly opened. The man backed out of it.

'Was he fat or thin? Or well-built?'

The big bottom rose in the air; the big top followed. He hurried off on bulky legs.

'Fat,' Carole whispered, using as much capacity as a roar.

Then Mr Fox appeared round the side of the car. He walked to the door, opened it, looked up and saw her. He gave a little sad smile and shrugged his shoulders. Then he did something astounding. He raised his hand to his mouth and blew her a kiss.

It wasn't a true kiss but it would have to do, it would have to carry her.

'I love him,' she whispered.

He got in the car, shut the door, the starting motor began to turn.

It wasn't the sea this time but upwards, high into the colourless sky of early morning. Towards nothing at all.

34

A girl in nurse's uniform and cloak came along the hospital corridor and took the chair next to Chapman.

'Excuse me?' she asked, as soon as she was seated.

Chapman turned towards her. She had an alert, busy face, and the overall effect was of rather unappealing inquisitiveness, despite her snub nose.

'Yes?' he asked in return.

'Are you a friend-and-relation?' The question was brusque in tone, making no allowance for the possibility that he might, for all she knew, be Nurse Shearer's grieving father.

'No.'

'I didn't think you were. You're a policeman, are you?'

Chapman grumpily agreed.

'I'm Nurse Sowerby. I hope you get whoever did it and put them through the mincer.'

'Thank you for the suggestion, but we have our own procedures.'

'That's what *I* believe in, an eye for an eye. Or in this case, bits for bits.'

Something in her very bloodthirstiness made him warm to her a little.

'It seems rather drastic.'

'What they did to Mr Fox was drastic. And to Carole.'

'Do you work with Carole?'

'I did, yes. Don't worry, I know what state she's in. Did's the word.'

There was a certain unlovely frankness about her remarks, as if it gave her some kind of satisfaction to get down to the nitty-gritty.

'So naturally you feel —'

'Oh, Carole's a lovely girl. Is, was. Always in the centre of everything. You know the kind. The life and soul, that sort of person.'

Suddenly Chapman felt sorry for Nurse Sowerby. There was a minimalness about her which told you *she* could never be the life and soul of the party. Even the generous testimonial gave you a sense of cattiness held at bay – she could be nice about Carole Shearer because Carole lay dying. It was necessary for her to feel that she had the edge over other people, because she didn't.

'It often seems to be the very alive people who come to a tragic end,' he said.

Nurse Sowerby gave him a sharp look as she followed the implication of the remark.

'It's ironic about her being blown up along with Mr Fox,' she said suddenly.

'Oh. Why?'

'Well, we all used to say she was in love with him. Just teasing her, you know. But I think she had a crush on him anyway. I don't expect he even knew she existed. He was a big-shot surgeon and everything, and she was just a humble nurse like me. But they died together anyway. More or less.'

'I see,' said Chapman, and they lapsed into silence.

After a quarter of an hour or so the door of Carole Shearer's room opened and a number of people trooped out. The simultaneity of their exit gave Chapman the odd impression that some sort of show had just finished inside. Nurse Sowerby stood up and began talking to the Sister who had stopped the door. A podgy man in a cheap suit walked towards Chapman.

'Hewitt,' he said.

'Hello, Superintendent. I'm Chapman.'

'Yes, I gathered that. I heard you scrabbling at the door.'

'I decided that with you in the room already, the Sister had a point.'

'The Sister's a pain in the bum,' Hewitt stated. 'Mind you,' he added, 'I'm not sure I understand what you're doing here myself.'

'Didn't you read that piece —?'

'For heaven's sake, you can't conduct investigations according to what you read in the daily garbage. Is that how you work up in Manchester?'

The complicated inappropriateness of the accusation kept Chapman silent for a moment. Then he gave the only reply that was possible: 'It's a matter of routine.'

'Routine!' Hewitt sneered. The sneer broadened into a triumphant smile. 'I've got the goods,' he went on. 'At least as far as *my* case is concerned.'

'Really?'

'Yes, the girl spilled the beans before she died.'

'What do you mean, the beans? What beans?'

'She's one of the bloody gang, that's what beans. She was in love with the bastard who planted the bomb.'

Chapman looked at him without saying anything for a moment. He felt stunned, out of his depth. Finally he managed, 'I don't understand how that could be.'

'Well, the heart operation finished early, didn't it? The patient took a turn for the worse. All right then, there's this Shearer girl, she's the inside contact of the terrorists. She probably told them, you know, when the operation was going to take place, where Mr Fox parks his car, all that. She watches the doings through one of those little spy-holes, knowing her accomplice is outside. It finishes early, she thinks, hell, what if Fox goes straight out to his car before pally's done his bit? She shoots out to the car park, runs up to the Mercedes, and just at that moment, bang. That's how I see it. What do you think?'

'For God's sake, Superintendent, the girl was Jewish.'

'So?'

'I understood the assumption was that this was an anti —'

'All right, so it was an anti-Semitic outrage.' He paused, and for a moment the chubby self-congratulatory features looked uneasy, even shifty. 'You know as well as me that most murders are committed in the family.'

'What exactly did she tell you?'

'Well, I asked her what the bomber was like. You know, tall or short. Fat, thin, indifferent. She couldn't say a lot, she was on her last legs. But she finally got out "fat". So it *was* the bloke the Beeb interviewed. Bit of luck really.'

Chapman felt a sudden chill. Rostris had been right all along, Manley was vindicated. Why had he been so determined to disbelieve what his only witness said? Instinct, he'd told himself in justification; perhaps a better name for it would be anti-Semitism. No, of course not, how could there be any question of anti-Semitism when Manley wasn't a Jew?

But Manley had been right about the Fat Man. Perhaps he was right about his own Jewishness also. Perhaps in the sense *he* meant, he was one after all.

Anyway, it was time to redress the balance in various directions. 'Your evidence corroborates *my* witness's account,' Chapman affirmed.

'Come on,' replied Hewitt, 'what can this business have to do with *your* case? There are fat men everywhere.' With pride: 'I'm pretty fat myself.'

There was no point in arguing. He, Chapman, had taken his time before believing Manley; he could hardly expect prompt endorsement from the Superintendent.

'Did she say anything else?' he asked instead.

'She sort of paused. She was snoring as a matter of fact. You'd think for all the world she was taking a nap. Except that her lips kept moving. I bent over to listen and finally she said "I love him". Famous last words, eh? Then she passed on.'

There was such a thing as having paid your dues. 'Famous last words all right,' Chapman agreed. 'But she wasn't talking about the Fat Man, she was talking about Mr Fox. She was in love with Mr Fox.'

Hewitt glared. 'You what? What makes you say that?'

'I've been talking to one of her friends. That nurse over there. It was a bit of a joke among the nurses apparently.'

Hewitt followed his arm towards the back of Nurse Sowerby, who was just walking off down the corridor with the Sister.

'Hell's teeth,' he said, and set off in pursuit.

35

As far as Chapman was concerned, everything in his case had changed. Rostris's judgement had been proved correct and indeed Rostris's method was now called for: routine. Manley had noticed that the Fat Man had suffered an injured arm in his explosion, and what Chapman needed to do was to have the anti-terrorist squad double-check outpatient records for the day after the incident and to arrange for a couple of constables to undertake the mammoth task of ringing every doctor in the London area to ask if a fat man with a scorched arm had requested treatment. It was necessary of course to clear these proposals with Hewitt himself, and on the day after Nurse Shearer's death Hewitt wasn't about. He left a message claiming that he was out conducting his investigation; Chapman wondered if he was sulking.

It wasn't until late afternoon that he managed to track Hewitt down: a whole day wasted. They arranged to meet in a Tottenham pub called the Rose and Thorn.

The pub was large, square-shouldered, pre-war, built for the roadster trade. Now it had an air of being overtaken by events, a cut-price palace. Inside however it was still plush: revolving doors, wood-panelling, the smell of cinemas. The saloon bar was divided into three compartments, American-style, separated from each other by wooden partitions. Hewitt, with pasty face and stained suit, sat on the well-upholstered settee of the middle one, a glass in front of him.

Chapman walked up to him and asked, in what he hoped was a friendly and conciliatory tone: 'Is that a scotch?'

Hewitt looked up. He was obviously still sullen. 'Double. You won't have to pay.'

'Really?'

'They like to encourage the law. It keeps the place respectable.'

The place seemed respectable enough in its own right, but Chapman said nothing. He picked up Hewitt's glass and carried it over to the bar.

'A double scotch and a pint of bitter,' he said.

The barmaid was in her early twenties, wearing a pretty summer frock. As she passed the drinks over Chapman noticed that her right forefinger was in an ugly navy blue stock which seemed as out of place in the well-manicured sequence as a labourer at a cocktail party.

'That'll be a hundred and eighty-seven,' she said.

Chapman would far rather have paid, but he sensed Hewitt's eyes on his back.

'I'm the police,' he told her.

'A hundred and eighty-seven,' she repeated obstinately.

When Chapman arrived back at the booth Hewitt had thawed and become affable.

'They never charge me,' he said.

'Perhaps it's your charm,' Chapman suggested before he could stop himself.

'I *have* done them a few favours from time to time.'

'There's a favour you could do me.'

Hewitt, having exorcised the embarrassment of yesterday, was co-operative. Chapman described the arrangements he required and then they discussed their cases in a general way. Chapman mentioned Manley's Jewish fixation.

'I've got a lot of time for Jews,' Hewitt said, still in an agreeable mood. 'It's the jungle bunnies I can't take.'

Chapman followed his gaze around the bar. A number of customers had appeared in the last few minutes, all of them black.

'Get it from my mother, I think,' Hewitt went on. 'Those British Rail golliwogs used to make her puke.'

'For Christ's sake—' Chapman began, but it was too late. A black face, surmounted by a bright green cap, appeared round the side of the cubicle.

'You sayin' you better than me, daddy?' the young man asked in an irritating black sambo voice.

'Being your father's one thing I can't be accused of,' Hewitt replied, unabashed.

'You sure full of shit, that I do know,' the young man retorted.

Suddenly in sharp contrast came the educated accentless voice of a besuited black man standing at the bar. 'Why don't you leave the palefaces alone, Indian?'

'I'm no fucking Indian, man, who you accusing?'

The young man had turned away from Chapman and Hewitt and was walking towards his challenger at the bar. He was wearing a mauve velvet jacket, cut tight around the waist, and looked exotic and cockatoo-like by comparison with the citified aura of the other man.

'I suggest we bugger off at this juncture,' Hewitt said, rising to his feet. 'That could be a fight brewing up. You know how the police get blamed when this sort of thing happens. Look at Brixton.'

It wasn't until he was halfway home, on the Manchester train, that the thought struck Chapman that the police *were* to blame. He remembered Hewitt's free drinks and wondered what favours he actually did the Rose and Thorn. Not going into it too often, perhaps.

As he entered his house Chapman had an immediate sense that, despite the fact he'd only been away for two days, things had changed.

'I'm back,' he explained unnecessarily to Susan, who had met him in the hallway, radiant as ever. For some reason a sort of inertia descended on him, and he was loath to go further into the house.

'Come on in,' Susan said, giving him a quick kiss. 'You do live here, you know.'

He followed her into the kitchen.

'How's Margaret?'

'Tucked up in bed, not to worry.' Susan's tone was perhaps too soothing for comfort. 'Shall we have a drink?' She poured them both a scotch. As she handed his glass over she admitted: 'Margaret's in a bad way, Mike.'

'Really?' he replied. He was aware that he sounded only faintly curious, as if she'd told him his rubber plant was wilting.

'She's so much weaker all of a sudden. She didn't want to get out of bed today. She wasn't *able* to get out. She just couldn't. I didn't go to work, I waited in for the doctor. He says . . . she's approaching the end. He says it will all happen much faster now. A matter of days. He could put her in hospital but there's nothing they could do for her. She's not in pain.'

'That's good,' Chapman said. 'That she's not in pain,' he explained.

Susan was resting against the washing machine, leaning very slightly backwards and hugging herself just below her bosom, whisky glass casually tilted in her hand. She seemed so relaxed, so at home.

'I'd better . . .' began Chapman. He rubbed his nose and eyes, as if the news had made him sleepy. 'I'd better put in for compassionate leave.'

'No,' Susan said quickly. 'There's no point. There's nothing you could do here. And you've got your case. It's important. I'll let you know immediately . . . anything happens.'

'But how can —?'

'I phoned the station today and told them my mother's fallen ill.'

'*Your* mother?'

Chapman could have bitten his tongue as soon as he'd spoken. Margaret wasn't *his* mother, she was his wife. He suddenly realised that he'd reached the last stage of a long process. He no longer thought of Margaret as dwindling towards toddlerhood but as being, as her illness had implied all along, prematurely senile. Possibly it was because of the proximity of her death; perhaps because he was having an affair with Susan, who was so much younger. Margaret had gone from wife to child to mother.

Chapman had an intuition of the passing and replacement of the generations that was so poignant he wanted to weep.

Susan meanwhile took a sip of her drink and gave him a roguish look.

'Naughty, wasn't it?' she asked. 'Still, I don't mind lying for love. I do enough of the other sort of lying for it.'

They went upstairs to look at Margaret shortly afterwards. Her head, on the pillow, was bland, ball-like. She was snoring gently.

'She seems quite happy,' Susan whispered. Then she added: 'She's stopped speaking altogether.' She stretched out her hand and riffled through Margaret's hair. Chapman's heart lurched.

Susan gazed seriously through the dim light of the bedroom, her hand still resting on Margaret's head. 'We'll manage, don't you worry,' she said gravely.

That 'we'. Suddenly Chapman felt that he was being given the Wilkins case as a sort of diversion or consolation prize. Somehow a domestic conspiracy was being undertaken by these two women, dying wife, beautiful young mistress. It would have been like an opera if the dying wife had not gone, via stupidity, into stupor; if the beautiful young mistress had not been a police sergeant.

The reasons behind the conspiracy, its inner logic, Chapman could not even begin to fathom.

36

As if the initial decision to track him down was the only one that counted, Chapman found it unnervingly easy, once he started making enquiries at the Manchester hospitals, to draw a bead on the Fat Man. At least, on *a* fat man. Chorlton Hospital, the fourth on his list, had had an outpatient who corresponded to the description only two days previously. He was overweight, with a neglected and suppurating burn on his right forearm.

'I gave him a very thorough bollocking,' the small Welsh consultant said musically. 'It was disgusting, a grown man letting himself get in that state. I said, a big boy like you, frightened of hospitals.'

'And what did he say to that?' Chapman asked.

'Not a peep. I imagine he was trying to stop himself from whimpering.'

'Perhaps he was just being stoical,' Chapman suggested. The Welshman gave him a puzzled look. He obviously wasn't used to having his diagnoses challenged.

At least the Fat Man/fat man had left his/a name and address. Norman Colclough, 29 Waverley Avenue, Heaton Moor, Costford, Greater Manchester.

Norman Colclough did not, on the face of it, sound like the name of a mercenary terrorist, and indeed there were at least two ways in which it might not be. Mr Colclough might be a law-abiding, if overweight, citizen who'd happened to burn himself on his gas stove. Alternatively Norman Colclough might be of normal build, unburnt, a name and address the Fat Man had got from a street directory or the voters' register.

But at the same time Norman Colclough might be the real thing.

As he drove south towards the address Chapman wondered if the solution could really be as easy as all that.

Why not? Colclough was an excellent name for a mercenary terrorist; whatever the newspapers might say there was no percentage in calling yourself something memorable like Carlos. Moreover there was some evidence that the Fat Man felt disdainful about covering his tracks. He'd shot Mr Wilkins from the vantage-point of a noonday street in the centre of Manchester. He'd been interviewed on television following his assassination of Mr Fox. These were not necessarily manifestations of carelessness or incompetence; the Fat Man perhaps held the opinion that you could attract more attention by covering your tracks than by leaving them as they were, that observation was a quality in the witness rather than in the subject.

Chapman remembered an investigation he'd once conducted into the theft of rare books from the university library. The criminal – a student in all probability – had put on a nylon overall, obtained a trolley, and trundled it straight past the porters who were checking user-identity cards. He'd then filled his trolley with all the treasures he could fit into it and with equal aplomb trundled it past the library assistants who were stamping out the books of the honest users. He'd never been caught.

The Fat Man had been less lucky – there had been an unusual witness to the Wilkins murder in the shape of Anthony Manley. Nevertheless he would have been home and dry, given Chapman's own scepticism, if circumstances hadn't vindicated Manley. Even now, of course, he might be home and dry – or rather, not at home at all.

But Chapman had to assume he *was* there – assume the best, or the worst – and plan accordingly.

He decided to take a leaf out of the Fat Man's book, go right up to the front door of number 29 Waverley Avenue, and knock. The question then arose as to what he should say if and when the door was opened.

Suddenly he remembered something Anthony Manley had

gone on about: the anomalies of chief rent. He had complained that the vendor, in one of his conveyancing transactions, had forgotten to keep up with his chief rent payments, and as a result the completion of sale had had to be delayed. Therefore Manley had gone home for lunch; as a consequence he had seen the Fat Man being interviewed on television.

Chapman had had his own experience with chief rent and it was, indeed, exactly the sort of niggling technicality that you could forget all about, only to find it surfacing at an inconvenient moment (how incomprehensible it already seemed that he'd been so unsympathetic to Manley!). He and Margaret had been liable to it on their house, an almost nominal sum of two or three pounds a year which they nevertheless had to pay to the owner of the title despite the fact that in all other respects they possessed the property outright. A very high percentage of the houses in the Manchester area had the same lien on them. Eventually the Chapmans had exercised their right to buy the chief rent title themselves, just to eradicate their sense of being answerable to a landlord. But some years later a collector had still called, unaware that the property was now freehold. Chapman could remember his manner, a combination of the ingratiating and the suspicious, with great clarity.

29 Waverley Avenue was very typical of Heaton Moor, a large, tall, Edwardian terrace with four or five bedrooms and three floors, faced with rather rubbery-looking red brick and dark sullen windows, very respectable still although such houses were often turned into flats and occupied by students and other short-term lessees. This was the sort of environment that would suit the Fat Man perfectly. Its prevailing atmosphere was decorous, middle class, but nobody would question or even notice your comings and goings. People wouldn't necessarily know the name of their next-door neighbour, and if they did find out they would expect it to be just such a name as Norman Colclough.

The gate of number 29 was freshly painted; the lawn, though tiny, was scrupulously mown; the path was brushed;

the front door had a shiny brass knocker.

As he let the latter drop Chapman experienced a sudden twinge of fear. The Fat Man might come to the front door carrying a sub-machine gun. This was alien territory – you couldn't expect the etiquette of the small-time criminal. How ironic if Margaret were to outlive him after all. Here he was, still in the normal world – as Wilkins had been in the restaurant, as Mr Fox had been in the hospital car park – and at any second normality could be ended forever. A person could fall from a skyscraper and remain in perfect health an inch from the ground, heart beating, blood circulating, liver doing whatever it was livers did. It was that last inch which took it out of you.

The knocker struck. Chapman raised it and struck again.

I wonder how Margaret and Susan are getting on, he thought, teasing himself with irrelevant concerns as he waited for the door to open.

37

The moon-like head remained on the pillow. It seemed featureless, ancient, eroded, worn smooth by time. Margaret no longer resembled a swollen baby, anything but; but her head did look as if it had been painted by a child. It was a crude, pink, heavy balloon.

Beside the bed Susan's beauty was intricate and active, a matter of caught details and shifting planes. Expressions moved about her features with the delicate interplay of clouds. Two presided: the unafraid alertness of a nurse, or a policewoman, willing to look anywhere, at anything, totally able to cope; and the warmth of one who, having indeed seen everything, finds herself able to accept, and love, the *status quo*. A counterpoint of hard and soft; her bright eyes, full lips, bent towards Margaret.

Mute as a bulb that nevertheless receives messages about the state of the seasons and the condition of the soil, Margaret responded. Her blankness focused, while remaining blank: a message in invisible ink.

Susan read the response, and responded in turn. Even in the dimness of the curtained bedroom her cheeks pinked. A certain self-consciousness only intensified the bond between the two women, adding the warmth of humour, providing an underpinning of irony. The atmosphere was thick with their affection.

When Susan finally spoke her words seemed hardly to be spoken at all, they simply became part of the warm environment as a scent can become an inextricable part of a scene without even being noticed.

'We're all right, aren't we?' she asked gently.

Again the contribution was absorbed by Margaret, as a

plant is supposed to absorb kind words.

'I'll tell you something, Margaret,' Susan continued softly, and then she paused once again. Only at this point did the atmosphere begin to modify. Behind serene undergrowth something dark and ominous began to shift, pad, approach. And then quietly, gracefully, lightly as before, the gentle voice leapt on its prey: 'These men are full of hot air.'

After she stopped speaking the warm silence in Margaret's bedroom began slowly and inexorably to deepen.

38

At last the door opened.

The man in the aperture was not the Fat Man, though he was well-built. He was in his mid-thirties, with black hair, broad cheek bones, strong distinct features, although his overall expression was strangely blurred, as if he had just been woken from a deep sleep. This impression was confirmed by the fact that his clothes, an open-necked shirt, rather tight cord trousers, one flip-flop, had obviously been pulled on hastily. He smelled strongly of women's perfume. He looked suspicious, indeed hostile, but when he saw it was Chapman he relaxed and even sighed with relief.

'Thank God,' he said.

'I'm sorry to —' began Chapman, but was immediately interrupted by a strident woman's voice from the depths of the house.

'Is it him? For God's sake!'

The man turned round to face her, and Chapman was able to make out, at the far end of the hall, a plumpish woman as unkempt as her companion was. She had straggly hair, a big loose bosom within a very faded green tee-shirt, a drab ethnic skirt, bare feet. Chapman suddenly realised they'd been in bed together – she was the source of the man's perfume.

He also realised something else. The relief that was almost tangible in the air was because their expectation about what lay on the other side of the front door had been the same as his. The Fat Man.

'I told you it wasn't,' the woman said self-righteously. 'For a start he'd have let himself in.'

The man walked down the hall towards her. Their argument got underway as if Chapman, not being the Fat Man, was nobody at all.

'He might have forgotten his key.'

'He doesn't forget things.' There was a pause and then the girl continued in a harsh voice: 'And anyway, do you think he would think twice about finding your bum in the air?'

'For Christ's sake, it's no joke, you know. He would —'

'You don't know anything about him. You haven't learnt anything in all this time. He's not possessive, you know. That's what he's about, not being possessive. That's his whole belief, for Christ's sake. Not. Being. Possessive. Own. Er. Ship. Can't you understand? He doesn't own me.' The voice lowered from aggression to utter contempt: 'He doesn't even own *you*.' The contempt broadened into an unpleasant wheedling tone: 'You belong to the household as a whole. You're our chicken-chicken.'

Chapman, in the limbo of the front doorstep, found himself analysing every aspect of what was being said. The subject of discussion was the Fat Man. The woman, despite her definiteness, didn't believe her own argument; she was as grateful as the chicken-chicken that it hadn't been the Fat Man at the door – she was being testy because she'd been frightened, she was being forceful because she'd felt vulnerable. It was amazing what you could work out, just by listening carefully, even when you were a stranger to the situation. The woman had a Belfast accent, that was significant.

The subject of the discussion was the Fat Man. Back to that, the most important item of information, or at least detection. Every instinct told Chapman it was true.

For a moment he wondered if he should just walk away, go back to the station, ruminate on the set-up, formulate a plan. The two. . . lovers seemed hardly the word, the two people, wouldn't even notice he'd gone.

No, it would be a wasted opportunity. Whatever happened he couldn't come back here under the same cover. They might be treating him cavalierly, but it would be madness to treat them in the same way. This was a terrorist cell after all. While he was here he ought to find out what he could.

'Excuse me, sir,' he called out politely in the direction of the squabble, 'are you the householder?'

The argument did a rapid fade, to be replaced by silence, perhaps embarrassment. Could terrorists feel embarrassed?

The man turned away from the girl and walked back down the hall towards the front door. He looked suddenly slope-shouldered, despite his solid chest, as if the altercation had loosened a string in him somewhere.

'No, I'm not the householder,' he said tiredly. He gave Chapman a sad, bored look, and then abruptly turned on his heels and walked rapidly away, brushing against the woman as he did so. She approached and stood leaning against the door-frame. The man went through a door at the far end of the hall and shut it heavily behind him.

'What do you want?' the woman asked. She impatiently rubbed at one of her breasts, giving an odd rippling effect to the flesh beneath the tee-shirt.

'I'm looking for the householder,' Chapman replied in the bright tone of a petty official on unsavoury business. 'A Mr Colclough, I believe.'

'He's not here.'

'Oh, I see.'

They looked at each other for a few moments, the woman's eyes candid in their unpleasantness.

'What did you want him for?' she finally asked.

'I've come about the chief rent, as a matter of fact.'

It worked: the woman looked baffled.

'The chief rent?'

'Yes. My company has just bought the chief rent title to this house. Along with lots of others, of course. Hundreds. Thousands, as a matter of fact. It looks as if there's a bit of a backlog. Nothing to worry about. It might be an administrative muddle anyway. The last title-owner made a complete cock-up of his records.'

There was a pause. The woman, thank God, was still totally uncomprehending.

Chapman took a chance. 'Shall I come back later?' he asked in his most patronising tone. 'Perhaps it would be better if I discussed this with Mr Colclough in person.'

Again, success.

'No, no, I'll deal with it,' the woman said, suddenly almost animated. 'Mr Colclough's got a lot on his plate.'

'In that case, can I step in a moment?'

Grudgingly: 'I suppose so.' She stepped back to let him come in.

The hallway was well decorated, nicely carpeted, complete with a set of coat-hooks and a small table on which rested the telephone. The woman obviously didn't intend that he should get any further into the house. Chapman wondered if he dared ask for a drink of water or suggest that he wanted a pee. In the meantime he improvised for a while on the subject of chief rent.

And then the telephone rang.

The woman picked it up.

'Oh, I'll see if he's in.'

She put her hand over the mouthpiece and called out: 'Mark! It's that. . . John. You know. Him. Are you in?'

From some room at the back of the house the chicken-chicken replied in a muffled voice: 'Fuck.'

'Yes,' said the woman to the telephone. 'He's in. Hang on a minute.'

The chicken-chicken returned sulkily to the hall, skirted Chapman as if he might be infectious, and picked up the phone.

'Half a minute.' He too then placed his hand over the mouthpiece, but he didn't say anything. He simply gave Chapman a dour look and transferred his gaze to the girl.

'All right,' she replied grudgingly. Then, to Chapman, she said: 'Let's go into the other room a minute.'

Chapman, heart pounding, followed her to the doorway through which the chicken-chicken had just reappeared. He walked through it into a different world.

The floor was uncarpeted and grimy. There was a broken-backed jumble sale three-piece suite, so filthy that you couldn't even tell what colour it was intended to be. The walls

188

were as smeary with dirt and grease as a neglected cooker, except that in this case the sludge was presumably human in origin rather than animal or vegetable. Decorated in people-fat; the very notion gave Chapman a chill, as if he'd walked into a Nazi concentration camp. Of course in this case you were only talking about nicotine, palm-prints, hair-oil, sweat: voluntary deposits. Nevertheless there was a psychopathic suggestion in the squalor. A bald electric light was burning, although the room was full of sunshine from a window over-looking a neat, if small, back garden. The lamp fitment was clogged with spiders' webs. Strangely there was a television set in one corner, looking glossy and technological.

'We haven't got round to doing it up yet,' said the woman, sharing his gaze at the room at large. Chapman suddenly wondered if she'd ever noticed its state before. He'd once had to break into an old woman's flat when her neighbours had become worried because she hadn't switched her blaring radio off for three days. She'd been lying on the floor with a broken hip, hypothermia, incipient pneumonia, but she still contrived to be plucky, self-deprecatory, civilised. All around her was a seething morass of cockroaches and maggots. There were cat turds, the accumulation of months if not years, over all the furniture. The old lady was perfectly unaware of the state of her flat, or rather she was unaware that the state was anything unusual. She had lost her reference point. It wasn't until she encountered the cleanliness of a hospital ward that she cracked up, and died. Her radio had been tuned to a Mozart opera on Radio Three.

'Oh, that's none of my business,' Chapman told the woman at 29 Waverley Avenue, trying to hide his exuber-ance. This wasn't Norman Colclough's sitting-room, but the Fat Man's lair.

It was still possible, just, to make out some of what the chicken-chicken was saying into the telephone. So Chapman now embarked on the task of spinning out his chief rent yarn to the woman while trying to pick up a one-sided conversation from the hall.

CHICKEN-CHICKEN (*angrily*): you *what*?

(*angrily and authoritarian*): Not at this stage you'd better not.

(*somewhat mollified*): I see.

(*businesslike*): Concert Inn at [*the time was indecipherable, or rather simply lost, as Chapman's whole concentration flicked for the moment, in response to a sceptical look in the woman's eyes, to what he himself was saying*] o'clockish.

The phone went down with a clonk; immediately, the woman lost interest in Chapman.

'Look,' she said, 'how much are we talking about? Hundreds of pounds?'

'Heavens no. Ten, twelve, something like that in all. I've not got the exact figure on me.'

'In that case, why don't you just send us a bill and we can all stop worrying about it?'

'A bill is on its way,' Chapman said plausibly. 'I just thought I'd look in to prevent any misunderstanding.'

'Fret not.' The Belfast in her voice was harsh and relentless. 'We're very understanding here.'

The hall was empty as Chapman was ushered out. The chicken-chicken for the moment had obviously gone to roost.

39

The Concert Inn would have been an end-terraced house in a side street near St Peter's Square, the very heart of Manchester, except that the terrace had recently been bulldozed down leaving the shored-up pub standing alone, like a single stump in a gum. The analogy was intensified by the reddish colour of the exposed soil, and the tracery of foundations that was still visible, neglected roots. Coarse, sparse grass, the sort you find on sand-dunes, was growing from the clay.

Chapman parked on one of the improvised car parks that were only too available, now so many buildings had been demolished, with a view of the front of the pub. He took out his notebook and fiddled with it. Any passersby would assume that he was a salesman updating his order-book, if they bothered to notice him at all through the Manchester downpour that had replaced this morning's sunshine. Puddles, like car parks, gathered and encroached.

Chapman had arrived at 5.15, a quarter of an hour before opening time. It could be a long wait.

In the first hour only half a dozen customers went in, all workmen. Chapman sat and listened to the rain clattering on his roof and watched it run in thick streams down the windscreen. The low pressure started to affect him too – he began to lose confidence in the hunt, to wonder if after all he hadn't succumbed to Anthony Manley's fantasies, dreamt the same dark dream.

And then the chicken-chicken scuttled down the street and vanished into the Concert Inn.

The problem was that if the person from the other end of this morning's telephone call, the man called 'John', had arrived already, he and the chicken-chicken could be conferring in the Concert Inn at this very moment. They could then leave separately and Chapman would never be any the wiser as to 'John's' identity.

He ran through his memory of the men who had already gone into the pub. Labouring types, men in overalls, hardly revolutionaries, surely. Hopefully 'John' was still to appear. He sat and waited while the rain drummed and ran and the interior of his car developed a damp chill, despite the fact that it was early evening in the height of summer.

And then after another twenty minutes or so somebody rather different arrived.

He was a lean man in his late fifties, dressed in a smart gaberdine mac. His hair was white, whiter than the age of his face, and he had intelligent, even distinguished, features. It was his body, somehow, that receded. He moved his arms jerkily, and twice, as he strode through the rain towards the pub, his head twitched sideways. He was being followed.

A hundred yards behind him, out of sight even of his more extreme twitches, another mackintoshed, emaciated form hurried through the weather. Chapman knew instantly that he was on 'John's' tail; something in his bearing and manner marked him out, gave him a familiar quality.

The second man neared. Of course he seemed familiar – it was Rostris.

'John' entered the Concert Inn. Rostris, clearly not expecting him to do so, stopped in his tracks and stood for a few moments in the middle of the pavement. He was hunched, with rain or indigestion. Then, obviously making up his mind, he continued towards the Concert Inn and followed 'John' inside.

Chapman continued to sit in his car – what else could he do? He wondered rather bitterly why Rostris had muscled in on his case. He speculated even more resentfully about what might be happening in the pub. He felt left out, cocooned in the rain.

After just two or three minutes however 'John' and the

chicken-chicken left the pub. They were obviously going to do their talking elsewhere: that was a bonus. After a discreet pause, Rostris followed. Chapman let them all go past his car and he followed also. The great advantage in tracking a tracker was that he was unlikely to look back.

The leading pair crossed the road, went up Portman Street, near the back of the Midland Hotel, took a narrow access road that sloped up towards another muddy car park, and walked across it into the entrance of the derelict Central Station. Rostris stopped by the entrance, peering round a brick pillar at the cavernous space within. Chapman approached softly and placed a hand on his shoulder.

Rostris tensed, twisted around; then, seeing it was Chapman, relaxed.

'In heaven's name,' he whispered, 'you don't want to play tricks like that.'

'What I'd like to know,' Chapman whispered back, 'is what the hell you're doing in the middle of my case?'

'I should think you'd be grateful,' Rostris replied grumpily. 'There's two of *them*, perhaps you've noticed.'

The argument would have to be shelved for the time being. Chapman and Rostris, one each side, peered into the entrance of Central Station.

All that remained of the station was the vast, basic building, purged of tracks, booking offices, platforms. It was an airy structure of girders and glass, floored with compacted dust, Manchester earth that had not been rained on for more than a century. It had all the grandeur of a steam cathedral; what do you do with such a structure when function and theology have withered away? The council had argued for years. Cut off from the railway grid, relieved of utility, it hung in limbo, a station for the after life.

'John' and the chicken-chicken were still walking across the interior, heading towards its very centre. Since they had no identifiable trade, profession or class, since by definition they were outsiders, they made appropriate commuters for a nonexistent terminus. In any case, the station was a perfect place for them to talk. From the vantage point of Chapman and Rostris they could be merely suspect wheeler-dealers wondering whether to take a chance and speculate on the site.

They arrived at the very centre of the floor-space, and began their negotiation. And then the great disadvantage, or rather from Chapman's point of view, the great advantage, of Central Station became apparent. He and Rostris could hear an extraordinarily large proportion of what the two men were saying.

It was as though they were a matter of feet away instead of a hundred yards. The effect was that of a whispering gallery, a random property of the intricate spider's web of girders, and of the particular configuration of the emptiness all around. His sense of dislocation was so strong that Chapman at first could hardly believe the words he heard were actually being spoken by 'John' and the chicken-chicken, and he turned around to see if anyone had approached them across the car park. But no: just a sea of mud, the silent metal vehicles, the hissing rain. He and Rostris were in the lee of the station, and relatively sheltered. He turned back. The effect still seemed to be, quite literally, unnatural, as if they were watching a long shot on television and listening to voice-over dialogue. He remembered how Manley had described the strangeness of seeing the Fat Man commit murder on a busy noonday street while nobody else seemed to notice. This time the hallucination was of sound rather than sight. No hallucination: Rostris could obviously hear them also.

'JOHN':   no business to undertake another contract while ours

CHICKEN-CHICKEN: his business

'JOHN':   think that totally irresponsible

CHICKEN-CHICKEN: his own way

'JOHN':   portant thing for now the bomb always uses a rifle to fame

CHICKEN-CHICKEN: discretion *your* business

'JOHN':	for God's sake next time
CHICKEN-CHICKEN:	it's up
'JOHN':	got to
CHICKEN-CHICKEN:	if he is, so what
'JOHN':	damn lab of petrol
CHICKEN-CHICKEN:	I'll tell him the blue touch-paper and retire
'JOHN':	the point at all the petrol microbes in the heat
CHICKEN-CHICKEN:	be good, would have thought
'JOHN':	talking about a *plague* how many kill
CHICKEN-CHICKEN:	[*silence*]
'JOHN':	the Fat Man himself and all probability
CHICKEN-CHICKEN:	[*silence*]
'JOHN':	hundreds ands don't know
CHICKEN-CHICKEN:	I'll tell him then I
'JOHN':	urgency tomorrow remember

At this point the conversation finished. Without a farewell, without a backward glance, the chicken-chicken began to walk towards an opening in the far side of the station.

'That bastard's trotting off,' Rostris whispered. 'I'll go round the outside and clobber him while you wait here and keep an eye on the other one.'

'No,' Chapman replied baldly.

'Now look, let's leave —'

'It's my case.'

'And I'm the Super. If —'

'It's my case. I take responsibility.'

'This isn't —'

'If we pull in the chicken-chicken, we —'

'The who?'

'The chicken-chicken. I haven't been sitting on *my* backside either, you know. If we pull him in, we'll have no line on the Fat Man. The chicken-chicken's not going to spill the beans, is he? We're dealing with pros. The only way we could make sure that the Fat Man doesn't take half the city with him would be to publicise the whole issue in the press, and then he'll go into hiding and we'll lose him. This way we can make sure that he's warned off doing anything foolish with high explosive, and lay a trap to get him. The chicken-chicken's nobody, he's the go-between,' he concluded authoritatively.

'He'll have skedaddled now in any case,' Rostris said, in sceptical resignation.

They waited.

'John' stood quite still in his place at the centre of the station area, and remained there for some minutes, obviously not wanting to be in circulation at the same time as his co-conspirator. Then, as luck would have it, he turned briskly about, and came towards the station entrance where Chapman and Rostris, tucked behind the pillars at either side, were waiting for him. As he walked through they stepped quietly to each side of him.

Nervous he might be, but he neither bolted nor twitched. He looked at the men grasping his arms with mild surprise on his countenance, and then seemed to accept the new situation without any regrets whatsoever.

40

At about the time Chapman began to take Manley seriously, Rostris had set off in pursuit of ecology, with similar success. So Chapman discovered in their brief discussion in Rostris's office while John Outram, as he called himself, was being guarded by Sergeant Stebbings in the interrogation room.

Murgatroyd's cavalier attitude to the health risks implicit in his research had suggested a line of enquiry to Rostris. This might not have been the first time disaster had struck; and a previous incident might yield evidence which would implicate the callous bastard more readily than anything which could be gleaned from the accident that wouldn't stop happening.

It didn't take long to discover that a Hautbois worker had indeed died in mysterious circumstances several years before. Dennis Barlow, the victim's son, unfortunately proved to be sullen and unco-operative. However, Rostris's questions turned up an unexpected clue. He suggested that Mr Barlow Senior had succumbed to an allergy; Dennis indignantly retorted that he'd been 'infected'.

How on earth had the lad, who seemed almost slow-witted, managed to find out what the Hautbois organisation was so determined to conceal? The line of enquiry was perhaps more relevant to Chapman's case than his own, but Chapman was out pursuing his own investigation. Rostris put a tail on the youth at once.

The same afternoon Dennis went to visit a large former vicarage in south Manchester. Rostris himself followed the owner of the property when he left it a couple of hours later, and accordingly paid his visits to the Concert Inn and Central Station.

'Anyway,' he concluded, 'I think we've let that character

stew in his own juice for long enough. It's time we went in and gave him a bit of a grilling.'

'*I'll* go in,' Chapman said flatly. 'It's my case. They were discussing the murder of Dr Murgatroyd, remember, which arises out of the Wilkins killing. That tanker business is another issue altogether. If anything crops up that'll help you with it, I'll let you know.'

'But surely —'

'My guess is that this Outram won't be intimidated anyway. He'll either tell me something or he won't. Another copper won't make any difference.'

Chapman was right, it was his case. Rostris realised there was no rejoinder he could make – even his stomach remained silent. In point of fact there was another reason why peace was beginning to descend on the digestive front.

'Perhaps we should start with your name,' said Chapman, sitting down opposite Outram, and taking out his notebook.

'My name,' Outram replied, 'is Gordon Chamberlain.'

For once in his life he was glad to admit it: the time had come to get down to ultimate issues.

'Gordon Chamberlain,' said Chapman, writing.

'I am prepared to make a very complete statement,' Chamberlain went on, 'subject to one condition.'

There was a pause.

'A lawyer?' Chapman asked.

'A journalist. I want a journalist to be present. I know of one, a man called Ed Pointon. He works for the *Morning Sky*.'

'I see.' Chapman had dark, thoughtful eyes. There was likely to be a great deal of sloppiness and incompetence in the police force – the organisation as a whole was too big to be anything but flaccid, and no doubt its particular aura as a profession would encourage many criminal types to apply, by the same confusion of ends with means that caused adventurers to try to enrol in the SAS. The latter organisation, being small and finely tuned, was in a position to insist on the sort of rigorous screening the police could never run to. All things considered Chamberlain felt he was fortunate to have come across a policeman with whom he could feel some rapport. 'It's rather funny that you should say that,' Chapman went on.

'Oh?'

'I don't suppose reporters are ever thought of as the policeman's friend. But they're really persona non grata here. Policy from above.'

'Really?'

'Not that we've got anything to hide,' Chapman explained. 'I mean more than any other police station.'

'Of course not,' Chamberlain agreed.

'And Pointon is particularly – well, we've had our difficulties with him.'

'That's very unfortunate,' Chamberlain stated. The quiet definitiveness contrasted with a peculiar nervous tugging at his nose, as if he were frightened it would retract. 'Because Mr Pointon's presence is a flat condition. I'm not prepared to negotiate with you on the subject.'

Chamberlain knew he was in a strong position. A statement to the press was now the most effective way of shutting the Pandora's box that Murgatroyed had opened. Perhaps in some ways it would prove even more effective than the planned assassination. Experience showed that the papers were more interested in the sensational aspects of events than in the considerations from which they arose; now, in the absence of gory details, Pointon would have to concentrate on matters of principle, of Green Principle.

Moreover, Chamberlain himself had nothing to lose, no price to pay. Except freedom, of course, and he'd never had much use for that. You didn't join the SAS if you wanted life to be a holiday. If you anything. If you.

'All right,' Chapman said finally. 'We haven't got time to play the fool with each other. If my superior doesn't like it he can lump it. In any case, we owe Ed Pointon, in a sense. Which reminds me. There's one condition *I* must make.'

'Oh yes?'

'Pointon will have to agree not to publish the story in

tomorrow morning's edition. After that he can do what he likes. Shock-horror. Exclusive interview. All the rest of it. The reason's obvious. We have to make our own arrangements for tomorrow.'

'That's all right,' said Chamberlain, 'as long as I can give him the whole story.'

Actually Chamberlain had no intention of giving Ed Pointon the whole story. Or perhaps, to put it another way, there were two stories. One, the one the *Sky* would be given, was operated by the mechanism of cause. Indeed, now that the assassination of Dr Murgatroyd had been prevented, there was a superabundance of cause, and a certain paucity of effect. It was effect that really interested the press; in its absence, however, they would have to make do with its progenitor.

But cause, of course, was not the same as motivation.

The first cause: Chamberlain's discovery, under the alias of Frobisher, of what it was that Murgatroyd was brewing in his bleak asbestos laboratory under the protection of his acolyte, henchman, hanger-on, James Wilkins.

His primary motive, however, had developed on separate, if parallel lines, while he stood by the shore of Bellingshausen's Sea, vomiting into the vacuum that had been left by Nicola. It was only then that he fully intuited the evil that had begun to breed, after ice ages, at the bottom of the world.

The second part of the unreportable story, the second stage of motivation, had occurred nearly five years later. Chamberlain had left the SAS, a young man's profession, and retired to his family house, a former vicarage on the south side of Manchester. He and Nicola had sold their own house when they got divorced, and split the spoils. There hadn't seemed any point in buying himself another – it would have been a mockery to own a house when he didn't have a home.

The vicarage wasn't a home, despite the fact that he'd lived in it as a child. All he could really remember was sitting in a shabby dining-room, just him and his father, and eating food served to them by a grudging housekeeper. Now there seemed a certain appropriateness in its gloomy associations.

No job presented itself. He had turned down the opportunity of teaching at the SAS Training School in Herefordshire. He had never believed in staying on when the party was over. Nor was he willing to take a post as security officer to a corporation, the obvious alternative, preferring to be a nothingness than a Wilkins.

It was the hot summer of 1979. Chamberlain was sitting in his garden reading a detective story. The flowers had shrivelled up, the grass was brown, even the trees seemed to be wilting. The baked garden made no demands; Chamberlain found himself relishing its diminishment. The thought had occurred to him, since the start of the heatwave, that he should sell up and buy a villa in a place that was hot all the time, basking like a lizard on a rock. Intense heat created a stillness in which he no longer felt uneasy.

Then, suddenly, Nicola was in the garden beside him.

'I knocked and rang,' she said apologetically, 'but I couldn't get any answer.'

In the years since Chamberlain had last seen it, Nicola's figure had developed a boxy quality which her limp summer frock did nothing to alleviate. After all my mourning, he thought, such jaded plainness. There seemed a bitter irony in the fact. Of course it was a cruel way of looking at her, but he had nothing but cruelty left.

'I thought you'd be out here,' she continued anxiously.

He scrambled to his feet. 'This is a surprise,' he said. He wondered what on earth to say next. 'Sit down and I'll get us something to drink.'

Brightly: 'All right.' She looked about the patio as if expecting another deck-chair to materialise of its own accord.

'I've only got one deck-chair to tell the truth.' He couldn't avoid a touch of revenge: 'One of everything. You have it and I'll bring something to sit on from the house.'

Nicola obviously felt the niceties were getting too complicated and decided to go straight to the heart of the matter. 'I wonder if you can guess why I've come here?' she asked.

Chamberlain stood looking at her. He had a long experience of feeling unreal, but now his sense of unreality was stronger than it had ever been, was strong enough indeed to have become a kind of reality in its own right. He felt as if the two of them were characters in a play under brilliant lighting.

Needless to say, he was familiar with the lines – he knew why Nicola had come. Her barrister in his turn had reached a certain age and needed to have some visible symbol of his worth at his side. Because he knew the answer, Chamberlain didn't reply.

'He's left me,' she finally admitted.

'Oh yes?'

'No point in beating about the bush, is there?'

'No.'

'The thing is, Gordon, it's brought me to my senses. It's made me realise something I should have realised all along.'

Once again he was one step ahead of her and the thought of what she was about to say made him shiver, despite the heat.

Suddenly she clutched the top of his arm. A faint pinkness overlaid her habitual pallor – the sun perhaps, or the stress of emotion. The extra weight that had accumulated on her face had kept wrinkles at bay but at the price of making her eyes seem more minimal than before.

'It didn't mean anything, Gordon. It was meaningless right from the start. I don't understand how I could have been so blind. I know this would sound more convincing if it was me who'd left *him* and not the other way round but it's still true. It wasn't love, there was no love involved from beginning to end. I just had a thing about him, I suppose. You've got to believe me, Gordon. You're the only man I ever loved.'

She looked at him beseechingly under the raw sun, her eyes visibly dwindling in the intense heat. He remembered how maternal she'd been towards him when she left; now he was supposed to offer paternal consolations on her return.

'It was all a delusion, Gordon,' she insisted, still trying to force him out of his silence.

At least he didn't feel as if he were acting any more. His emotions – fear, despair, desolation – were as solid as stone. To have spent the last few years coping with emptiness was one thing; to be told that it had all been unnecessary was quite another. And as for the *thing* Nicola had described, with its imperatives, that didn't bear analysis. Or rather he couldn't bear to analyse it.

'Go away Nicola,' he said quietly.

'Oh Gordon,' she wheedled, misunderstanding his tone, 'don't be bitter. Let's try —'

He almost hit her. Instead he turned on his heel and walked into the house. He didn't turn back; he didn't even allow himself to look out of the window into the garden until it was almost evening, by which time of course she was long gone.

He went for a walk. The evening sunshine was still strong. He walked for several hours. At one point he bought an evening paper, just for the sake of the small transaction. A little later he noticed he was hungry and stepped into a hamburger bar.

The café smelled of meat fat and was even hotter than the street outside. There was a gang of youths in one corner, wearing studded leather jackets, and talking and laughing noisily. They seemed like creatures from another world, they were so young.

As Chamberlain ate his hamburger he flipped through the newspaper. After a few minutes he became aware of a sort of flicker out of the corner of his eye and, looking up, he realised that a girl who was sitting by herself at the next table was smiling at him. She was young, dyed-blonde, wearing a bright pink cotton frock. As she caught his eye her smile vanished and she tilted her head towards the door, suggesting they should both leave the café. A prostitute. For some reason his spirits, low to start with, sank so abruptly that he could have wept.

Instead, he turned back to his paper. He had reached the business page. And there it was.

SHAKE UP IN HAUTBOIS NORTHERN DIVISION

Mr James Wilkins was to take charge of administering the Hautbois Manchester interests; Dr Leo Murgatroyd was to establish a fuel research division in order to look into the possibility of developing new forms of energy.

It was at this point that motivation and cause gelled into a single commitment. Chamberlain's inner crisis had come to a head with Nicola's reappearance and the prostitute's smile. While Nicola was gone their marriage had at least possessed a retrospective value from suffering; now she'd attempted to come back Chamberlain understood it had always been worthless. Or rather that it had deserved the sort of meagre price-tag the prostitute no doubt placed on herself. The girl's speedy transition from unexpected smile to predictable pro- position seemed to encapsulate the whole long process of his relationship with Nicola. That sense of vacuum which Cham- berlain had experienced by the shores of Bellingshausen's Sea intensified; now there wasn't even a world to stand at the bottom of.

In a void, revenge was at least something: a free act in a dimension where everything cost and nothing had value. And the obvious candidates were those individuals who were pre- pared to sell their own world for profit.

That was where the evening paper came in. The informa- tion it contained on the subject of the Hautbois shake-up reinforced Chamberlain's motivation with a cause that was suddenly on his own doorstep. Just as, this afternoon, Nicola had been.

41

Shortly after coming across that item in the paper Chamberlain reverted to Frobisher and broke into Hautbois's newly established Salford laboratory. There he photographed a number of scientific documents which established beyond doubt that Murgatroyd was at work on an extension of his Livingston Island research. Frobisher then showed this material to some Iranian contacts of his.

They were interested; indeed, speaking as individuals, they were horrified. Not so much at the biological threat as at the prospective superannuation of their country's main source of income. As representatives of that country, however, their hands were tied: the xenophobia that had surfaced in the revolution of the previous year, and which was being kept alive by the issue of the American hostages, made it virtually impossible for them to co-operate with foreign agents. In any case it was part of their current ideology that the Islamic destiny was above such sordid considerations as the oil trade and global economic patterns.

Nevertheless, while his contacts hesitated Frobisher went quietly ahead with his preparations.

'I spent some time contriving an alibi,' he told Chapman and Pointon. 'Obviously it didn't work.'

'You mean you decided to set up that youth, what's-his-name, Dennis something. Barlow,' Chapman interpolated.

'It really *did*n't work,' Chamberlain admitted, obviously impressed. Then, ruefully, he took a handkerchief out of his pocket in such an unlikely fashion that Chapman thought for a moment his arm must somehow have been refracted, like a stick in water. Chamberlain could have been manufactured to a blueprint by Picasso: stammering movements, a double-jointedness of the limbs. His SAS past ruled out lack of co-ordination, although that was your initial impression. On second thoughts perhaps his facility for negotiating unexpected corners had been a positive advantage during his time on active duty.

Chamberlain explained how he'd come across a reference to the death of a worker called Barlow during his investigations into the activities of Hautbois's northern division. It occurred to him immediately that this could be a spare motive going begging, and he undertook some legwork. Sure enough he discovered enough rage and bitterness in Dennis to convince press, police, public, whoever might *need* to be convinced, that the deaths of Wilkins and Murgatroyd could well be acts of revenge.

'The ghost of Hamlet's father,' Pointon suggested.

Chapman looked at him in surprise; Chamberlain meanwhile went on to justify his intention to frame Dennis by the argument that the youth would patently be incapable of organising the assassination of Wilkins and Murgatroyd, and innocence would out.

'It outed too bloody soon,' Chamberlain admitted. He pronounced 'bloody' with the urbanity of an ex-officer.

The intention had been, of course, that Dennis's status as a red herring should be established *after* he, Gordon Frobisher, or rather John Outram as he decided to call himself for the lad's benefit, had reverted to Chamberlain again, and had placed himself at a suitable distance from events.

Outram had been forced to modify his plan before it even got under way. He discovered that Dennis had already found himself a co-conspirator of sorts, a marxist conservationist of the dottiest variety called Miss Clare. There was nothing for it but to change tactics and concentrate on helping the pair to develop their cranky little organisation. The evidence would point straight at all three of them, Outram included, but they would have shown themselves to be so patently hare-brained that no one would take them seriously. There was no better cover in all the world than an obviously false confession. The beauty of it was that the Green Principle would actually believe that it had organised the killings; its claims, though false, would be sincere. In reality of course it would have been Frobisher, acting with the backing of his Iranian contacts, who had dealt with Murgatroyd, Wilkins, the biological threat. And, in the non-publishable dimension, had exorcised the ghost of Nicola, eradicated the after-taste of aguila and seal-blubber, faded out the rhythm of Bellingshausen's Sea upon that narrow shore.

The Iranians had by now come back into the picture. By the first of two lucky coincidences the SAS had stormed their London embassy to rescue the hostages being held there by 'anti-revolutionary' elements at the very time when Frobisher was cultivating Dennis Barlow. For the briefest of moments this act cancelled out the malign influence on Iranian foreign relations caused by the holding of American hostages in Tehran. The flush of enthusiasm for the British in general and the SAS in particular lasted just long enough for Frobisher to extract a sum of money from his connections sufficient to finance the sort of operation he had in mind.

'It's my gratuity,' he told Miss Clare. The nobility and self-sacrifice implicit in the remark were meat and drink to her.

The actual placing of the contract resulted from Frobisher's second stroke of luck. He happened one night to feel like a drink and walked into a pub he'd never used before, near the city centre. It wasn't exactly prepossessing: a small, dismal terraced building called the Concert Inn. He chose it out of whim because he was actually on his way to listen to a Hallé concert at the time. At a table in one corner he discovered the chicken-chicken gloomily sipping a pint of beer. Or rather, not the chicken-chicken – at that stage Frobisher knew him as Mark Lindupp, lately a sleeper on active duty with the SAS.

This part of the story was not for Chapman or Pointon. Suffice to say that he'd managed to take out, through the offices of an intermediary, a contract on Wilkins and Murgatroyd. The police would no doubt catch the Fat Man in their trap tomorrow; and they had already spied on Lindupp during the negotiations at Central Station. Their task was simple enough; there was no need to help them unduly on their way. It was bad enough having to spill the beans on Dennis and Miss Clare, although in their case the consolation was that they hadn't actually done anything even if, benighted souls, they thought they had. But one had to draw the line somewhere.

Chapman meanwhile was perfectly aware of such distinctions. There was no point in wasting time trying to persuade Chamberlain to admit more than it suited him to do. In any case Chapman was already busy going through his own plans.

First he would have to report to Rostris. He was still determined to keep him at arm's length from the case, however. Perhaps it was a way of keeping him at arm's length in other directions. Nevertheless any connection with the accident that wouldn't stop happening was indirect, to say the least. His second task was to warn Murgatroyd to keep away from his laboratory tomorrow, and to glean from him sufficient information to enable the police to organise a stake-out. Thirdly of course came the stake-out itself, with the prospect of catching the Fat Man rifle in hand. It was fortunate, to say the least, that the chicken-chicken would by now have told him of the danger of using explosive.

While Chapman was thinking over these arrangements Pointon took his leave. He rose to his feet looking well satisfied. Why not? Chapman thought. Even with the prohibition on publishing his story in tomorrow morning's edition of the *Sky* he'd been more than adequately repaid for having to keep quiet on the subject of the Hautbois Project.

As he was leaving the interrogation room Pointon turned and spoke. His voice was carefully drained of emphasis and even volume, a flat reportorial voice: 'Oh, by the way, you can tell Rostris that I saw his point and left that rag I was working for. I'm on the *Northern Evening News* now. Got my own by-line. Guaranteed.'

'Oh yes?' replied Chapman. He was too busy thinking about the matter in hand to notice the implications of Pointon's remark.

42

As the chicken-chicken drove south from Manchester city centre after his rendezvous with Gordon Frobisher in the shell of Central Station the weather changed, as it so often did in the early evening. The rain stopped, the cloud cover rapidly broke up and dispersed, there was a sudden radiance from low sunshine on wet surfaces. He decided not to go back to the house immediately. Instead he drove into Didsbury and took a walk in Fletcher Moss Park. He needed to think.

The park was like a large rockery, flowerbeds grading down a steep slope, with a goldfish pool at the bottom and beyond, tennis courts, water meadows, the flat anonymity of North Cheshire suburbia. The chicken-chicken sat on a bench from which he could see the whole view, took out a cigarette, and allowed his mind to play over the last five or six years, over that long long sleep from which finally he was beginning to awake.

In 1975 the chicken-chicken was known as Mark Lindupp, and he was one of the SAS's élite Belfast operatives, assigned to penetrate the IRA. He was to be inserted in a cell and once inside, to 'sleep' until reactivated by his 'sponsor' or spymaster, Gordon Frobisher. Unfortunately by the time Frobisher pressed the appropriate button Lindupp was too deeply asleep to respond.

The preparation for his mission had been rigorous. Lindupp was provided with a Northern Irish identity, background and accent, the product of eighteen months' special training at the SAS centre in Herefordshire. He knew the streets of Belfast like the back of his hand, even though he had never been there in his life before. One of the qualifications for this branch of SAS work was a total lack of Irish experience. This was to guard against the possibility of reverse infiltration, and also to ensure that the operative, when installed, couldn't be recognised and his cover blown. Of course Lindupp was given a number of introductions when he arrived, although he wasn't told which, if any, were in the know. He had to act his part all the time.

As he sat watching the evening sunshine eradicate a wet afternoon in Manchester, the chicken-chicken thought of those first weeks in Belfast, while he was waiting for something to happen. It had rained almost the whole time. His experience condensed to a scene on Belfast docks, grey rain falling into brown water, the wet steel hulls of moored container ships, little frog-like people scurrying by, dockers, sailors, port officials, passengers, businessmen, their heads squashed into their necks as a retreat from the incessant rain. Lindupp was tall in most company, but people here seemed particularly short, perhaps because he was an outsider who didn't belong with them.

After he had been in Belfast some weeks Lindupp was invited to a party. He had gone to a number of functions already but nothing had happened and he'd developed a sense that the real party was going on elsewhere. Certainly in the distance there was often the dull rumble of an explosion or the puttering of gunfire.

This party began in the usual way, people standing around chatting, a fiddler and tin-whistle player doing their bit, some sporadic and nervous early evening dancing. But just as things were at last getting underway, and people were beginning to feel relaxed, two more guests arrived, and the atmosphere changed completely.

They were normal-looking boys, strutting cheerily in like everybody else. But the hubbub in the room ceased abruptly, as if someone had turned the volume off. Then it resumed again more loudly than before, everybody talking busily to show how nonchalant they were. A young man near Lindupp nodded his head in the direction of the newcomers and said, in a voice that had been miniaturised by fear and caution: 'You-know-what-ers.'

Lindupp made sure he never got near them during the half-hour or so they were in attendance. Nevertheless he observed them sidelong, with care and in detail. Their ordinariness was almost tangible: it was a quality he could recognise, having been trained intensively in the same discipline during the last eighteen months. One was tall and rather ungainly in his movements, the other shorter and more wiry, with a way of looking about him with bright non-demanding eyes, like a bird. Ordinariness was more than second nature for them, it was their world, the very medium in which they operated. Lindupp had a sudden image of when they were small at school. They wouldn't have been naughty, or bullies, because to be those things was to do what the establishment expected of its trainee do-ers, its incipient tough persons, its apprentice SAS men. They would, on the contrary, have sat quietly and patiently in class, watching everything that went on, totting it all up. Around each of them would have been an area of silence. Once again Lindupp felt the association with birds. They would draw nourishment from their surroundings, they would gradually take shape, and then, one day, peck, they would break out and Christ knew what they would do to you.

As they moved through the party, Lindupp noticed how grateful and gushing people were to them, trying to show that they were pleased to be still alive. He, meanwhile, experienced the sudden calmness you feel when the task you have been born to do is at last underway.

'See you later, dar-r-lin,' the taller one said to the hostess when they'd made their brief rounds. The short one merely twinkled his fingers at the room in general, and they walked out. There was an audible sigh of relief.

Lindupp waited a few moments, so as not to look too obvious, and then left himself.

He didn't bother with his car but walked straight on to the

empty street. The lights were so dim they seemed to illuminate nothing but themselves, so he waited a few moments until his eyes grew accustomed to the night and a façade of terraced houses and shops opposite came into view. There was no sign of anybody about. The streets of Belfast tended to be like that at night, as though the world had come to an end.

Nevertheless Lindupp began to walk, slowly but without actually dawdling, down the silent street. He hadn't been walking more than a few minutes when a car suddenly drew up beside him and the front passenger door swung open. He stepped unhesitatingly inside and they drove off.

The small one was driving; the gawky one sat in the back. The small one said: 'Where we're going is to the Fat Man's,' as if Lindupp would understand the reference. He grunted something affirmative in reply, as if he did.

The Fat Man lived in a small detached house in a respectable residential – albeit predominantly Catholic – area of Belfast. The street was well-lit and there was a porch light over the front door which illuminated a tiny well-tended front garden. It looked, every inch, a place that had nothing to hide.

The outside effect encroached inwards as far as the hall, which was chilly and uninviting but wallpapered and neat enough.

'We keep it like this for the benefit of the gas board,' the Fat Man was to tell Lindupp later. 'The meter's under the stairs.'

They had been let in by a girl. She was chubby, freckled, attractive in her way, though she had a rather sulky downturned mouth. She was wearing faded jeans and a tee-shirt in bright lime green through which her unsupported breasts showed as individually distinct as tropical fruit. She took no notice of him, of any of them, but simply led the way along the hall to a room at the end.

The room was lit by a naked bulb. The wallpaper was beginning to peel and there was a greasy smear all round the walls, about four feet from the floor, as though some enormous filthy person had just taken a bath there and left a tidemark behind. The Fat Man, sitting in a chair by an old gas fire that had been set in the chimney breast, was getting on for enormous but he wasn't in the least bit filthy. In fact his balding head shone as if it had been polished, and his suit, a light-weight summer one despite the fact that it was November, looked expensive, if not exactly smart. You were conscious of the sheer yardage of material.

The girl stood leaning against the wall. She hadn't glanced at the Fat Man, any more than at the rest of them, but Lindupp was aware she was in his orbit. He was suddenly struck, despite the crisis which he was facing, with an incongruous, hilarious thought: she's the girl-friend of the fat bastard!

'You know why you're here?' the Fat Man asked.

'Yes,' Lindupp answered shortly, hoping he was the only one who *did* know.

'What I mean is, at this point in time.' The Fat Man had only the faintest of Belfast accents, like an acidic film on the surface of his voice. Below there were depths of plumminess. Altogether he was an oddity in the lean and hungry IRA. He seemed old for his role, around the late thirties, and he generated an atmosphere of someone who had been to university, who was used to middle-class comforts. In due course Lindupp was to discover that the sordid, ragged surroundings reflected not the Fat Man's predilections but his ideology; and within a few months the contradictions in the man's character were to resolve themselves into a strange synthesis of left-wing and capitalist elements, when he went free-lance to become a mercenary terrorist.

'I heard you needed someone,' Lindupp replied vaguely.

'That we had a vacancy?'

'Yes.'

'And that's all?'

'That's all I heard.'

'I wish those people who arrange things wouldn't be so coy,' the Fat Man grumbled. 'They have us dancing round each other in circles. Bad as bloody civil servants.'

'Haven't you got a vacancy then?'

'We will have by tomorrow evening.'

Even SAS men can feel fear; Lindupp had thought he was experiencing it already. Now, suddenly, he was.

'They didn't tell me that,' he said softly.

'That we had sprung a leak?'

'No.'

'I suppose they didn't want to put you off your vittles.'

In God's name, how am I going to get out of it? Lindupp wondered. Without getting killed myself?

'Do you mean —?' he asked. The one consolation was that anyone was liable to talk broken sentences when faced with such a prospect. The less said the better.

'It's the way it's always done, you know. It's the best way.' The Fat Man gave him a hard, assessing look. He had a large mole on an otherwise scrubbed, well-shaven cheek. 'Why don't you sit down?' He pointed to a kitchen chair a few feet to one side of Lindupp. Perhaps he suspected that his new recruit's legs were buckling. The pointing finger, the hand altogether, was small and delicate, as though the outposts of the Fat Man's body weren't fully inflated. Lindupp sat down.

The girl was still leaning against the wall, preoccupied perhaps with her own thoughts. Certainly, despite the tenor of the conversation developing in front of her, she still seemed to be basking in the glow of the Fat Man's authority.

'It's much better on reflection,' the Fat Man continued, 'for you to know nothing about the whole sorry business. You can rest assured that the formalities have been gone through, that it's all above board.' He paused. 'What I mean is, there's been a tribunal. The whole business was beyond any doubt, reasonable or unreasonable. You know as well as I do that in a case of this sort there's no choice. And it's much better for an outsider like you to do the dirty work, so to speak. It makes it impersonal. There's no place in this set-up for being vindictive or revengeful.'

'No,' Lindupp agreed. The Fat Man was quite right, of course. What he said conformed to everything Lindupp had learned about the conduct of revolutionary cells in his course in Herefordshire. Any guerilla group, urban or jungle, right or left, would operate in exactly this way.

'Think of it as your membership fee,' the Fat Man suggested.

'Yes.' There was another way you could look at it, and Lindupp wondered if the Fat Man had thought of that too. He looked up at the big complacent face, the swollen cheeks forcing his mouth into a pout, reminding you that a mouth was just an orifice. Of course the cunning sod had thought of it.

Lindupp wasn't just being asked to pay his dues, but to prove his eligibility to join. It was as simple, and as neat, as that.

And he wasn't eligible.

43

Lindupp lay on his bed for many hours that night, looking out of the window. He hadn't pulled the curtains and as his eyes became accustomed to the dark the night sky grew paler, with an orange haze from the street lights rising into it from below.

It was time to think clearly; he was sharing a house, an IRA cell, with other people who did just that. There was nothing anarchic about their behaviour, it was well-ordered, even legalistic; his must be the same.

As he lay he put a number of points to his own tribunal.

1. Whoever it was who had been sentenced to death by his IRA colleagues was doomed. No intervention, no appeal, was possible. You could put the man in prison, you could send him to Argentina with a false beard, it would do no good, he was dead in any case. The greater the lengths you went to to save him, the more determined they would be to polish him off. And to keep somebody alive required non-stop attention forever; but to kill him you only had to do it once, for the space of a second. It was an unequal struggle. The way to look at it was to regard the man as dead already, as only alive in some technical sense – the functions of his body were continuing for the present on the same sort of basis that the hair and toenails of people continue to grow for several days after they've been executed. The condemned man wasn't alive in the context of life.

2. Given that nobody could save the victim he, Lindupp, could save him less than anybody. He was after all in the same trade, liable to the same fate. His status, as far as the SAS was concerned, was that of a sleeper. That is to say, he had to co-operate, to behave correctly as a member of the cell, and wait for his sponsor to contact him when the time was ripe.

That was the safest method, as his instructors had made clear. If you were blown, or through some indiscretion, blew yourself, you wouldn't be able to give anything away because you wouldn't know anything. Once again, a simple, universal procedure: a practice of the profession. The long and short of it was that as a sleeper he was specifically required not to use his initiative – except insofar as a member of the IRA Provos on active duty was required to use his initiative anyway, which might be quite far. He had enough on his plate.

3. The victim in any event didn't necessarily have his heart in the right place. It was highly unlikely he was in the SAS – they surely wouldn't infiltrate the same cell twice over. That way lay madness, they could end up with IRA gangs entirely staffed by SAS imposters. No, it wasn't likely. Given that the Fat Man would certainly be as discreet as the superiors he complained of, the chances were that Lindupp would never find out who the dead man was working for. They would be ships that passed, or rather collided, in the night.

4. Lindupp would be no more to blame than the trigger which he pulled. That was precisely what he would be, a larger-scale trigger.

5. He had known that he was likely to get involved in crimes and atrocities from the outset. That was part of his cover. But those events would take place anyway, with or without his participation. (See item 4 above.) And by participating he was helping to put a stop to them in the longer term. But. But. But. But what? But he hadn't expected this problem to arise straightaway. It had caught him on the hop. But that should make no difference.

He lay and thought through these points, one after another. They made up a convincing case. It didn't convince him.

There was one solution which he came across in the depths of the night, a horrific solution. He didn't dare confront it until nearly dawn. The risk of failure was acute, and the penalty would be torture and death. The penalty for success was nearly as bad.

However, it was the only thing he could do.

Having convinced himself, he slept. At least that was a form of escape, however temporary, from the dirty bedroom in the respectable house where, unbeknown to those who had trapped him, he was trapped. And sleeping was what he'd been assigned to do.

He woke up to the usual greyness of November Belfast. He went to the window and looked out. A pile of leaves was being riffled by the wind in the Fat Man's well-tended garden; a few stray ones skittered about in the street beyond. Some drops pinged on the clean window. A wet, Irish wind was obviously blowing from the west.

He turned back to his room. What sort of satisfaction did the Fat Man get out of creating this contrast between inside and out? In one place there was actually a handprint on the scratched plaster of the wall. It reminded Lindupp of what you saw in public lavatories when somebody lacking fore-thought found himself without paper and wiped his bum with his hand, then cleaned his hand as much as he could on the cubicle partition. Lindupp dressed quickly and went down-stairs.

In the room where he had talked with the Fat Man the night before, the girl was sitting on a ricketty and uncomfortable-looking kitchen chair watching television: a repeat of *Upstairs Downstairs*. Lindupp glanced at his watch. It was gone two in the afternoon – when he'd finally slept, he'd slept. The girl was slumped as far as she could be on the minimal chair and she wore yesterday's clothes. While he watched she scratched one bright green breast lazily, as much as to say, for our purposes this breast is just something one might happen to scratch. Finally she raised her eyes from the lords and ladies at their banquet and said: 'There's an egg in the kitchen if you want one.'

Her accent was far more Belfast than the Fat Man's, each word as flat and sharp as the blade of a chisel. Lindupp real-ised he hadn't heard her speak before.

'Thank you,' he replied noncommittally. He didn't particularly feel like an egg. 'It's a business we've got to do today,' he suggested.

'It's got to be done,' she replied, cutting each word firmly into the flesh.

There was satisfaction in her tone and Lindupp wondered for a moment if she were some kind of sadist. But there was no excitement in the atmosphere. Her eyes had found *Upstairs Downstairs* again, and she was still slumped in the chair. He realised her satisfaction lay simply in the thought that the thing was to be done, that the Fat Man would have cleaned his nest.

Christ, Lindupp marvelled, as he had last night, what a thing to find in the IRA: true love!

44

Lindupp drove one of the cars – not the one with the condemned man in it: that was possibly his compensation for
having to do the deed. They left at a little after four o'clock, as
dusk was falling but before the night-time security arrangements of the city were in operation. They would have to talk
their way through check-points when they returned, but by
then the evidence would have gone.

They went by separate routes, but Lindupp had been given
a map to study beforehand. After some miles on the Antrim
road he took a fairly narrow turn-off west, just beyond a
ramshackle village garage called Murphy's, and drove down a
country road for miles towards the night itself, which slid
down the windscreen as the road rose towards high land. He
saw nothing of the Ulster countryside save signposts picked
out in the headlights, and the occasional wintry-looking rabbit. There were few other vehicles, and after he'd forked left
twice in succession, there were no vehicles at all, despite the
fact that the final road he found himself on was rather wider
than its predecessors, and well-metalled. He could sense,
rather than see, woodland accumulating on each side of it.

Beside him, at the front, was the gangly Provo, known as
Jerry. On the back seat was Isle, presumably short for Eileen,
the girl. Neither had spoken for the whole journey. At this
point, though, Jerry said shortly: 'There's a lay-by a bit ahead.
Turn into it.'

Lindupp had been navigating for himself and this was the
first indication that Jerry knew the route. Once again he got
the impression that he had been tested. Sure enough, a small
lay-by, complete with litter-bins, appeared at the side of the
road. He turned into it and pulled up.

'Turn off your lights,' Jerry ordered.

He turned them off. They sat in silence for a few moments. Lindupp became conscious of the scent of perfume coming unexpectedly from the girl, as though to fill the void left by driving and the headlights. The smell was heavy and sophisticated, no doubt to the Fat Man's taste. Apart from the perfume all was very still. The trees to the left, a section of the road ahead, gradually became distinct as his eyes grew accustomed to the dark. The night seemed to have retreated several yards, leaving paler, intermediate air behind.

'All right,' said Jerry after a while, 'drive up over the kerb, just beyond the bin there, and into the wood.'

Lindupp said nothing, but started the engine and obeyed. He swung out into the road a little, to give himself an angle, and mounted the kerb. The car bucked and clonked as they went over a patch of rough ground and then they entered the trees. A branch came down like a huge hand and touched the windscreen. Then the car wheels found the grooves of a woodland track and he was able to drive almost normally.

'Put your lights on dipped,' Jerry said, when they'd been going about a minute, 'we're well off the road now.'

Another few hundred yards, and the Fat Man's car was suddenly ahead, parked on the track without lights. Mark pulled up immediately behind it.

Jerry opened the door and got out.

'Keep your lights on a minute,' he told Lindupp, and went on towards the other car. The girl got out of the back, and went up with him. Lindupp stayed where he was. He picked up the pistol that had been slid under his seat before they began the drive. It was a precision job, a Westing automatic, .33 calibre, able to kill at very long range: its ammunition would hardly slow down to notice a candidate for execution. Lindupp had been trained on the gamut of firearms in Herefordshire, and could handle a Westing efficiently enough.

Jerry opened a rear door of the Fat Man's vehicle and helped someone out – Lindupp realised the man's hands were tied in front of him and he couldn't manage by himself. Christ, he thought, what would have happened if they'd been stopped at a roadblock?

He suddenly had an eerie intuition that the man would have said nothing, that he would have kept his bound hands out of sight on his lap.

Nausea began to rise in Lindupp's throat. He'd not been briefed on how to accept death passively – the SAS inculcated the notion that you struggled forever. It might be to no avail but at least it would take your mind off dying. So nothing in his training or indeed in his experience had prepared him for seeing the IRA victim approach his end so co-operatively, perhaps even affirming the set-up which he'd already betrayed.

Lindupp found it difficult to be passive; but he did have the compensation of practicality. The moment of nausea was not to be wasted: develop it, cultivate it, build on it. He remembered his sponsor, Gordon Frobisher, describing a meal he'd eaten during a recent mission in Antarctica. What was it? Aniseed spirits and seal-blubber, think of that. Let your mind dwell on every detail.

The Fat Man manoeuvered himself out of the front of the car and walked towards Jerry, Isle, and the victim. The short Provo, Sean, followed, looking over his shoulder once or twice as if under the impression that even here the security forces might be lurking amongst the trees, perhaps disguised as gnomes or leprechauns. They *are* here, realised Lindupp bitterly, here I am. Much good may that do.

As he joined the others, the Fat Man took out a cigarette, lit it, removed it from his lips, and placed it between the victim's. Christ Jesus, thought Lindupp, how corny can you get? It was almost funny. Incipient laughter created a drag in his throat and chest; brought nausea nearer to the surface.

Jerry stepped over to the boot of the Fat Man's car, opened it and took out an emergency lamp. Then he trudged up to Lindupp's window and said:

'You can turn your lights off now. We'll just go over there a bit.' He nodded towards the trees. The Fat Man, Isle, Sean and the victim were already going in that direction. 'Bring the tool,' Jerry added and went after them, switching on the lamp as he did so. Lindupp doused his lights, put the gun in his pocket and followed Jerry's shifting beam.

Jerry put his lamp on the ground in a small clearing. The Fat Man walked with the victim to a large tree and put him in position in front of it, adjusting the stance as if he were dealing with a piece of furniture. Jerry shifted the lamp so that its beam lit the condemned man up.

The latter was still offering no resistance; and he didn't seem interested in saying anything. No famous last words – at least that part of the charade didn't have to be gone through. The cigarette was removed from his mouth by the Fat Man and thrown away. The victim just stood there, looking fed up. Fed up to the final degree.

'All right,' said the Fat Man, walking over to Lindupp. Everybody had stepped tactfully to one side. 'How you like,' he added in an undertone.

Lindupp knew what that meant: head or heart, take your choice. It was another test, of course, he understood that. The head was the professional option, so quick and final. But one might blench at opening such a definite box. The heart was the alternative for the second-rater.

He took the gun out of his pocket, weighed it calmly in his hand, checked that it was ready for firing, and took several paces towards the victim. Then he raised the gun, and levelled it at the man's forehead, from a range of about two yards. The man kept his eyes modestly downcast. After a few seconds, Lindupp lowered the gun until it was pointing towards the heart. I'm sorry, you poor slob, he said silently, I'm sorry to lead you such a dance, but with the room I've got to manoeuvre in, it's the only one I'm capable of.

Lindupp stood quite still in that position for what to him seemed like ever, so what it seemed like to the condemned man at the other end God alone knew. At long last he allowed himself to lower the gun to his side.

'I can't do it,' he said.

For the first time the victim looked – not hopeful, certainly, but at least interested, as though finally something was going on that concerned him.

Jerry came up and took the gun out of Lindupp's hand. Lindupp immediately turned to one side, bowed his head, opened his mouth and retched. He retched and retched again. And then, to his joy, he found what he was looking for, and vomited. Even while he was being sick he watched from the corner of his eye what was going on in the vicinity of the tree.

Jerry raised the gun; at the heart, interestingly enough. Surely *he* wasn't a second-rater? No, after all the pussyfooting that had gone on, it was more likely a form of executioner's etiquette, Jerry not wanting to rub home what a big bad boy he was to a folded-up colleague.

Jerry fired twice. The silencer didn't eradicate the sound altogether but the sharpness was taken out of it: dob dob.

The victim seemed to hiccup twice, just out of synchronisation with the gun's noise, and then he relaxed, as though his body had already come to terms with the tracks of the bullets. He slid gently down the tree and settled into a heap at the bottom.

Lindupp was aware of the Fat Man approaching, so he switched his eyes to the ground and concentrated on throwing up. A delicate finger and thumb, unrepelled apparently by the proximity of vomit, gently pinched his cheek.

'What shall we do with him, then?' the Fat Man asked in a soft maternal whisper.

Lindupp looked round at him, lips blurred, eyes full of tears of strain. There was a pause; a pause in which his whole future, his very destiny, twisted round on itself.

'I know what we'll do,' the Fat Man went on, answering his own question, 'we'll let him be my chicken-chicken.'

He said it as if it wasn't an insult at all but a term describing a definite household function; as if you could keep a chicken-chicken as a pet.

45

The chicken-chicken, sitting in the evening sunshine of Fletcher Moss Park, didn't dwell for too long on what had happened since he received his designation, because so little had. About six weeks after the execution the Fat Man had informed his superiors in the IRA that he was getting a bit long in the tooth to remain on active service, and he had been amicably retired. Jerry and Sean were assigned to other cells; Isle and the chicken-chicken, as the Fat Man's personal retinue, had gone with him to London, where in flat contradiction to his claim to the IRA chiefs of staff, he set up in business as a contract killer for left-wing causes anywhere in the world. Isle provided the domestic infrastructure: watching television, not doing housework, going to bed with the Fat Man when required. The chicken-chicken acted as go-between, administrative assistant, initialler of contracts. When his sponsor, Gordon Frobisher, finally pressed the button, the cell in which he'd been planted no longer existed.

Of course he could have walked out; he could have knocked on the SAS's door. But for what? To announce that his mission had failed? To inform them that he could be of no further use because the Fat Man would be in hot pursuit and would bump him off as soon as he caught up? It was highly unlikely the chicken-chicken would have been able to get the authorities interested in hunting down the Fat Man himself. He was merely a contract killer; if he were removed from the scene somebody else would simply take his place – the market was buoyant enough. It was the organisations which laid the contracts that the SAS was interested in.

There was another reason for the chicken-chicken's inertia. He felt as you might do in a marriage which no longer has anything to offer you except boredom, boredom which saps your energy and therefore makes it impossible for you to extricate yourself. The sleeper had fallen asleep.

The marital analogy held in several respects. There was the Fat Man's ominous nickname for him, which implied the sort of affection you might feel for someone you knew was your inferior in every way, someone who was dispensable. There was also the fact that the chicken-chicken had begun to have sexual relations with Isle.

Not that this affected his status. Indeed he suspected that she believed it would make him less important and impressive if she had sex with him than if she kept him at arm's length. The implication was: I'll keep faithful to the Fat Man. Oh, except for the chicken-chicken, of course. As she'd informed him only this morning, 'You belong to the household as a whole.'

Six months ago they'd all moved up to Manchester. The Fat Man had accepted an important and lucrative London contract and he didn't like to work too close to home – so they'd changed homes. Not long afterwards the chicken-chicken happened to go for a drink to a somewhat dingy pub near Manchester city centre called the Concert Inn. And who should walk in but his former sponsor, Gordon Frobisher?

The chicken-chicken experienced all sorts of emotions in quick succession: fear, guilt, regret. But that in itself was a breakthrough – it had been a long time since he had experienced emotions of any kind. The presiding one, distilled like a clear liquor from rotting materials, was the awakening of hope or, what in his case amounted to the same thing, the hope of awakening.

When he had told his story it turned out that Frobisher had a use for the Fat Man's services, as so many had before him. But even the fact that once again he was acting as a go-between couldn't demoralise the chicken-chicken. He couldn't escape a sense that the wheel had gone full circle.

He got to his feet now. The sun was turning red and dropping down towards the horizon. As he walked towards his car he realised what he had to do. The time had come to act. The Fat Man had run into a number of difficulties recently, signs that he was approaching the end of the road. He had decided somewhat greedily to accept the Manchester contract the chicken-chicken had brought from Frobisher, despite his almost simultaneous commitment in London, and the fact that it would be on his doorstep. The chicken-chicken guessed he had decided to accumulate a rapid pile before announcing his retirement. If that was his intention his recent run of luck would only serve to confirm it. His technique of bulky invisibility had failed him during the Wilkins assignment, and a witness had actually told his story to the *Morning Sky*. Even more spectacularly, the Fat Man had found himself being interviewed on television immediately following his assassination, by car bomb, of Mr Frederick Fox in London.

If the Fat Man were to cut and run, where, if anywhere, would the chicken-chicken be? Unlike Isle, he would suddenly find himself without a function; also, of course, he would know too much. Yes, it was time to act.

Or rather, keeping to the spirit of so much of his past, it was time not to act. He would fail to pass on Frobisher's message about the dangers of Murgatroyd's laboratory, and the necessity of using some other means for the assassination than explosive. Let the Fat Man stew in his own juice. The chicken-chicken pondered once again on his tendency to linger casually in the vicinity of his own explosions, that strategy of transparent obesity. It had begun to let him down recently; perhaps tomorrow he'd be more than simply scorched by the blast. Even if he weren't he would have enough on his plate without turning his attention to the chicken-chicken.

And the consequences? The consequences would be nothing to do with the chicken-chicken, that was precisely the point. He would no longer be involved, he would have relinquished the role of go-between.

It was gone ten when he arrived back at 29 Waverley Avenue. The Fat Man, he knew, would be in the garage, making his bomb. He would be there all night: he believed in made-to-measure explosions. It was amusing to think how little he understood the dimensions of this one.

The chicken-chicken went straight up to his bedroom and put his things, all of them, into a small suitcase. Then he went downstairs again, placed the suitcase in the hall, and stepped back to put his head round the living-room door.

Isle was watching television but she looked up when she heard the door open. Her arms were folded under her bosom and as he watched she raised them slightly, still folded. Of course. The Fat Man had other things on his mind, and Isle was at a loose end.

'I'm going out,' the chicken-chicken said bluntly.

It was the first time he'd ever refused the invitation. For a second her breasts held their position, green demanding spheres, emblems of the Fat Man himself. Then, astonished, Isle let them drop, as someone else might let her mouth sag open.

Mark Lindupp closed the living-room door, walked down the hall, picked up his suitcase, and stepped into the night. He had broken out of his coop at last.

46

After the sopping afternoon, it was a sunny evening. Chapman had insisted on being a prima donna as far as the interrogation of Outram was concerned. He was actually hostile on the subject, and Rostris had an unpleasant suspicion as to the source of that hostility. Can you, he wondered once again, be jealous of another man's fart?

There was nothing for Rostris to do at the police station but at the same time he wasn't all that keen on going home. He knew himself too well. He would wander in, start to potter around the house, and then, before he knew it, as if in a trance or a fit of absent-mindedness, he would find himself gobbling a sandwich. Lumps of cheese, whole gherkins, slices of onion, great wedges of bread, the sort of sandwich that is only held together by the sheer ferocity of mastication, top and bottom pressed towards each other by the action of jaws, the raw edges sealed smooth by the passing flash of teeth.

Rostris hadn't eaten for three days. That was one way of looking at his predicament. The other way, the way he was insisting on, was that he hadn't had sexual intercourse for almost three years, ever since the fiasco with Susan Hopwood.

The only way to stop farting was to stop having indigestion; the only way to stop having indigestion, as far as he could see, was to stop eating. He was perfectly aware that as a solution it was rather like being decapitated to cure a headache, but there didn't seem to be any alternative.

And it was beginning to work: the winds had gradually dropped. True, he had been rocked by the occasional wave; small whirlpools would whish and gloop; the receding tide sucked vainly at the shore. But since this morning, when his

stomach had given a kind of dying squeak during the interview with Dennis Barlow, there had been silence.

To keep away from food and alcoholic drink he went out
for a walk – not a pastime that normally had much appeal. But
at least it was a sunny evening. The smell of warming rain, of
cooking dog-turd, rose from the pavements as he walked
through the seedier parts of south Manchester.

His motivation wasn't entirely negative: he was also hoping,
in an obscure way, for something unexpected and sexual to
happen, as though the vacuum left by the cessation of wind
would mysteriously fill itself with female opportunity. The
truth of the matter was that since his arrangements and relationships had collapsed after the Hopwood débâcle he'd
somehow forgotten how one went about making a casual
foray. That is to say, he could remember the circumstances in
which such occurrences had taken place in the past, but for
the life of him he couldn't think how those circumstances had
been brought about. He walked for hours.

The sun set. He passed teenagers groping in bus shelters,
middle-aged couples walking home from the pub, individuals
taking their dogs for a walk before going to bed. He began to
feel maudlin, as if he were the only person in the world who
was entirely on his own. His life was empty; his career was
empty; his stomach was empty. At last, walking through the
centre of Fallowfield, he found himself surrounded by the
scent of hamburgers and unable to bear it, to bear anything,
any longer, he stopped and turned back to the small café from
which it was coming.

He bought himself a hamburger and a cup of coffee and sat
down at a small plastic table which was furnished with tea
rings, food crumbs, a plastic tomato full of ketchup. His
heart's desire. He looked around him for a while, prolonging
the expectancy of the moment before he dived into his meal,
as a swimmer might wait on a hot day before plunging into a
pool.

The café was unexpectedly busy, almost seething with life
after the quietness of the evening street. The clients were

mostly youths, reptilian in leather jackets. At the next table though, a girl sat alone. A woman rather – she was thirty or more, but was dressed in a blue and white striped mini-dress and had brightly dyed blonde hair. She looked up as she became aware of Rostris's gaze and a smile immediately erupted on her pimpled, rather pretty face.

Rostris's heart pounded. He could hardly believe, after all that lucklessness, his luck. At the very moment when he needed one most, a whore had appeared. She was a bonus, an omen, a sign that you needn't write life off after all. Ignoring his hamburger he smiled back.

The woman's smile vanished immediately, as if his had neatly cancelled it out. She stood up and, leaning towards him on her high-heeled shoes, walked to his table and sat down. Then she gave him a rather anxious look. Rostris tried to calm himself down by looking at her carefully. She was somewhat gaunt, with bad skin and makeup which looked as if it belonged on another face altogether, a bigger one where it wouldn't be so noticeable. And yet she was pretty. Or perhaps, on second thoughts, it wasn't that she was pretty but just that she was there.

'It's fifteen pounds,' she said finally, obviously worried in case she hadn't gauged his price correctly. Too little and he might be put off; but you couldn't charge much to a customer in a place like this.

'All right,' Rostris said.

She immediately relaxed. Their bargain struck, the atmosphere between them became friendly, as if they'd known each other for a long time.

'My place isn't far,' she said in a co-operative tone.

'Really?' Rostris replied. He had a sudden picture of a dismal room, steam still rising from the bed.

While he paused for thought she spoke up again: 'You may as well eat your hamburger, there's no hurry.'

He looked regretfully down at the seductively glistening meat in its soft bun. 'I don't think I'll bother,' he said.

She gave him a disapproving look and for a moment he

thought she might be finding him insufficiently carnivorous. Then realisation dawned.

'If you fancy it,' he offered. 'It'll save waste.'

'I suppose it will,' she agreed, as if her main concern was to do the hamburger a favour. While she ate, Rostris put his mind to work. Certain sarcastic headlines appeared in his imagination: POLICE OFFICER FOUND IN BROTHEL, Belt snapped, court told; PIMP BLACKMAILED COP, Defence claims; VICE GIRL CASE. Accused Officer Says 'Just Friends'. The alternative of course was to suggest she came to his house. There were dangers there too: POLICE SUPER TOOK SEX GIRL HOME, but they were not as great. There could be no concealed hangers-on, no videos or tape-recorders, no coincidental raid by the vice squad. And when it was over he would tell her he was a policeman and she wouldn't be seen for dust. Particularly if he gave her five pounds extra.

'We'll get a taxi and go to my place,' he said, as she finished off the hamburger.

'You're the boss,' she agreed, obviously pleased.

It was nearly midnight when they arrived at his house. The neighbourhood was dark and discreet; as they approached the front door he wondered what on earth he'd been worrying about. Police officers weren't expected to be gods; they were only human; if not, in certain cases, sub-human. The long interval since the last occasion, and the disaster that had occurred then, must be making him nervous. Silly really; sex was like riding a bicycle, you never forgot how to do it.

They went straight to his bedroom. The woman wasted no time. She kicked off her shoes, pulled her dress over her head, unsnapped her bra, slid her pants down, and climbed on to the bed. She wasn't wearing perfume and the faint smell of sweat reached him from her nakedness, human and pleasant. This was the level of contact he'd wanted to achieve on that long-ago occasion with Susan Hopwood.

He took his own clothes off, glancing down at his stomach when he'd done so. It was firm, flat, above all silent. Fancifully he thought of it as a kind of launching-pad, all prepared for lift-off. He got on the bed beside the girl, and within a few moments, he entered her.

And then the telephone rang.

'I thought you'd want to know how things stand,' Chapman's voice said.

'Yes,' Rostris answered in an emotionless tone. He was naked in his hallway.

'I'm going to try and catch the Fat Man on the job.'

Still trying to keep his voice as dry, as desiccated, as possible, Rostris replied: 'Are you then?'

'Don't you think it's a good idea? He will already have been warned off about the use of explosive. And I've told Murgatroyd to keep well away, so there's no risk. I thought I'd install myself in the lab and wait to see what happened. Have the place surrounded outside of course but not so as you'd notice. Luckily there are a few derelict warehouses around there. Murgatroyd doesn't open up the lab until one o'clock on the dot on Fridays. It's very much a one-man operation, and he spends the morning writing up his reports in the Hautbois office in the centre of Manchester. Security reasons apparently, following a break-in a year or so ago. He doesn't want to chance leaving the documentation and the bugs together and have someone half-inch the complete package. Murgatroyd's very regular in his habits. I expect the Fat Man knows all about his comings and goings but just in case I thought I'd install myself in position about eight o'clock and wait for him to turn up. What do you think?'

'It's your party,' Rostris said, unable to keep a certain bitterness at bay.

'I think it's the most sensible arrangement.'

More placatory: 'I'm sure it is. Look, let me know how it turns out. All right?'

'Yes.'

'And good luck.'

'Thank you.'

Clonk, the phone was down. Rostris swore reflectively and then consoled himself. All was not lost. He had just experienced sudden unexpected aggravation, had his long-awaited coitus interrupted, and here he was still in the clear, not a rumble, not a bloop, not a fiss, not the faintest symptom of indigestion. He thought of the woman waiting for him upstairs and for the second time that night he experienced a stirring of optimism. You couldn't have indigestion without eating, but tumescence was gratuitous. Perhaps when life was taken as a whole, the pros did have the advantage over the cons after all.

Scrawny, naked, nursing his rediscovered erection with the careful pride of a savage balancing his spear, Rostris mounted the stairs to his bedroom.

The prostitute had fallen asleep.

Strangely Rostris took it in his stride. The woman's over made-up eyes looked open, shut, but her thin spotty face was already suffused with the warm pink of sleep. She had eaten his hamburger, fallen asleep in his bed; she must live so near the edge of hunger and exhaustion. Why worry? There was always tomorrow morning.

He slipped into bed beside her and slept also.

He awoke early but there was already sunshine beyond the curtains. The woman was still asleep, her back towards him. He stretched his arm around her and placed his hand on her warm breasts. She responded cosily, as unsurprised as a wife or a whore can be, and turned towards him.

Back at the police station Chapman sat for a moment in stunned silence. Then, slowly, like a swimmer in deep water, he reached for the telephone and dialled Rostris's number.

47

Rostris was at his most dour and unsympathetic. That was odd really, considering that he'd always gone against the grain of his nature and shown understanding about Margaret's illness. Also last night he was doing everything he could to elbow his way into the case; and now here was his opportunity to take it over completely. Chapman felt both mystified and irritated as he put the phone down.

And then he remembered his dying wife, as you remember a much-dreaded appointment which you've never in fact forgotten, and other feelings took over.

It was like a huge railway terminus, endless people scurrying about shunting and bumping not luggage but letters. Every few minutes, like a train, a successful sentence clacked off into the distance and disappeared.

Margaret watched from the sidelines: Ladies' Waiting.

She didn't feel left out any more – Susan, discernible in the midst of the scramble, carried her load for her. It was lovely to watch her flicking in and out of the busyness.

In out in out, the activities of everybody, apparently sporadic and individual, conformed to a pulse. As soon as she realised that, Margaret became aware of the whole environment throbbing like a single organism, some microscopic form of life.

The heartbeat grew fainter, became simply a beat, sustaining no tangible burden, like the lessening plink of a radar scanner as the object moves out of range. As she progressed further into death Margaret's world became still.

But the stillness was charged: not a void but an abstraction.

There, down below, Susan was the word; here, above, Margaret was the meaning. She was, she realised in a swoop of joy, in heaven. Her past, freed from its words, returned to her in its infinity of detail. Poor Susan, diminished and physical, manhandled existence in all its bulk; she, Margaret, lay bathed in the intricate radiance of an entire lifetime that had unexpectedly dawned on her afresh.

And then, abruptly, Susan was replaced at the bedside. Like two black suns rising over the horizon, Mikey's eyes came into focus.

In the ending, after all the words: let there be darkness.

Margaret had been taken away. Chapman and Susan sat in his sunny kitchen. There was silence. Chapman was aware that he was shaking. Susan put a hand on his arm to quell it.

'Come on, tough guy,' she said. 'You're a policeman, remember.'

'At least I was there when she died. I wish I'd. . .' His voice tailed away. He wasn't sure *what* he wished.

'There was nothing more that could be done. There never is. When you die you die. It's the way it has to be.'

Her voice was quiet and warm. For the first time since that business about Rostris Chapman felt near her again. He also became aware that it was a beautiful day, that the room was full of light. He could feel the sun's rays through his clothing. Susan's face shimmered before him like an effect of the light itself.

'You've had so much to put up with,' Susan was saying.

'And you.'

'All right, *we*'ve had so much to put up with. But that's in the past now. We can make a fresh start. Both of us.'

Yes, Chapman was certain now. Rostris had disappeared along with Margaret. The way was now clear for Susan and himself; they could indeed begin anew.

For some inscrutable reason, perhaps out of a need to give precision to an ultimate moment, Chapman found himself glancing at his watch. It was seven minutes past one.

48

'I've got to go out straightaway,' Rostris told the prostitute.

'Oh yes?' she replied, rather scornfully. She swung her legs around so that she was sitting, naked, on the edge of the bed. Her breasts were narrow and somewhat limp, but to Rostris their soft whiteness was unutterably inviting. They seemed a graspable form of that liquid which he bought from the chemist's, and which would fall on his stomach like warm snow, to blank out the acid for a while at least. He pulled his pants and trousers on quickly and then picked up his jacket from the floor where he had thrown it in his hurry last night. He pulled his wallet out of the inside pocket, took out four fivers, and handed them to her.

'Services rendered,' he said. 'Or not rendered. Sorry about that.'

She brightened up immediately. The sort of trust and intimacy that had developed round the consumption of his hamburger and the sleeping in his bed was triggered off again by the receipt of his money.

'You're a nice fella,' she said softly. 'It makes a change.'

'I'm a cop,' Rostris said from inside his shirt.

'It doesn't worry me,' she replied, standing up and beginning to pull her clothes on also. 'And, you know, the other thing doesn't worry me either.'

'What other thing?' Rostris asked.

'Us not making it.'

'Oh that. It bloody worried *me*, I can tell you. Sometimes it's worse than being a doctor, the phone going.'

'I know,' she said sympathetically. In bra and pants she stepped over to him and patted his cheek. 'I'll tell you something,' she went on, looking at him closely with smeary eyes, 'and I should know. You don't have to be able to get it up to be a man.'

'You what?' asked Rostris in amazement.

'Where's the loo?' she asked sweetly in return.

While she was gone he thought about what she'd said. Did the stupid bitch imagine he was using the telephone calls as an excuse? That was rich, that was. He had arranged last night in the hopes of boosting his morale after three years in the dumps, and had ended up being comforted by a prostitute for not being able to make it.

He thought back to that business about his fart and Susan Hopwood's virginity. He'd recently come to some kind of understanding about what had been in the poor girl's mind. She'd been offering him herself, in all its complication, and, as far as she was concerned, he'd responded with a raspberry. It was as if he'd made a nasty joke about her private parts: the case of the pristine woman and the male chauvinist police-man. And now here he was, three years later, being told by a whore not to worry about being a chinless wonder.

She came back into the bedroom and pulled on her dress.

'Listen,' he said, 'I would have been only too happy to make out with you. But it's my job, it's urgent. I'm in a hurry.'

She didn't listen, dim cow. 'I'll tell you what,' she said, sliding on her shoes, 'what I think about, about the ones who come in a hurry, I think well, at least they've got plenty of juice in them. Those big studs, who bang away on you for half an hour, it's the next best thing to dry balls in my opinion.' She was ready for action. Her face looked very much as if it had been slept in, but presumably that was no disadvantage. 'Goodbye copper,' she said, 'and I'll tell you another thing. It makes a nice change to go back to work not feeling shagged out.'

She turned and left the room. He heard her trotting down the stairs and out the front door.

'Bitch,' he said.

He arrived at the police station at a quarter to seven.

Chapman had already gone, but Sergeant Ankers, who was organising the arrangements outside the laboratory, briefed him on the plans that had been evolved during the night. He then signed on for Chapman's pistol. It was now seven-thirty, not quite time to leave for the laboratory.

Suddenly, almost before he realised what was happening, Rostris found himself in the police canteen devouring a fried breakfast. The sun was shining through the barred canteen windows; his egg looked like a miniature sun itself. Never, never in all his life had he eaten anything so delicious. All round him the scraping of steel, earthenware, aluminium generated a single, intense metallic note, the song of a canteen on a beautiful summer's morning.

It only took a few minutes to eat breakfast, and then Rostris left for Murgatroyd's laboratory.

The laboratory itself was quite small, a windowless box suspended in the centre of the cavernous space of the warehouse. There was a tiny ante-chamber outside it where, ever since a break-in some time previously, a guard would be stationed to keep an eye on things. Security arrangements had been kept to the minimum, in accordance presumably with Murgatroyd's theory about keeping a low profile. The guard clocked off at eight in the morning in any case, which was the time when Murgatroyd arrived to start work on every day except Fridays. The guard was just leaving as Rostris arrived.

Sergeant Ankers switched on the near light. The tanks, boilers, piping of the room sprang towards Rostris.

'Inspector Chapman had planned to conceal himself behind that,' Sergeant Ankers said, pointing towards a squat cylinder in one corner. 'A bit cramped, I'm afraid, but you won't be visible.'

'That'll be all right,' Rostris replied. He went over and wedged himself into the gap behind the cylinder. He had to sit with his knees forced up in front of his chest. Just enough movement was possible to peer round the edge of the cylinder at the Fat Man when he came in.

'Can you get hold of your gun and your torch all right, sir?'

Ankers asked, looking down at him and obviously luxuriating in the senior point-of-view.

'Go and teach your grandmother to suck eggs, Sergeant,' Rostris suggested.

'Yes, sir.' Ankers walked over to the door. 'Shall I switch the light off now, sir?'

'I'm not frightened of the dark, Ankers.'

'No, sir. Good luck, sir.' The light was switched off. Ankers and the room disappeared.

'Thank you,' Rostris told the darkness. The door briefly shone open, and shut, as Ankers exited.

It was a long wait, hour after hour. Rostris didn't dare leave his position because the Fat Man could walk in at any moment. It took only a short time before the discomfort of his back and legs was supplanted by the glow of his breakfast when it reached his stomach. Soon the ache extended from the clot of bile in the top of his chest, to the knot of piles round his anus, with every inch of the enormous, convoluted gut in between sharply illuminated by acid pain. As he suffered Rostris thought of all that cool geometrical piping in the darkness around him, and the seething sinister mess that was going on inside it, and he began eventually to feel slightly delirious, imagining that all the problems of the world could be put down to a sort of indigestion in the very nature of things.

The pain became so acute that he didn't know how he could bear any more of it; and then, as it always did, the intolerable became boring. Rostris's mind, giving it a wide berth, began to wander in other directions. He thought of the prostitute again, this time in a more disinterested fashion, concentrating on the sex that might have been. Then he thought of Chapman's wife dying, and he accidentally edged closer to his indigestion for a moment. In all the suffering of the last year or so he'd consoled himself with the thought that at least Margaret Chapman was worse off than he was. Now, with her death in prospect, he wasn't so sure. He retreated rapidly from that problem to the fact that the way would soon be clear for

Chapman and Susan Hopwood to pair off together formally. He wondered again if – no, surely not, surely she would never spill the beans. She would be hurt as much as him and it was animal recoil to skirt pain, that was what he was trying to do himself, although once again he'd taken an inadvertent step in the wrong direction. It would be better if he thought of. . .

At twelve thirty-eight, by the luminous dial of Rostris's watch, there was the scratching of a key in a lock and the door shone open again, to reveal the unmistakable silhouette of the Fat Man. One arm rose; the neon went on, its miniaturised tube reflecting suddenly on the Fat Man's shiny pate. He stood there, taking a long calm look at the room; Rostris didn't even breathe. Then he waddled in and placed a thin, elegant-looking attaché case on the work bench that ran down one side of the laboratory.

Rostris knew what would be in that case: a screw-together, assassin's rifle.

The Fat Man flipped open the catches on the case and peered inside as if to check the contents. Then he closed it again and stood there thinking. He was a cool customer. Rostris didn't want to take him at this stage unless he had to. At one sharp, Murgatroyd's time, a decoy would begin to let himself in. By then the Fat Man would have his rifle assembled and ready for use. It would be dangerous but Rostris would have the advantage of being behind him. At best he would catch him red-handed; at worst he'd have to shoot him, which would be good riddance.

To Rostris's surprise, the Fat Man, leaving the case where it was, walked to the door of the laboratory, turned off the light, and went out, shutting the door behind him.

Presumably he was going to peer out through a window at the front of the warehouse, and wait to spot Murgatroyd approaching. Why turn off the light, though? He'd need it on when he came back to assemble his rifle. Maybe he was just the sort of tidy person who always switched the light off when he left a room. Perhaps Rostris would get the opportunity of asking him in a few minutes.

Meanwhile Rostris waited.

The Fat Man stepped out into the sunny street. All was peaceful. There was nobody about except a newspaper seller, waiting by his empty box. The Fat Man took a deep breath and was just about to walk away when a van appeared at the far end of the street, approaching at speed. He paused to see what it would do.

The van screeched to a halt beside the newspaper vendor, a bundle of papers was thrown out on to the pavement beside him, and then the van continued on its way. The newspaper seller, an old man, bent down and with some difficulty lifted the bundle on to the top of his box.

The Fat Man looked at his watch. Twelve forty-five. It would be the noonday edition of the *Northern Evening News*.

He began to walk slowly down the street towards the vendor. There was still nobody else about, and he couldn't help wondering who, in this drab, declining area of Salford, would actually purchase the papers that the old man was now arranging in front of him. Well, he would, for one.

He would be noticed if he scurried past, trying to make his getaway. Anyway, he didn't have the build for those sort of tricks. There was nothing more anonymous than behaving exactly like everybody else. He stopped at the vendor's box.

'A nice day,' he suggested.

'Fourteen pence,' the man replied, folding up a paper and passing it over.

'Thank you,' the Fat Man said, giving him the required money and walking on.

It would do no harm to glance at the front page. Anything to keep his pace and appearance casual.

He unfolded his paper. Its whiteness glared in the sunshine and some moments passed before the black print surfaced into focus. When it did however, the Fat Man stopped in his tracks, casualness forsaken.

SECOND HAUTBOIS KILLING FOILED
REPORTER ATTENDS POLICE INTERROGATION
by
Ed Pointon

... three weeks ago, like a ringside seat in hell ... any journalist worth his salt but that oh so bloody scoop ... last night happier privilege of being present, this time as a representative of the *Northern Evening News*, as a second brutal tragedy was averted ... questioning of suspect by his own invitation ... to discover another chilling murder had been arranged by the fanatical clique calling themselves the Green Principle ... can now reveal information I previously had to hold back, on police insistence, in the public interest ...

A CITY OF SIGHS AND DYING

... Hautbois laboratory developing fuel based on germ warfare procedures ... microbes more or less lifeless at normal temperatures, but like creatures in a late-night horror film, go on the march when their surroundings hot up ... irony, the planned assassination originally involved the use of explosives ... set off, a plague bomb which could have infected half Manchester, causing illness and death to countless innocent men, women and children, a city of sighs and dying ... changed tactics in nick of time ... authorities believe a shooting is now on the cards.

DEADLY SANTA

... police this morning preparing to ambush British Jackal ... but a well-rounded genial figure, a Santa Claus of death and destruction, identified by a witness, through the agency of your reporter, as the author of the heart transplant outrage, when surgeon Mr Fox ... apprehension will bring Hautbois threat to an end ... does take place this morning, in later edition ...

The Fat Man remained perfectly still. Around him lay the sunny desolate street. It was still, apparently, empty, except for the newspaper vendor, but of course it was not empty at

243

all, it was secretly swarming with police, there would be rifles trained on him at this very moment. He had that sense, as you would when cornered by an animal, that the only possibility of survival would be to make no unexpected movements, indeed no movements at all.

But that was impossible. If he remained here the invisible forces of law and order would slowly manifest themselves, seeping out of the buildings, accumulating on the road all round him. There would be all the cumbersome mechanics of an arrest. He could try to hurry things up, embark on an explanation, but nobody would believe him.

He tried to work out what the time was. He didn't dare look at his watch, the action might be misinterpreted. It had been a quarter to one when he left the laboratory. Then plod plod plod he'd walked over to the vendor, say forty-five seconds, things never took as long as you thought, then the transaction, twenty seconds, then plod plod off for a few paces, then stop in his tracks, perhaps another twenty seconds, then the skim read of the front page, then this pause for thought, how about two and a half minutes in all? Call it three. That made it twelve minutes to one.

The bomb would go off at five past.

He had a choice. If he let himself be arrested, assuming he didn't get shot in the process, he'd still be arguing with the constabulary when the plague exploded all round them. On the other hand, he could try to defuse the bomb. He knew how long that would take: something over eleven minutes. In his business that was the sort of information you needed to have to hand. No, call it thirteen, to allow for his bandaged arm.

If he continued to walk away he would be shot; if he stayed where he was any longer he'd be arrested. But what if he began to walk back? That would take them by surprise. If in a slow and relaxed manner he returned to the scene of the crime? Certainly it would confuse them. And while they waited to see what he'd do, perhaps he'd get the opportunity of doing it. Their motive would be to discover whether he would incriminate himself any further: his would be to produce an act of general benevolence at the last minute. Since he couldn't get away he might as well be arrested on an up note.

He turned and began to walk slowly back towards the laboratory, along the quiet street.

He'd spent, it must have been a minute, thinking, and now this leaden purposive walking, this slow hurry . . .

The one thing to be thankful for, Rostris realised, was the state of his legs. They had now been folded up, the knees pressed against his chest, heels tucked up against his buttocks, for nearly five hours. A number of sensations had passed through them, in particular two: pins-and-needles, and a kind of shrieking of his thigh muscles. But for the last couple of hours the legs had been totally without feeling, as if they'd succumbed to rigor mortis.

Not so his internal organs. They glowed, pulsed, dilated, seethed, did everything but burst. His attention had returned to them since the Fat Man left the laboratory. For much of the morning his mind had managed to concern itself with other things, but now as the confrontation neared, he thought perforce of himself.

The door opened once more, the light went on, the Fat Man re-entered. He must have decided it was time to prepare for Murgatroyd. He went over to the attaché case, opened it, and began to fiddle with its contents, obviously screwing together his rifle.

As Rostris sat in taut silence he felt the pressure begin inexorably to build up in his lower bowel. The Fat Man, despite fast and nimble movements, was taking a long time with his gun. Three minutes to the hour, two, one . . . There was the sound of a key in the lock outside, Murgatroyd's substitute had arrived.

Rostris rose to his feet.

Rostris remained in a squatting posture.

It was extraordinary. He'd given the instruction but it simply didn't happen. He tried again. Again he stayed exactly where he was.

The door opened and Sergeant Ankers, pistol in hand, stepped warily in. Rostris, unable to wield his gun in his cramped position, couldn't cover him. The Fat Man didn't turn round or even look up, but continued to work at his attaché case as busily as before. Nevertheless, he spoke.

'I know you're not Dr Murgatroyd,' he said, 'I know you're the police. This is a bomb. I'm in the process of defusing it. Otherwise it will explode in just over three minutes. I doubt if there's time to evacuate your men out of range of the explosion. Certainly there's no time to get them clear of the effects of the plague. So I suggest you remain exactly where you are and say nothing. Just leave me to get on with it.'

Ankers looked towards Rostris's boiler. Slowly his eyes tracked down till they reached his level. Rostris tried to shrug acquiescently. Ankers turned back and gazed at the Fat Man. Rostris thought frantically about the dimensions of the explosion that could take place so soon. The bomb itself: probably enough to destroy this laboratory. That would account for himself, Ankers, and the Fat Man. But it was worth remembering that what was being developed in the laboratory was a substitute for petrol. That should add fuel to the fire. Say, take out half the street, including twenty-odd policemen and a surly newspaper seller. But then of course one had to account for the bugs which would be sparked into activity by the intense heat. My God, how much of Manchester would die at the same time? The one thing you could never discern from the centre of an explosion: its boundaries.

Rostris had endeavoured to think on the rather abstract level of the explosion in order to keep his attention away from even more pressing details. But now, as the full horror of the situation dawned on him, he became aware that the fuse on his own bomb was dwindling with terrible rapidity.

The policeman was behind him, slightly to the left. That was all right, thought the Fat Man, as long as I know where I am. The point seemed to have struck home, that was the important thing. You couldn't necessarily rely on the intelligent co-operation of the constabulary.

As he worked the Fat Man thought of other things. He'd seen films and television programmes about bomb disposal, but they were rubbish. Men concentrating until beads of sweat appeared on their foreheads. If your head was sweating what in heaven's name would be the state of your fingers? For them to operate with the requisite clarity and deftness your head had to be elsewhere, on some other subject. The subject that came to mind was his own failure to be aware of the dangers of using explosives for this assassination. The cause of that failure was obvious.

The chicken-chicken had been a cuckoo in the nest.

Fifteen seconds, fourteen, thirteen. He'd put his watch on the laboratory table beside the attaché case when he began work. His fingers were a blur now, he marvelled at them disinterestedly, as one might those of a concert pianist in full flight. Eleven, ten, nine, eight –

Suddenly: whiss, steeb, blinch, farb, proob.

He thought for a fraction, however irrationally, that the explosion had begun. The noises came from his right, low down, on the other side of the room. Before he could stop himself his head had turned in that direction, his fingers had extricated themselves from the maze of wiring. . .

In those last seconds, Rostris's thoughts moved in another direction. He thought of how strange it was for a form of life to inhabit that most inhospitable and sudden environment, the explosion, and wait for its superheated moment as seeds in a desert wait for generations for rain. Much good may it do them, he said to himself, remembering what had happened to *his* long-awaited moments. Susan Hopwood and the fart; the prostitute and the telephone; this morning's long wait and another fiasco.

And now the final moment came, and all Rostris's bitter, sharply-etched brooding, turned white:

POSTSCRIPT

At five minutes past one, the ten twenty-two train from Manchester arrived at Euston. The first-class carriages were at the front, of course, so that the well-to-do and the business clientele wouldn't have too far to walk.

Dr Leo Murgatroyd stepped out of his first-class compartment. He was carrying a black leather briefcase inside which was a small lead flask, lined with a shiny laminate. A minute thermostatically controlled heater, battery-operated, kept the liquid contents of the flask at exactly the right temperature. Dr Murgatroyd was on his way to see Ronald Saunders, Chairman of the Hautbois Company, to discuss what should be done next.

Mark Lindupp stepped out of a second-class compartment some forty or fifty yards further back. He was not on his way to see anybody, which was exactly what suited him.

Dennis Barlow was near the far end of the train, although he'd made a number of expeditions forward to the buffet car during the course of the journey to buy beer. He was only coming to London for the day: he thought, after yesterday's visit from the police, that he might as well make some gesture in the direction of an alibi. He'd suggested to Miss Clare that she should come too, but she just made a pompous reply about the appropriateness of remaining at home since her commitment was to what was at hand, 'to the local'. Dennis imagined her doing some knitting: they'd read *Tale of Two Cities* once upon a time in class.

On the journey he reflected upon failure. The police would intervene; his father would remain unavenged. Taking a philosophical leaf out of Miss Clare's book, one of her books, he consoled himself with the thought that we all become packet-soup in the end. Luckily he was too far down the platform to see Dr Murgatroyd walk past the ticket collector at Euston Station, or his philosophical solution might not have held.

In a compartment even further back than Dennis's, in fact several million miles further back. Finn Malke had been listening to static for over four months, ever since that last abrupt message from Patricia Hughes on Earth. He was waiting for the message to be completed, for that pink, firm-toned, full-fleshed voice to speak to him again and convince him that he was not alone, that there *was* a sexual dimension, that he participated in a community: that discourse, like the physical world from which it derived, had a landscape of its own.

There was no landscape; only space. And no message, except static.

Static was a good word. For an unbearable time and distance, while Malke sounded previously unimaginable depths of loneliness, there had been nothing from his onboard receiver but a flat, consistent plateau of sound in which no detail was discernible. Static. The months that had gone past had not happened, since nothing had happened in them. And the distances... He'd travelled through such distances that distance itself was stretched thin and became irrelevant. A voyage to stasis.

Malke had a squirt of corn on the cob and resumed his watch through the portside observation window. The starry vista occasionally seemed to align into an image which was evanescent, filmy, seductive. For Malke the shimmering form was a beautiful Englishwoman, suggestively implicit amongst the harmony of the spheres. But as soon as she came she went, like faces which appear amongst the patterns of the wallpaper, or animals that take life from the movements of the clouds. Malke lapsed back into his long trance, a stasis of the mind.

And then something came through.

ssssssssssssssroonssssssssssssssssssssssss

It was embedded in static, but distinct. A sudden hiatus, no, more than that, a sound in its own right, but one he couldn't quite make out.

Malke sat upright, put his corn on the cob tube down, turned up the volume of his receiver, and began to listen intently.

sssssssssssssssssfridididididdssssssss

Something else definitely, he couldn't understand what, but something.

sss guyowroop ss lardybeena

His heart began to pound, sweat broke on his forehead. It was deeper in tone than Patricia Hughes, deeper than a man even, but something. It was something.

snortup lugmiff flamooj

And then Malke realised. Such a long time had passed since he'd heard words that the significance took a time to sink in. They weren't words he could ever understand, they weren't for him, they weren't from home; they were from some other place, they were for some other person altogether. Or some other thing.

What was clear, from this perspective: home had nothing to say to him any more. He had known all along, but he needed to be told. And now his radio had told him.

Slowly Malke rose to his feet. He dropped the cob tube into the garbage holder, placed his last bags of pee and crap carefully in their respective storage units, and then went to the medicine compartment and took out the remaining pill.

He did understand those distortions of the static after all. As banal, as disinterested, as meaningless, as the high-pitched gabble of a disc jockey, or the monotonous drone of a news bulletin, or the strident argument of a political manifesto, they could be interpreted, at least in their practical effect, as an incitement to self-destruction.